I0761356

The Fury and Cries of Women

CARAF Books
Caribbean and African Literature Translated from French
Renée Larrier and Mildred Mortimer, Editors

Angèle Rawiri

The Fury and Cries of Women

Translated by Sara Hanaburgh

Afterword by Cheryl Toman

University of Virginia Press *Charlottesville and London*

Originally published in French as *Fureurs et cris de femmes*

University of Virginia Press

Printed in the United States of America on acid-free paper

First published 2014

ISBN 978-0-8139-3602-4 (cloth)
ISBN 978-0-8139-3603-1 (paper)
ISBN 978-0-8139-3604-8 (e-book)

9 8 7 6 5 4 3 2 1

Library of Congress Cataloging-in-Publication Data is available from the Library of Congress.

Cover art. Clive Watts/Shutterstock

Contents

The Fury and Cries of Women

I dedicate this novel to my friend Rita Berthier,
who died before giving birth to the baby
she was carrying and so desired.

1

Disintegration

She rolled over onto her sore belly. Despite the fact that time was passing, immobile on this rainy and gloomy morning, she wrapped herself in her sheets, dampened by a nightmare-ridden sleep. Forgetting her abdomen for a brief moment, she thought of how many job applications were piling up in her office. Then, with a wave of her hand, she swept aside a thought so extraneous to her growing anguish.

She stretched slowly, as if that would suppress the panic progressively invading her. An ironic smile pursed her lips, dry and sore from being bitten, and she massaged her belly nervously. For she knew perfectly well this suffering that inevitably preceded the flow of large gushing blood clots. After two weeks of delirious hope, it almost always happened like this: the fetus absorbed itself, and when it did, she would withdraw in complete silence, which would intensify with her foul mood. All of her senses would then tune into that part of her body which, like a well-regulated clock, announced with precision the fatal hour when the foreign body would expel itself.

Once again, the child that Emilienne had so desired these past twelve years refused to form and to implant itself in her womb.

Her wide eyes turned toward the ceiling, as if she were staring at a haunted place, she glided her right hand over the side of the bed where her husband usually slept. A humiliating chill ran through her arm, which she pulled back with a sense of dread. In order to warm it, she wedged it, like a distended lump, between her thighs, pulled the sheet back over her head with the other hand, and, as if it were a cumbersome object, placed it awkwardly against the other.

Curled up like the little girl she wanted to be again, Emilienne felt shivers darting through all her wounded limbs. Her eyes, suddenly stinging, moistened. Spitting with rage, she clenched her teeth, a movement that only aggravated her state of mind, unable to hold back the stream of tears which in the past had poured silently down her ravaged cheeks over two premature wrinkles. This morning, a nervous twitch took hold of her eyelids, starting the flow with one treacherous tear from each eye. The two tears now joined, forming one large warm drop, and streamed slowly down her neck, then separated again, each one settling into a wrinkle. Emilienne, who for an instant had had her head propped between two pillows, abandoned herself to her grief.

How long had she been crying? She didn't know. And did not care. Besides, nothing mattered to her now, not even the time that had passed while she had been waiting . . . the time! The time! How long it is to wait for the one thing you most yearn for when you believe you no longer have time . . .

She jumped when someone knocked at the door. Before opening to that look of curiosity, to that face she hated more than anything, she had just enough time to run to the bathroom and splash water on herself. It was definitely her emotional state that the other's half smile seemed to peer into questioningly. Emilienne shot her a look of fury.

In order to get rid of her, she pretended to have a bad migraine and closed the door, not waiting for any comment. Overcome, belittled, and disgusted by the walls and objects in her room, witnesses to her emotional defeat and the deterioration her body had undergone, she had the feeling she no longer belonged to this world, as though she belonged to another. As when she suffered her bouts of depression, her troubled and agitated thoughts always brought her back abruptly to the one thing that was certain: she had to safeguard her marriage. No matter what the price, she needed to win back her husband who was drifting away from her.

She lay down again, this time on her left side, her tears flowing over the hollow of her ears before they fell onto the sheet. It was the tick-tock of the clock that brought her back to herself, reminding her that outside, life carried on. She stretched out again, but this time cracking her knuckles, and at last managed to drag herself out from under the sheets, pulling through this painful torment she was allowing to eat away at her like a person surrendering to a death sentence.

Emilienne tottered toward the window, drew the curtains, and raised the blinds. A misty rain was falling delicately upon the leaves of the almond trees along the fence. After last night's storm, dead leaves and almonds were strewn about the lawn.

To this day, Emilienne could not figure out her husband's attachment to these trees, so messy they needed cleaning up after almost every day. It must be the shade they provided. Though, if the company that employed her didn't tend to the maintenance of their villa, they wouldn't have been able to afford all of their domestic help. The way of life in Kampana required executives to have their own household staff and security. The high-level executives didn't think twice about hiring, in addition to the cook, a gardener and a driver for school-aged children. Emilienne and her husband had all such help working for them, except the driver. The gardener took care of garbage collection and watered the vast lawn during the dry season. Twice a week, the landscaper and his helpers came to mow the grass and trim and care for the plants and the various flowerbeds.

"What good is all of this to me?" the young woman asked herself, moving away from the window. "I live behind the walls of my problems, and all the rest is nothing but décor."

She scanned the room with a melancholy gaze before stopping on the triple mirror that covered an entire wall and reflected, on the opposite wall, two large wedding photos and a nude by a mysterious painter who hadn't thought it necessary to sign his work.

She raised her eyes and imagined it was night. At the same time, a soft, filtered light shone in from the false ceiling covered with gathered fabric spread out like a fan. Emilienne lowered her head and turned, with regret, toward the hollow left in the mattress by her body. The flowered bedspread in shades of green matching the fabric on the ceiling trailed on a pale green, fluffy carpet. A miserable smile formed on her lips when her eyes considered the nightstands, the bed frame, and the chest of drawers all made of white lacquered particle board with polyester varnish: an order placed with Furniture France to mark the "spectacular" significance of their first paycheck. For everything to have matched in their room, they would have had to change the wood frames of the windows and closets and painted them glossy white.

Emilienne searched her failing memory feverishly for the pallid ghosts of the passionate love they'd once shared, which had sometimes brought tears to her eyes and at other times provoked cries of passion. Sadly, only fleeting images of these intimate moments—now so distant—remained. A few, however, were more vivid. One night, in the elevator of a small hotel, Joseph, who was only her lover at the time, had ripped off all her clothes in a fit of passion, and, covering her with sensual kisses, carried her into an anonymous room decorated entirely in white. He had then placed her delicately on the carpet before demonstrating all his talents as a lover. The pleasure was so intoxicating it almost brought her pain.

During the following months, Emilienne had such a glow that her close friends watched her with wonder. Her complexion was more radiant, her health sound, and her energy contagious. She took on an enchanting self-assurance. "Only love can bring about such a transformation in a woman," her college friends noted observantly. These remarks made Emilienne feel on top of the world. She not only thought but knew that nothing could threaten her happiness, not even death. To reassure herself that this intoxicating love was real, she would literally jump on Joseph and kiss and touch him all over each time they would meet. Like a cat on its mistress's lap, he would coo and purr and shimmy all over.

Emilienne shook her head vigorously in an effort to blot out the devastation these memories brought upon her; she turned away from the bed and headed into the bathroom. In the shower, the cold water revived her body. She would have stayed under the water if she hadn't had to get to the office. And so, with reluctance, she stepped over the edge of the tub. And even before she had managed to bring her other foot over, her weight had nearly sprawled her out across the tile floor. How many pounds had she gained since she married? Each time she looked at the scale, she was seized with anxiety. The scale had become a toy on which the children hopped on and off, those rare times they entered her room. She would have thrown it away long ago if her husband hadn't objected.

With vexation she faced the mirror framed with spotlights and fiddled with the soft, fatty flesh hanging from her arms, belly, and thighs. She truly could not bear the sight of this other self, with whom she did not identify. She moved away from the mirror, a bad taste in her mouth, and went to get a white pleated skirt suit from the closet. Turning her back to the wall-length mirror, she undid her braids, combed her hair back to the nape of her neck, and rolled it up, holding it in place with small hairpins. The feel of this dull, dry hair, which at one time had been a major asset, worsened her mood. It didn't matter whether the bun was tied neatly at her neck; she didn't want to see herself again in a mirror for the rest of the day. Quickly she applied a layer of lipstick, put on her black shoes, and took a shoulder bag of the same color out of the closet.

As she opened the door, she found herself face to face with Eyang, her hand raised, about to pound on the door. A habit she was not about to break in spite of her son's reproaches, which always ended on the same note:

"Good grief! You really are deaf. Don't you ever hear us when we answer? One of these days I'm going to have to bring you in to get your ears checked."

"Oh, but you are going to work, aren't you! Your silence made me worry."

She managed to poke her head through the half-open door just as Emilienne, infuriated, was closing it again.

She looked at her cunningly and replied in a dry tone, "He didn't come home last night. Didn't you notice earlier? Just take a look in the garage."

Eyang retreated, shoulders back, giving an elusive look. "Why, it seems she wants to avoid the conflict this morning!"

Emilienne slammed the door and locked it, then, with an angry spring in her step, left the house.

Once inside the car, she placed her hand again on her belly. The pain was worsening near the navel, more acute, as if a razor blade were cutting into her inner organs. "Between now and this evening it will have completely disintegrated," she grumbled to herself. "There will be nothing left but my useless uterus." With her elbow on the car's windowsill and her other hand absently stroking the steering wheel, Emilienne waited patiently on Charles de Gaulle Boulevard for the light to turn green.

The dense fronds of the majestic coconut and date palms lining the boulevard were swaying gently and with an irregularity in sync with the wind and a misty, capricious rain. The first morning customers and late workers, hunched under their umbrellas, were running swiftly across streets and past storefronts. On the road, the line of cars stretched endlessly, as happened each time it rained. The most impatient drivers honked restlessly, causing a racket that aggravated the young woman's already tried nerves. Luckily, she forgot the traffic and noise quickly, locking herself into thoughts of her past, which did not take long to emerge clearly in her mind. Her love story streamed before her as if projected on a giant screen. She had fully retrieved the memory.

After dating for a year during their university studies in Paris, the young couple had decided to get married. In accordance with custom, they went to each of their families during vacation to announce their news.

The bride- and groom-to-be, having planned to meet in a bar in the city, went first to the home of the widow Eyang. She was about fifty years old at the time, full-figured and full of vitality. She dressed simply but wore her clothes with a dignified grace. Besides, she was naturally distinguished, a refinement noticeable in the way she held her head, the way she walked and gestured with slow and steady movements. Her facial features, offset by a page boy cut, were rather ordinary. Her husband had just passed away, and she clung desperately to her son, who, up to that point, had been purely a source of great pride and fulfillment.

Joseph adored her, and if he performed well in his studies, it was in part to keep from disappointing her. She was living in a working-class neighborhood with her daughter, five years younger than Joseph. The wooden house had good ventilation and was neat and tidy. The furniture, modest yet well maintained, took on a certain value in such a setting. After Joseph introduced his fiancée to her, she reacted in a fit of rage that her son had never known her capable of.

"You will not marry a girl from *that* ethnic group as long as I live!"

To emphasize her disapproval, she'd hissed loudly, directing her disdainful gesture at the inside of her son's legs. The lovers had exchanged stunned looks.

"If it is truly I who created you and carried you in this belly for nine months," resumed his mother, vigorously tapping her midsection several times, "I forbid you to see that *person* ever again. Do you not know that those people look down on us and believe they are more sophisticated than us? I wonder sometimes if they're not sick in the head. We have pretty, well-educated girls, too. They're waiting for you to take an interest in them instead of setting your eyes on that . . ."

The incomplete sentence barely out of her mouth, she'd looked Emilienne up and down and with a brisk gesture pulled the flowing fabric of her dress between her thighs. The chair she was sitting on creaked each time she shifted her weight. She resumed her knitting furiously.

Emilienne, who understood their language perfectly well, could barely contain her exasperation. She blinked her eyelids heavily. Joseph smiled and gave her a knowing wink. She composed herself. Teeming with rage though remaining outwardly calm, Joseph responded:

"Such disgraceful behavior is beneath you, Mother. I am ashamed. I'll marry Emilienne as soon as we get back to France. Do you realize you've just lost a son? Unless you apologize, I will no longer speak to you. Don't worry; I'll continue to live at home until I leave, for appearances' sake."

For a brief moment Emilienne had thought she'd seen Eyang's short hair stand on end and her hands shake. When she was about to turn back toward Joseph, she saw the old woman brandish the knitting needle and hurl it at her son, who dodged it in the nick of time. The needle had pierced the wooden wall.

On the side of the road, where they were waiting for a taxi, the young woman, still deeply unnerved, snuggled up to her fiancé.

"If she wasn't your mother, I would have given her a good slap." Then, altering her tone, she asked, "What are we going to do? What if she curses us?"

"Don't worry; she can't do us any harm. I love my mother a lot, but I had to react the way I did. Let's see your parents instead. Were they at home when you left?"

"They were there at two o'clock. In any case my mother will be there. She hardly ever goes out."

"I hope they aren't cantankerous as well."

THE TAXI had dropped them at the entrance to the doctors' residential community, which was surrounded by a wire fence. The villas were enormous modern constructions. Brick footpaths separated rows of houses. Some tenants had planted a hedge of flowers in order to create a sense of privacy for their homes.

The kitchen door, which faced an outdoor courtyard, was wide open. Passersby could see Rondani crushing bananas with a pestle and mortar from outside. Emilienne entered the kitchen alone; the aroma of wild boar stock simmering on the stove filled the air.

"That smells good!" the young woman exclaimed, opening the lid. "I have a feeling I'm in for a treat tonight. Can you wash your hands and take off that apron for a moment, Mama? I want to introduce you to someone."

"It's not the time to receive company, my child; and who is it you want to introduce to me?"

"My fiancé," Emilienne announced, bearing an enigmatic smile.

The mortar had slipped out of her mother's hands and rolled onto the floor.

"It's about time, my child. I was beginning to worry about your lack of interest in marriage. Have him come in through the other door. He mustn't see me like this."

Rondani washed her hands quickly, wiped away the sweat that beaded her forehead, and carelessly threw the apron on the stool she'd just gotten up from.

Joseph, all the while, was familiarizing himself with the things around the house. Everything inside seemed to date back to another era: the armchairs with bamboo vines drooping along their contours, ceramic plates dulled by time, and hazy photos in plastic frames.

"Hello, Son." Rondani held out her hand to Joseph.

A glimmer in her eyes and a wide smile lit up her face, making her look a good ten years younger.

RONDANI RAN OVER to an old wooden cabinet, opened it with a clatter, and took out a bottle of whiskey and three glasses. When she bent over to place the tray down, she stumbled on the foot of the small serving table. She lost her balance and would have ended up flat on the floor if Joseph hadn't hurried to catch her. The glasses and bottle clinked against one another but did not break.

The shot of whiskey she served Joseph spilled on the cloth embroidered with butterflies that covered the table.

"Excuse my clumsiness, dear children, it's not every day that I host a future son-in-law," she said ironically.

Emilienne smiled at her mother and squeezed Joseph's hand gently. Rondani began the process again, this time with more control over her movements. She asked the two newly engaged to raise their glasses. She drank hers in one gulp—she never drank alcohol when she was alone but didn't hold back when she had visitors.

Calmly, the young man began to speak:

"I am very happy to meet you, Mama Rondani, and am sorry that Papa Openda is not here. I don't know if we should wait for him to come back from work or save this conversation for another day."

Perked up by the alcohol, Rondani studied Joseph closely. "This young man is very fine," she concluded, rubbing her hands together conspicuously.

"As you'd like, my child, but I believe he'll be coming back late tonight. Since he became a doctor, he sees certain patients at their homes after his work at the hospital. He doesn't even rest on the Lord's Day anymore. One thing I don't agree with him on. Anyway! My daughter has just told me you want to get married. What is your name, Son, and which part of the country do you come from? It's becoming difficult these days to distinguish between those who come from the North, the Central region, or the South. You speak only French these days, even with family." She smiled at Joseph as she settled comfortably into the armchair.

"My name is Eyang Joseph, and I am from the North. My mother . . ."

He stopped speaking when he saw Rondani's shoulders slump. The look in her eyes, confident and full of delight a few moments earlier, became shifty. The smile frozen on her lips made her look dazed. Her only response to what he had said was to get up and order her daughter curtly to follow her into the bedroom.

"What is wrong with you? Has he cast a spell on you or what?" she began after she'd shut the door and flopped on the bed. "Don't tell me that you want to sully our lineage by marrying a foreigner. None of your ancestors married a woman from that region. Even my grandfather, who couldn't keep his pants on and left bastard children all over the country, didn't go that far. He never, do you understand me, ever unbuttoned his fly in front of a woman from that region. As you can well imagine, that would be known; it's perfectly simple, he would have been the first to tell. And you, my daughter, a university-educated young woman, you're the one who wants to poison our pure blood! Do you know that the children you have, if you have children with him, wouldn't even be yours?!"

Faced with her daughter's mocking smile, Rondani went on: "For those people, children belong to their fathers and uncles. You see, my daughter, it's better to forget this idea right now and not get into such a degrading situation. And that's not all; I'm going to explain something else to you: they marry our daughters out of revenge. Yes, yes, it's no laughing matter; they're retaliating for having been our slaves. My great-grandfather had hundreds of them. It's not by . . ."

"Stop, already," Emilienne chided, standing up. "Tell me,

Mama, wouldn't that make you yourself the great-granddaughter of a slave? And, anyway, do you even know where you're from? Maybe from a grandparent who supported the slave trade by trading his own brothers for bad tobacco and a gun with no ammunition? You don't know what you're saying anymore. It's because I am a woman of my time that I don't want to get caught up in these issues straight out of the Middle Ages. We're in the 1980s now, and *you* are still talking to me about the slaves your great-grandfather might have had. We have got to move on!"

She was pacing around the room, her arms crossed behind her back—a habit she got from her father.

"You're in a good position to know that men from here are very authoritarian—which, I'd like to point out, is not true of Joseph—and they have the unfortunate habit of walking all over their women. Such behavior in no way implies vengeance on their part. I don't understand you."

Before continuing, she went over, sat down next to her mother, and stared into her eyes.

"Can you tell me what your precious ethnicity has that is better than any others'? In the social setting that you defend so aggressively, constantly extolling its so-called virtues, I see nothing but a superiority complex fed by selfishness and jealousy. The children we will have—and we will have them, whether you like it or not—will be ours. I am determined to marry a man and not a family. I want you to understand once and for all that I love him and that it is with him that I intend to share the rest of my life. What is the problem, then, that you and Joseph's mother have? She is suffering from an inferiority complex, while *you* look down on other citizens of your own country, propped up on a pedestal that you've created in your head. There is something really wrong in our society. And to say you call yourself a Christian! You make me want to throw up."

EMILIENNE WATCHED her mother, who with each sentence she uttered was gradually reaching her breaking point. Never before had she been so bold and disrespectful toward her. And she already regretted having gone so far. It was vital, however, to set forth her view with a compelling argument.

Rondani swallowed her saliva noisily and answered with unwavering resolve.

"If I've heard you well, the mother of your *fiancé*"—the word was pronounced in a disdainful tone that made her daughter's head spin—"is also against your marriage! Well, I am not surprised. Anyone in her right mind would not go against her beliefs and customs and abandon her pride simply in the name of love."

Unlike her usual demeanor in such circumstances, Rondani had remained relatively calm. It was not a good sign. The calm she maintained was more cause for alarm than if she had broken out in a fit of undue anger. Emilienne wanted to finish this conversation as quickly as possible.

"Listen to me carefully. I will marry Joseph despite everyone's objections. It's about time we change our attitudes. If you're surprised that we continue to be exploited by all the foreigners who come to this country, attitudes like yours provide the reason. If we aren't even in a position to build solid bonds between citizens of our own country, how can we hope to see a nationalist sentiment emerge in our capital city of Kampana? How can we find people motivated by the same spirit in the interest of our country? I wonder why I say all these things to you if you can't even understand. I am saddened to have to go against you, Mother. I don't expect Father will approve either. When you change your mind, you'll know where to find me, if I haven't gone back to France. Good-bye!"

She rushed out into her bedroom, throwing her clothes pell-mell into her suitcases. Her heart throbbing, feeling hurt and powerless, Rondani watched her daughter make her dramatic exit.

Emilienne's eyes glazed over as she recalled this long string of bitter memories. "The least one can say," she thought, "is that my marriage was doomed from the beginning." She parked her car in the garage reserved for administrators at the National Headquarters for Administrative Building Maintenance (NHABM). This large office building essentially oversaw the maintenance and repair of all of Kampana's administrative buildings. Consequently, it had local branches in all the big cities. No need to point here to the large sums of money that filled its coffers. Of course, all the company's managerial directors enjoyed hefty financial and material benefits.

To be a director at the NHABM was to have made it professionally and socially. The general manager was better paid than a secretary of state. As in all state-run companies, people were hired by presidential decree and released by another decree, either to be promoted to a higher—usually political—position or to lose everything and become a complete nobody.

Emilienne had gotten her job as managing director of administrative affairs through her connection with an old university colleague, originally from the region where she was born, who had become a government minister. When a new general manager was named a year ago, company output fell slightly and, consequently, so did revenue. When replacement of lower management with members of his own family and protégés of influential men wasn't enough for him, Monsieur Poutou embezzled money from the company and slowed business down. Some had said that in a few years—or even a few months—the company would be on the verge of bankruptcy. While awaiting the petition for bankruptcy, the supervisory staff, well aware of the situation, was helping itself to the money while naturally taking all necessary precautions.

As Emilienne passed through the halls of the NHABM, she noticed half of the offices were closed. Only the expats were at their desks. Clearly, they'd left their doors open intentionally. The locals always came to work an hour or even two after the official opening time.

In her managerial capacity, the young director had tried, in vain, to institute discipline among the personnel by leaving memos and warning letters.

One day, a company executive came to see her and roughly said the following:

"It is entirely to your credit to seek to reform the employees. I, too, had principles when I arrived at this office. I firmly believed that each employee was to carry out his task with discipline and work efficiency for the good name of our company. In addition, I used to tell myself that I was working not only for myself but, more important, for the nation, which needs the help of all its children. Favoritism and the injustice of our leaders taught me a lesson quickly, however. Now, I am happy doing my work without diligence and without doing more than I have to. I learned that I alone would not change people's ways. And neither will you. Let me to give you some advice: file your good intentions away in one of your desk drawers."

Two days later, Emilienne was the object of intimidation. The higher-ups barely even attempted to mask their threats. They made sure she understood it was in her interest to look the other way, shut her mouth, and close her ears to certain situations that had no impact on her own duties. As the old adage goes, *a single finger cannot wash the whole face.*

After serious reflection, Emilienne decided it was better to keep her position. Unemployment of the university-educated workforce was no longer limited to industrialized countries; it was already affecting the Third World. This fact got one of the company's employees going, his comments seizing Emilienne's attention so firmly that she reflected upon them for a long while. The gist of what he said was this:

"What would our states do if those with a head well filled and a hollow stomach waved placards in the streets? One thing's for sure: such a protest would paint the sociopolitical landscape a different color, and many a country would suffer grave repercussions no one wants to see."

SHE SAT DOWN in her office. The room was large with a bay window. The beige textile mural, the furniture, and the brown carpeting all contributed to the sense of a rigid work environment.

She leafed through the letters and memos her secretary had typed up. Speaking of her, a year after being hired, the secretary had come by her office one night before closing and recounted an anecdote that made Emilienne smile. When a few employees had gotten together in one of their offices, the youngest made the following comment:

"Don't you have the impression that our manager's work consists solely of writing memos?"

"So I'm not the only one who noticed!" exclaimed another. "She's up to her nine hundredth memo. We will have to suggest a party when she reaches the thousandth."

Quickly, Emilienne signed the few letters that were typed correctly, put the others in a file folder, and opened the voluminous dossier of job applications. To each, with a few short sentences wrapped up neatly with some polite formalities, she had to express her regrets and advise the applicants to reapply at a later date. Even though she knew that the new positions, if ever one were to open up someday, would be distributed discretely among those who were already close to the company's group of managing directors.

Very quickly, she composed a form letter. It was up to the secretary to personalize each version by adding the name of the applicant and the desired position. While she wrote, she half-heartedly ate a croissant, which her secretary had left on her table a short while ago, as she did each morning. And before the weekly meeting with the other managers, she called her secretary, who came right over, swaying her hips and walking on her tiptoes even though the heels she wore didn't really make her any taller. Stuffed into a snug, see-through white dress, she put on a big smile and stood immobile in front of her boss.

"Good morning, Madame!"

"Good morning, Dominique. You couldn't find more decent clothes to wear this morning?"

"Oh, Madame! I was in such a hurry that I grabbed the first outfit that jumped out at me," she replied in a shrill voice.

Only this morning Emilienne couldn't help herself from looking with awe at this young woman whose complexion and body were so nearly perfect her traits and silhouette would inspire more than one photographer.

"Dress more decently from now on," she said abruptly. "We are not here for a fashion show. Here, all these texts must be retyped," she added, passing her the heavy file folder. "Type this text up for me quickly."

She handed it to her, already absorbed in the local paper.

"Will do, Madame. I wanted to tell you I won't be coming back to work this afternoon. I have to take my daughter to the hospital."

Emilienne looked up, her mind elsewhere, then brushed this news aside and sent her secretary on her way. She had hired her on the urgent recommendation of her husband, who had explained that he needed to repay a very good friend who had helped him out in the past. He didn't give any further details about why he owed him, nor did he mention who this friend was.

Helping out this friend, who until then she didn't even know existed, was the first important favor her husband had ever dared to ask of her, and she couldn't refuse. And anyway, she thought, absolving herself of any guilt about it, what would be wrong with pulling a few strings on *her* application in light of the arbitrary hires she witnessed so regularly?

To avoid any ridicule for her choice, she took charge of the young woman's training. Although the result was not outstanding, she was satisfied with the efforts her protégée had made. She certainly had not become an excellent typist, nor was she any better a secretary. Her work was often careless.

Emilienne arrived in the conference room just as the general manager walked in. She took her seat between the director of human resources and the head of finance.

Having difficulty speaking over the loud drone of the air conditioner, Monsieur Poutou, in his thin, reedy voice, announced the day's agenda, which everyone knew already: to review personnel promotions by rank—despite the report the HR director had already prepared. Having never been able to speak in front of more than two people, he shook as he presented each employee's career plan, with both hands wedged between his legs.

Distracted, Emilienne listened with half an ear, scribbling notes on her notepad as her colleagues commented on the quality of personnel performance. She knew by force of habit that half of what was said would not go on record. Then, just as she decided to speak, a horrible pain jolted her, as if she had been pricked with a long needle piercing through her navel. With a violent thrust she bent over in her chair, put two hands over her belly, and held back the cries of the pain that were rising inside her. A distressing sensation quickly overcame her entire pelvic area. Her forehead was beaded with sweat.

"Uh . . . are you okay, Madame?" the human resources director asked, leaning over her.

"Are you sick?" inquired the general manager in turn. He stood up; then his colleagues did the same.

"I am not feeling well," Emilienne muttered, still doubled over, her teeth clenched. "Please allow me, gentlemen, to excuse myself," she managed to add as she stood up with great difficulty.

"Of course," Monsieur Poutou continued, "go home. You are clearly having a malaria attack. Take good care of yourself, and don't forget that this illness can still be fatal these days."

Her teeth and fists clenched, she stood up courageously and left, her legs unsteady. She was upset at herself for having been the object of such a spectacle. Through the day, everyone would learn that she'd felt ill at this meeting. The managers were known for a certain lack of discretion. That was how they kept up on idle gossip around the city.

The pain was spreading—to her pelvis, spinal column, and knees. Emilienne arrived at her office right as Dominique was placing the work she'd just finished on the table. With one last effort she gave her secretary some tasks to do and shut the door.

Seated on a folding chair in the garden, Eyang had dozed off under a pale sun. When she heard the sound of the car, she quickly scurried over to the hallway leading to the bedrooms and hid behind one of the doors. She placed her hand over her heart, which was beating loudly after such a hurried walk. Once she regained her calm, the old woman walked toward Emilienne as she headed straight for her room.

"Is it already noon?" she asked, surprised, standing in front of her daughter-in-law.

"Let me by," Emilienne murmured as she opened the door.

Eyang entered the room with her. Completely sapped of energy, she grabbed onto one of the closet doorknobs to support herself. Without waiting for her mother-in-law to leave, she unbuttoned her jacket, fingers trembling, and then stood facing Eyang, who, seeing her face contorted with pain, took two steps back.

"You still have your migraine?"

"Yes," the young woman said harshly, through clenched teeth.

"That's not all," Eyang went on brusquely. "The children

have got to eat when they return from school." She carried on, her feet planted firmly on her spot on the carpet: "The cook and the housekeeper didn't come this morning. There is no food ready. I did the housecleaning and, believe me, with my rheumatoid arthritis, it isn't easy for me. I don't know why Joseph wastes money paying those people."

EMILIENNE'S ONLY ANSWER was to show her mother-in-law the door. Once she was alone again, she let go of the door handle and locked herself in the room. The sound of a saucepan crashing onto the floor filled her ears as she slipped on a nightshirt. As she headed slowly toward the bed, she tripped over the clothes Joseph had left strewn across the floor. She hadn't seen them when she came in. "Well!" she actually had the time to think as she stumbled, "He came home to change, anyway."

In thirteen years of marriage, her husband still hadn't learned to put his clothes away. At the beginning of their marriage, his sloppiness had really irritated her, and she had tirelessly called him on it. He had made a noteworthy effort for a few years, but the old bad habit had crept back since he'd been spending time with his mistress. It seems a lover's role is not to mold a man. In any case, Emilienne made up her mind. She picked them up when she felt like it, and when she was in a rebellious mood, she asked the housekeeper to do it.

In pain, she gripped the bed's headboard, then knelt down in order to regain her strength. She managed to grab the pillow, burrow her head down into it for a few moments, and, still on her knees, put her head—still sunken into the pillow—on the bed.

Her stomach was heating up and burning at the same time. Her limbs, chilled, tingled. She was uncomfortable in this position. It only accentuated her pain. She had to move, and her feet refused to comply! The messages her brain was sending were not reaching her limbs anymore. Would she be able to climb onto this bed? Who would have thought that she, Emilienne, would find herself one day in such a state of physical affliction? Why was she suffering so? *We must never mock the misfortunes of others,* her father always said. *The same thing could happen to us when we least expect it.*

The memory of a terrible act she had committed as a carefree child brought a grim smile to her face! One day, while playing with her friends on the riverbanks of the village where she'd been born and raised, a puny old man with a proverbial hernia passed by. You could see the weight of this heavy load—unusual for a man—dangling back and forth at the crotch of his pants as he walked along. Emilienne ran to find a sharp twig, then, approaching the old man, stuck it in the ground and used all her might to break it. The old man jumped about three feet in the air, holding his intimate parts with both his hands. Doubled over in agony, he wailed a distorted cry of pain. That was one of the sorts of malicious acts kids would innocently perform in the village. How he must have been miserable, how he must have suffered, Emilienne thought.

She moved one knee forward, then the other. They were against the bed now. Picking herself up, she gently raised her left foot, placed it on the bed, then proceeded to do the same with the other, and forcefully heaving her body, shifted toward the middle of the bed.

The effort she'd just made caused her to sweat profusely, and the sweat absorbed instantly into her pillowcase. She remembered she had some sedatives in the drawer of the nightstand. She needed a glass of water to swallow them. Too bad! She would have to endure the pain. After all, didn't she deserve this suffering? Doesn't the saying go, we reap the seeds we sow? What seeds could she have sown so badly in her life to deserve such a rotten harvest? Her torment was not a result of the excruciating pain a woman feels giving birth, one that disappears and is replaced by the sense of extreme joy the mother feels when she holds her child in her arms. No, her torment was barren and left her only with a feeling of insurmountable guilt. It was the kind of pain that makes a woman uglier, makes her wither, makes her bitter and mean because she has failed where others have succeeded.

Once again, overcoming her pain, Emilienne asked herself the only questions that would take her mind away from her body for an instant. "What do I have to do to get him back? Would the birth of a second child make him abandon that woman? Oh, God! What wouldn't I try to straighten out our marriage, to make it pure and everlasting! I am lacking in strength and shrewdness. How do I fight when I am unaware of what the end of this battle will look like and how it will come about? But yes," she told herself nodding her head ardently, "that's exactly it." She tossed and turned and wrung her hands in despair. "I must give him a son who looks like him." She rubbed her forehead against the pillow as if it would destroy the sharp pangs in her stomach. "So how do I bring him into the world when I am incapable of facing and fighting whatever it is that seems to be crushing my innards and every fetus that forms inside of me?! I've tried every imaginable concoction prescribed by the best traditional doctors in this country: I've had my fill drinking and eating all their potions." The very last one she'd gone to see, at her mother's behest several years ago, told her after six months of fruitless treatment: "My child, your enemies have more strength than my plants. There is a devouring animal inside your stomach, and as soon as you begin to form children, it gnaws them to bits. It would be dishonest of me to continue your treatment. Try to go to Benou. Most women who come back from there become pregnant within a month or two."

That evening, Emilienne had come back home determined never to spend another cent on her stomach. But now, the need to procreate was once again becoming a priority. And hidden behind that need was the relentless desire to win back her husband. Although it wasn't even clear whether she herself knew which took higher priority.

SUDDENLY, A VIOLENT wrenching brought her back to her body. Was it her uterus or her cervix? She couldn't tell. *It doesn't matter,* she thought, biting her lips to stifle the scream mounting in her throat. She felt a kind of heaviness descend in her, and before she could find a comfortable position for this expulsion she'd felt coming since the morning, the warm, sticky liquid flowed dully between her thighs, stiff and slightly apart.

In a movement of restless revolt, Emilienne folded her knees and crossed her feet. The sticky liquid continued to seep out ceaselessly, covering the area around her vagina and anus and spreading on the sheets. Panic-stricken, she thrashed about, kneaded her belly, which would betray her to the very end. Yet nothing could stop the flow. Her strength diminished and her nerves at their end, she finally relaxed her body and allowed herself to empty out. The room began spinning around her. For a brief moment, the bed appeared to be suspended from the ceiling, her head turned toward an abyss. Keeping her eyes closed, she clung to the edge of the bed, when, all of a sudden, she jolted as vomit made its way up from her chest, came rushing into her throat, and, finally, invaded her mouth. She forced herself to open her eyes and make a run for the bathroom. She did not make it in time. The acidic liquid spurted out of her mouth all over her sheets. Small chunks of croissant mixed with her blood on the sheets made her vomit deep brown in color. The odor gave off a putrid and foul stench she could not bear, causing what seemed an endless cycle of continuous nausea and vomiting.

Emptied out at both ends, Emilienne allowed the bubble that was blocking her throat to burst, and she bawled. And long after her tears had dried, she continued to moan. From time to time, she used the back of her hand to wipe away the mucous drizzling from her nose toward her mouth. She had a sallow look in her eyes, which fell indifferently onto her soiled sheets, spattered with the debris of fetal remains.

She stayed there for a long while, sitting with her knees still scrunched up by her chin, tapping and caressing her legs with her fingers. As she raised her head slowly to stifle this pitiful image of herself, she was seized with great panic. She did not see herself in the mirror. She rubbed her eyes vigorously, opened them wide. No! The curves of her body, hunched over, did not appear in front of her. Did she still have a body, an image, a reflection? Was everything within her in the process of disintegrating, disowning, and repudiating her? Her blood, her tears, the content of her stomach, and even her image!

Observing this void, Emilienne had the impression she was floating, disappearing. She had become what she had never ceased being without noticing: an ethereal body. At that moment she had the distinct sensation that her soul was abandoning her physical body. It was not that her spirit was rising so that she would reach a state of utter happiness. Was she dying? She remembered stories about certain dead people who had come back to life after their spirit had hovered for some time above their body. Hers, she didn't even see. Nor did she have the feeling of being happier or more serene. Quite the contrary; she now had the impression she was struggling, fighting off frightful forces. And what if she were one of these wretched souls destined to wander eternally in a whirlwind of anguish? At least she would be able to boast of having known hell, not only on earth, but between earth and heaven! As if one can take pride in suffering . . .

After that unending moment of drifting, of struggling, the young woman, little by little, regained her five senses. She could once again feel her flesh. In turn, the objects around her returned to normal. As she could not stay sprawled out on her bed for the rest of the day, she decided to get up, drew the drapes, and, staggering, headed toward the bathroom. A thick, blackish blood clot poured out of her onto the floor tiles, leaving her with a feeling of emptiness in her stomach. She felt lighter, though, very light, like a dry leaf. With a detached and resolute air, she took a cloth out of the cabinet to clean the floor and wiped up the slimy puddle. For the second time, she stepped over the edge of the tub, and this time sat down.

"What is the use of taking care of my body when it can't carry out its most fundamental task?" she grumbled as she adjusted the water faucets. "Everything in me is emptying, drying up and falling apart. Soon, I will be the mere remains of my reflection. And to say in spite of it all that I should take care of this barren flesh. For whom and for what must I put up with all these petty annoyances? The man I love no longer even notices my shadow. In such circumstances, how could he even describe the clothes on my back when in the rare moments we've actually crossed paths in this house he has turned his back on me? Am I not merely part of the décor now, décor that he is so used to seeing that he no longer pays attention to it and could just throw away without thinking twice about it!"

THE THOUGHT that it wouldn't be long before he got home made her jump. For she knew he would come back. Every time he came back to change clothes in the morning after spending several days and nights at his mistress's, he picked up the kids at school and brought them back to the house. A good way for him to make himself—or make himself think he is—useful. "Why aren't they back yet? So, it isn't 1:30pm yet?! Fine, I must hurry. For nothing in the world will I let him see the sheets soaked with my decomposing feminine waste." Very quickly she dried herself off and ran to remove any trace of the waste expelled from her body. The mattress, luckily, was not soiled, thanks to the rubber sheet protecting it—Joseph had been against this measure, which reminded him of his childhood. His mother had put it on his bed until he was fourteen.

Rummaging through one of the dresser drawers, she found an old plastic bag and hurriedly stuffed the stained sheets in it. Still racing around, she threw on a housecoat, remade the bed, and went out to throw her bulky package into the trash.

Joseph's car idled in front of the gate.

II

Nameless Despair

Leaning against the kitchen door by the garage, watching him get out of the car, she was suddenly overcome with emotion. Everything around her faded away.

Emilienne's eyes examined every part of his body. A beige gandoura from Senegal draped naturally over his six-foot-one frame, leaving visible only the bottoms of his pants of the same color. Beige rubber sandals protected his delicate feet. He had been wearing African garb for a long time now. "It makes me feel cooler," he liked to say, "and it is my way of returning to our roots." His short, wavy hair had a brilliant sheen.

When he raised his eyebrows, three creases would form on his forehead, making him look virile and irresistible. His grey eyes fell coldly upon his wife, his short, straight nose flared, and his full lips quivered. Emilienne, on the watch for this look, grew tense. Nevertheless, she gave him a sincere smile, because she was truly happy to see him again, although she was also still a little annoyed.

They had last seen each other three weeks ago, and only for two hours. He had made love to her like a drunkard throwing himself at a prostitute he'd picked up off some obscure roadside. Emilienne didn't hold it against him. There are some humiliations that only a woman can withstand, with stubbornness, if she wants to achieve a specific goal she has set for herself. All she had wanted was the physical contact that, as it turned out, had just now resulted in some blood clots on a couple of white sheets thrown into a small plastic bag, now at the bottom of a waste bin.

Oblivious to her welcoming smile, Joseph asked point-blank:

"Didn't you notice that your daughter isn't with the other children?"

Emilienne continued to smile, but this time scornfully. "Unbelievable. Where does he get this confidence?" she thought to herself before responding:

"Seems like you are not happy to be home, Joseph. As for Rékia, no, I don't think she's back, or she'd have come to my room to give me a hug."

"That's all you have to say. You're not even worried. I can't believe this. I must be dreaming!"

"Come on, that is not the only thing I have to do!" Emilienne hurled back.

"She hasn't come home," Eyang added, following the couple's quarrel intently from the kitchen.

"I can see that you're taking good care of your daughter," Joseph bellowed. "As a matter of fact, I really wonder *what* you still care about in this house. Your daughter hasn't come home, and you in your haughtiness don't seem to care. Your self-centeredness is seriously starting to get on my nerves."

Emilienne's heart beat so fast it was almost deafening. Even though she recognized the truth in her husband's remarks, she could not help striking back:

"I find it unacceptable that you would use this tone with me in front of your nephews and your mother. And besides, you are not in any position to tell *me* what I should be doing," she retorted and turned away, her blood boiling from his fierce look.

Joseph, scandalized, slammed the car door, which until that moment he had held ajar, and came over and stood in front of his wife.

"I wonder what would become of the children if I were not here. Every time I come home, there's some kind of problem."

He avoided brushing against her as he entered the house.

"Oh *please*!" his wife cried, "how egotistical!"

The Joseph who returned in a few minutes was calmer, concerned.

"Where can she be at this hour?" he worried aloud, stroking his head.

Emilienne, who up to this point had not moved, turned

toward him, her face also marked with worry and concern. Their alarmed looks weighed on one another, each with a gaze that penetrated the other and turned away. The pale sun that had loomed a moment ago went down. A thick veil of clouds passed over the house. Their dog, as if sniffing a threat, curled up between the legs of his mistress.

"Well, what are we waiting for?" his wife said, breaking the silence. "Let's look for her. Mama Eyang, give the kids something to eat!"

As though aware of the general sense of panic around her, Roxanne left Emilienne and went over to her master, nuzzling his pant legs. His forehead wrinkled with worry, Joseph half-opened his mouth, then thought better of it, seeing the look of dread on his wife's face. "I hope nothing's happened to her! She is the only thing still holding us together," he thought to himself.

"Let's go," he said aloud.

Roxanne turned in circles, whimpering.

"Come, Roxanne," Nomé called, drawing her attention to him.

Finally happy that someone in this house was showing her some attention, Roxanne pawed at him teasingly as the little boy petted her tenderly.

In this family, the dog held an important position. She was the silent witness to their sadness and quarrels, the confidante who would listen as they poured their hearts out and the beneficiary of all the tenderness that men, her masters, no longer knew how to give one another. Of course there were also times, like today, when she was ignored, but such indifference never lasted long.

No sooner had Emilienne sat down next to Joseph in the car than they were off. They headed toward the high school in silence, each lost in his and her thoughts, which eventually brought them both back to their child. As if imploring the heavens to return her child unharmed, Emilienne raised her eyes toward the somber sky just as lighting streaked it, followed immediately by the rumbling of thunder. Soon large drops of water were pelting the roof of the car as they drove through deserted streets.

They passed several vehicles of high-ranking state officials and business executives who were returning home. Finally, they parked in front of the imposing entrance to the high school grounds.

"Wait for me in the car. There's got to be someone inside who can tell me something."

He opened the gate and ran toward the first buildings to take shelter from the torrential rains. His clothes, now dripping wet, clung to his skin. With a worried look, Emilienne followed him with her eyes until he disappeared inside the school.

ALONE, HER PANIC MOUNTING, her face tense, she stared so intently at the gate that two little tears sprang from her dilated pupils. She tried with all her might to convince herself that Joseph would bring back their child, or at least tell her she was being kept in by the teacher or simply delayed by the preparations being made for next month's national holiday parade.

Her second trimester grades were not good. Her mother could not understand this dip in her school performance, as she had been among the brightest students in her class ever since elementary school. Her presence and her success at school had softened the despair of the mother, long neglected by her father. For many years, Rékia had been the only person who brought her bursts of joy, reinvigorating her with new energy each time. But this did not keep her later from blaming the girl, deep down, for not being a boy. She reasoned with herself, knowing that it was too idealistic to believe that the birth of a child could substitute for the love and presence of a man.

Emilienne adored the baby who had brought her joy and pride those first years after she was born. She had also grown closer to her husband, whose surges of affection melted her heart just as much if not more. For her, and although she didn't realize it right away, the intensity of the love she felt for her child depended on how much love she was getting from her child's father. Looking back, she fully understood that her affection for her daughter had been tinged by a certain reserve the day she realized her husband had a mistress, though, at the same time, she also became her refuge. This also explained her fits of aggression when her daughter sought her attention. She realized with bewilderment that the child did not truly hold the place in her heart she should have.

"Oh! My God! Have I been a bad mother? While many mothers seem to find their happiness in their children, I look to find it instead in a man. Am I abnormal?"

How happy they were when she was born! Her birth ten months after the wedding had dissipated the fear that their parents might have cursed them. Since no one had approved of their union, the young couple had closed themselves off in a cocoon that kept them safe. They had lavished their daughter with all the affection and love they were capable of giving.

In part because of this affectionate protection in her formative years, Rékia had been a cheerful child, stable and well behaved. By the time she was two years old, she was able to express herself better than most children her age. The only gloomy period of her childhood had begun with the arrival of the first dog her parents had gotten. Jealous of the attention they were giving the animal, Rékia became short-tempered and began wetting her bed; eventually, she even fell seriously ill. Emilienne and Joseph had to leave them both alone, and gradually the child became attached to the dog. Her attachment then became so strong that she would sometimes let it sleep in her bed.

One by one, as if by common agreement, Eyang, Rondani, and Openda made up with their children. Openda, more than the others, became especially fond of his granddaughter, who, he constantly repeated, resembled his deceased mother.

SEEING HER HUSBAND come back alone, running through the rain, Emilienne clenched her fists. Her nails dug deep into her palms.

"Where is she?" she yelled opening the door.

As he got back into the car, he replied calmly:

"No one has seen her since she left school yesterday," he said as he closed the gate. "So she must have disappeared this morning after bringing her cousins to school."

Furious, Emilienne retorted dryly:

"I have always been against your idea that letting them take the bus was a learning experience. Everyone, except you, knows that kidnappings are more and more prevalent. If something happens to my child, I am holding you responsible."

"You are sick in the head," her husband responded harshly. "And please don't forget that this child is mine, too. She disappeared between the school where she dropped off her cousins and the high school, a route she walks regularly. She did fine until now. And anyway," he added, changing his tone, "this is not the moment to rip each other apart. Instead let's put a missing persons alert on the radio and notify the police. We will find her," he concluded, attempting to sound persuasive.

"What will become of us if something has happened to her?" his wife shrieked, disoriented. "Do you think she's run away? For some time now she hasn't been talking much and has been eating very little . . . What if your double marital life has been getting to her! Maybe it's just puberty, or everything put together. Oh, how everything has changed!"

Emilienne shifted in her seat.

"Calm down. If any of your theories are true, I will gladly assume full responsibility for her running away." He took his wife's hand in his.

Emilienne felt herself melt. How long had it been since he'd touched her this way? Her eyes filled with tears! She was about to cry. "Rékia had to disappear in order for him to feel the need to come close to me," she thought.

The car came to a stop, and she found herself alone again. It was pouring. The water gushed down from the gutters onto the already flooded pavement, gathering all of the refuse from the street corners as it flowed along. Huge puddles had formed on the flat roadways. The cars drenched the passersby and hydroplaned at the slightest incline, spraying water and dragging everything in their paths. The visibility was very bad, and when Joseph had gotten out of the car, he had left the motor running and the wipers and AC on. So Emilienne could look around her and breathe easily.

They drove in silence from the radio station to the police precinct. The monotonous beating of raindrops on the roof of the car made the young woman doze off. Joseph squinted to see through the curtain of rain. The car glided occasionally across the pavement and at other times idled in the puddles.

THINKING THROUGH what he'd said about taking responsibility for their daughter's possibly running away, he realized he still refused to accept all the blame. When Rékia had been conceived, they had consulted every book and manual they could get their hands on about pregnancy and raising children. That was how they had learned that a child's upbringing begins in the womb, that a pregnant woman's diet and peace of mind, as well as her partner's attention and affection toward her, all contribute to the physical and mental health of a beautiful baby. Joseph did not fail in his duties, and he continuously encouraged his wife to follow the advice from those books. He even attended the birth—which was quite exceptional in this country. His wife's screams, despite the sedation of the epidural, pierced his heart. He was exhausted as though it had been he who had given birth that day.

Unlike his friends who abandoned their children to their mother, only showing up for brief moments before bedtime, he swaddled and bottle-fed his child. Only on this last point, in convincing his wife to breastfeed their daughter, had he been unsuccessful. "If we must have at least three children, I am not going to ruin my breasts with the first," she would explain untiringly. Often, he would leave the office early to be with his girls. The phrase "my girls" had a nice ring to his ears and held important meaning for him. At night, when Rékia cried and her mother was exhausted, he would rock her. The child slept more frequently in her father's arms than in her mother's, a bad habit that was difficult to correct later on. It was also he who led her around all the rooms in the house when she took her first steps.

"When did I start losing interest in them? Was it during the time I nearly lost my job, or when I took my first girlfriend? What was her name anyway? I don't even remember. There were so many after her! It's highly likely my apathy took root when Emilienne had her first round of miscarriages. How very odd a couple's life can be! Each passing day can contribute to strengthen the feelings and bonds that can either bring a couple together or draw them apart. We never realize it as it is happening. One morning, you realize that each spent the entire night alone doing his or her own thing and that this has been happening for several weeks. Searching frantically through our memories, we find with bitterness that many things are not going well. For example, for a long time now, we haven't even been telling each other about our days at work. One of us, just to annoy the other, gets the other's attention by hanging up the phone when the other is around or sharing important news with a friend while the other is within earshot. The other, while appearing to remain calm, is engulfed in jealousy and his pride is hurt.

"After several days of agonizing over the frightening discovery of our crumbling love, and after a minute analysis of our worsening relationship, one of us decides to solemnly put back the missing pieces and weave together the broken threads of our relationship. But then! That particular day the other is in a bad mood or quite simply isn't ready for this reconciliation at the same time. As if to discourage you, she launches into a monologue of complaints against you, and you are paralyzed. You file your good intentions away in your heart, so you can get them back out at a moment's notice to use against her if she reproaches you someday for your apathy. Hurt, you withdraw back into your pride and tell yourself that it takes two to make up. And if the other did not sense your good intentions, it's probably because she just doesn't care anymore. And yet . . . and yet all she had to do was be more perceptive that day, and read your face, detecting that glimmer promising to begin anew . . . What *would* actually happen if ever anything bad happened to Rékia? Touch wood," Joseph said to himself, tapping the steering wheel.

In spite of everything they'd just set in motion to find their daughter, their nerves were raw when they reached home. At least the radio would alert listeners all afternoon to their daughter's disappearance, and the following day as well if need be. A great number of children had already been found thanks to this radio station, so why not theirs? And the police, already on alert, must have begun their search.

They sat facing each other and ate their lunch reluctantly, only the occasional clattering of silverware on dishes breaking the silence. Outside, glints of a hesitant sun glimmered on the moist leaves of the plants in the yard. Seated nonchalantly on the folding chair on the terrace, overwhelmed by the somber thoughts that whirled around her old head, Eyang resisted the drowsiness attacking her this afternoon. Sprawled out next to her on a straw mat, Yvon snored. Roxanne slept with one eye open on the divan in the living room. From time to time she flicked her tail. In the bedroom, Nomé leafed through a comic.

"I'm calling the office to let them know I won't be in," Joseph announced as he got up from the table.

Meanwhile, to keep herself busy, Emilienne cleared the table. She also didn't want to bother the housekeeper who'd arrived just before the couple came back and was busy ironing. The cook's absence was a little troubling to the young woman given that since he'd begun working for them he had never missed work without letting them know ahead of time.

Instead of turning on the dishwasher, Emilienne decided to wash the few dirty dishes herself. It had been quite a while since she'd done such a chore, or any housework for that matter, except the weekend meals she continued to prepare to please the children, which they found tasted better than what the cook made.

For a little while, Joseph, too, enjoyed her concoctions. But now those same dishes didn't keep him home anymore. Just so the cook wouldn't outdo her with his culinary talent, Emilienne had bought Asian, French, and African cookbooks. Her tenaciousness could not possibly disappoint her husband, and had turned her into a cordon bleu chef. And because she was so able in the kitchen, she felt justified in her critique of a particularly skilled cook.

She would never dream of letting him go despite the fact that she found him ugly. To be so ugly was rare; he was perhaps even among the most repulsive of beings. In the beginning, his repulsive physique alone made her hesitant to hire him. "It's not a face you want to look at when you're pregnant again," her sister had commented back then.

This thought made Joseph double up with laughter. The young couple had just celebrated their wedding anniversary and were thinking about expanding their family with a second child. Only, here's the thing: Godwin had been working for them for over ten years, and still no second child!

EMILIENNE WAS DRYING the dishes when she distinctly heard Joseph in the living room: "Listen, darling . . ." Her heart began pounding. Her legs gave way under her body, suddenly heavy. Her husband's voice on the phone became more affectionate:

"I'm telling you, darling, my daughter didn't come home this morning. You can imagine my concern. Don't you think that you're going too far asking me to choose between my daughter and you? . . . Fine, fine, I'll call you tonight. No! I love you, listen to me . . ."

Emilienne clung to the kitchen sink. Her head was about to explode and her body became heavier. Leaning against the edge of the sink, the young woman brought both hands to her head. The deep disgust she felt for him along with the throbbing pain in her head made her nauseous. She spat profusely and turned on the faucet full force to drown out her husband's speech.

"How dare he call her darling, and in *this* house?! Is she so important to him that he needs to include her in our moment of crisis? And who does she think she is asking him to make a choice? I must be dreaming! I'm not hearing voices. It's definitely him on the phone!"

She shut off the water just as Joseph said:

"Kisses to you, you know where. See you very soon, my love."

Heavy tears of despair ran down the young woman's cheeks. "Just how far will he go to humiliate me? Isn't it enough that the entire city knows my husband has two homes? Must he now rub it in my face under my own roof?"

She gagged and ended up coughing up the little food she had barely managed to swallow earlier. "When am I going to stop emptying myself?" she muttered, straightening up. She wiped her face to remove any sign of her weakness and put the dishes away.

Walking into the living room, she found Joseph lying on the divan, his head resting on a pillow and his eyes closed. She knew him. If she dared ask him to explain his behavior, he would coolly deny that he'd called a woman—the nerve!

Emilienne stood watching him for a long time and concluded, to her astonishment, that he no longer belonged in this home. Was it the conversation he'd had earlier or the fact that he'd deserted their marriage that gave her this impression? Emilienne scanned the room; her eyes fell on each piece of furniture and then returned to her husband. No! He really no longer fit in with the décor, which, ironically, they had chosen together.

It was he, in fact, who had selected this three-seat divan and the three low armless chairs in white ribbed velvet, as well as this smoked glass shelf. And even buying the satin pillows in the colors of the national flag was his inspiration. Together they had selected the design for the living room in a catalogue: high windows overlooking a rectangular table and six chairs. They had then asked an independent contractor to build it all right there using local wood. The project matched the original design so perfectly that all their friends asked the name of the store that had sold it to them. The halogen lamps, however, came from France. The walls were covered with a softly patterned pale pink fabric. The curtain was made of veiled netting with a floral pattern on it, also made by a neighborhood tailor.

In those days Joseph found this part of the house particularly beautiful. Did he still think that now? Did he know that he had just shattered their intimacy forever by calling his mistress from what used to be their personal refuge?

EMILIENNE WENT OUT on the terrace, picked up little Yvon, who was still asleep, and brought him into his bedroom. Nomé had dozed off at the desk with his head resting on his comic book. She picked him up gently and put him on the bed next to his brother.

Standing over them, she watched as the two snored away in this room that had been destined for their second child. Nomé turned over and put his foot on his brother, who grumbled in his sleep. At their age, life had seemed beautiful and comforting to her, even though she was still somewhat troubled by her mother's laments for the brothers and sisters who had died. For a long time these moments of sadness hadn't affected her at all. She had felt protected and out of harm's way. But in this moment, she thought back on her mother's grief. In her own adult life, problems were building up at a troubling pace, not giving her a moment's rest. How long could she shoulder such heavy burdens? This evening, when her daughter came home, and she *would* come home tonight, she'd tell her how much she missed her and how much she loved her.

DEEP IN THEIR SLEEP, Yvon smiled and Nomé twitched his nose. Antoinette, Joseph's younger sister, had placed them in his care when the older one was five and the younger four. In fact to care for them was not exactly the proper term. Joseph had brought them over one night with an old dented cardboard suitcase containing their belongings. The next day, her sister-in-law, whom she always knew to be insipid and a little trite, came to thank her for agreeing to raise her children with an air of self-confidence and elegance that paralyzed her. She was sure, she had continued, that they would get a very good education. It was killing her to leave them, but she had to if she didn't want to lose her fiancé, a young man from a good family whom she was to marry the following month. Eyang, who was already living with them, had added that it was important for her only daughter to be among other children of her age until her daughter-in-law had other children. She had self-righteously drawn the conclusion that the two grandchildren belonged to their uncle, whose duty it was to ensure their education.

This theatrical melodrama plunged the young woman into a long silence. But the most contradictory thoughts kept running through her mind. She could, and she had every right to, make everyone leave her home. And then again, watching out of the corner of her eye her husband gaze tenderly at his nephews, she no longer knew what right she had in her own home. She no longer knew whether she should place her husband's obvious happiness above her own interests. Must she forgo her rights to please everyone?

Before she married, her sister had given her one piece of advice, which came into her mind now: "Whatever your reasons, never go against your in-laws. Even if your husband shares your opinion. You'll find yourself ostracized, unless, of course, they are nice enough not to push for your divorce. You'll be better off, believe me, if you let go of your principles of a liberated woman right now."

So Emilienne reassured everyone. Seeing the solemn gaze that fell from the eyes of the two young boys, she believed for a moment that she was their saving grace. Her tone of voice became condescending when she said she was flattered her sister-in-law would place such confidence in her and that she would not disappoint her. Her husband, who had grown taciturn awaiting her decision, began laughing like a little child and served drinks to everyone.

Emilienne was surprised at her own speech. Wasn't she becoming a hypocrite in order to please, and, at the same time, condescending in order to mask her game? Her sister called it the art of making her in-laws love and respect her.

"Why make enemies," she'd declared with an air of self-assurance, "when, with a little flattery and a hint of superiority, you can easily make allies of them? In my case, I can assure you that my in-laws are utterly devoted to me, and if it came down to it, they would band together against my husband to defend me. You see, hypocrisy is not a failing if it's used to stay on good terms with those who surround you."

EMILIENNE SHOOK her head. "How has all my willingness toward my in-laws served me? Is it because I am not a hypocrite? It's too late, I will never change." She watched her sleeping nephews for a moment. "Tonight when she comes home, I won't scold her." She left the room.

In the living room, Joseph was asleep. Feeling utterly alone, it was her turn to pick up the receiver.

"Eva, I need you—can you come right away?"

"What is happening?" Her sister's voice sounded alarmed at the other end of the line.

"Rékia has been gone since this morning."

"What?! I'll be right there . . . stay calm."

She called her manager and secretary. When she hung up, she turned on the radio just as the announcer read the notice of Rékia's disappearance. After the third announcement, she turned the radio off, took a book from the library, and went to sit on the lawn.

Roxanne ran over to lie at her feet. She petted the animal distractedly and lay down on the warm, moist grass. The dog came over to lick her face. Having kept from thinking the worst until now, Emilienne panicked. Her whole body trembled in terror. Her arms were covered with goose bumps. She felt cold, afraid, alone. Stubbornly, she tried to concentrate on her reading, but her gaze blurred. Eva found her staring at the words on the page which she was holding upside down.

"Still no news?"

"No!"

"What happened?"

She collapsed on the grass as her little sister recounted her daughter's disappearance.

"All we can do now is wait," Emilienne concluded, closing her book.

She was pale and looked as if she had lost weight since morning.

"Unbelievable! You don't think she went off with a stranger at her age! And, even if she was assaulted and abducted, there must be people who saw her struggle or heard her scream. At 8 a.m. there are so many pedestrians rushing around, and traffic is dense. Are you sure you've done everything you could? If they don't find her by tonight, Joseph should have the police question the students. They had to have noticed someone suspicious around the schools. By the way, I just stopped by to give Mama the news. She wanted to come with me, but her toothache has her bedridden. I'll stop by there tonight on my way home. I don't understand why phone lines are always down in their district when it rains."

She brought her hand to her head. In her rush she'd forgotten to put on her scarf, and her half-undone braids blew in the intermittent breeze.

Before running to meet her sister, she had hastily thrown on an old dress that gathered at the bust. If Rékia hadn't disappeared, Emilienne would have teased her, comparing her to a country girl on her way back from the fields.

When the phone rang, to Emilienne's ears it seemed like an ambulance blaring its siren. She ran into the house, her sister close behind, as Joseph picked up the receiver.

The creases on his forehead ran deeper than ever as he stared, listening intently to the voice on the line.

"I'll be right there," he mumbled and hung up.

Emilienne grabbed him by the belt.

"Who was it? The police? You're going to look for her, right? Did they say where they found her? Why won't you answer me? Why do you look so upset? You should be relieved."

She grabbed his sleeve. Joseph ran his hand through his hair and placed the phone down before muttering:

"They found a young girl's body; her description matches Rékia's. Of course, that doesn't mean anything. I am going to see."

Emilienne's grip tightened and remained pressed against her husband's sleeves.

"They're just saying any foolish thing they can come up with. You and I both know it can't be Rékia."

"You're right," her husband answered cautiously. "I am going to go see anyway. Don't worry. Everything will be fine, you'll see."

Eva ran toward her sister, whose arms fell limp at her sides. Her knees weak, Emilienne followed her husband into the kitchen.

"Head up, Emie," Eva mumbled, holding back her tears. "You're right. I don't think it's Rékia. She will be fine; she'll be back with us very soon."

She helped her regain her balance.

One grandchild in each arm, Eyang followed behind Joseph hurriedly until he reached the car. Then, with a grave look in her eyes, she joined the two women in the living room. Emilienne released herself from her sister's grip and slid down on the tile floor, her legs and body in a perfectly straight line.

Outside, it was dreary and cold, typical weather for the dry season. From the other side of the street, they could hear the first crows of the roosters as night fell surreptitiously over the city. A car revved its engine outside. The children got out and ran to join Openda and his wife. Rondani hurried to her two daughters, her arms raised.

"Emie, Eva, what is happening?" she asked in a hoarse voice, tears welling up in the corners of her eyes. "How could the child have disappeared? And where were you when this happened?"

"Calm down, Mama," her elder daughter replied. "Let's wait for Joseph. It won't be long before he's back. We still don't actually know anything."

"Why are you in such a state?" their father scolded, clenching his fists as he hunched over.

"We got a call from the police saying they had found a young girl's body . . ."

This time it was Rondani who collapsed on the divan and placed her hand over her heart. Eyang, standing a couple of steps behind her reached out to help her. An anxious look in his eyes, Openda, too, sat down facing his wife. Crouched in fear at the corner of the stone wall enclosing the terrace, the two boys looked into the living room with stricken eyes. Her tail between her legs, Roxanne scurried cautiously over to Emilienne, who immediately shoved her aside. The animal turned away sheepishly and went to curl up underneath one of the bougainvilleas in the yard. Hearing her neighbor scream at her daughter in the villa next door made Emilienne burst into tears, and she threw herself down onto the cold tiles of the floor.

"My poor child! I am sure they're mistaken. Eva, go see if she's coming."

Her tears clung to the subtle lines that marked her age and then streamed down her neck.

"Do you know, Mama," she screamed at her mother, "that she just got her period for the first time last week? Yes, she has matured. She is old enough to create life herself now. Soon you will be a grandmother because *she* will not be sterile."

Her mother rushed over to her as mute as a fish and wiped her cheeks dry.

"Please calm down, I beg you," Eva murmured under her breath. "You're going to make yourself sick."

She bit her lips.

Openda got up, left the room, and paced around the yard, his hands clasped behind his back. Eyang, her face contorted in pain, hobbled over to sit with the three women; just then the engine of the car sputtered outside.

"They are back!" Emilienne cried out, leaping out the door. "What did I tell you? Rékia! Where were you? You really gave us a scare!"

The young woman let out the cry of a wounded animal when Joseph took a bloody body wrapped in a white sheet out of the backseat. The young girl's head and face were bruised, and there was a deep cut above the arch of her left eyebrow. Holding her inert body tightly in his arms, Joseph walked slowly toward them. Emilienne threw herself onto them and fainted. Everyone started screaming. The children covered their faces with their hands.

With great difficulty, Eva lifted her sister and brought her to her room. Eyang, who was following behind, took a step back, grabbed the two boys, ran to the left then to the right, finally found the kitchen door, and rushed in. The kids were running behind her, bumping into the walls before finding themselves locked in their room. As for Rondani, she circled the table, her arms stretched out ahead of her, knocking over the chairs in her frantic rush, and hurried to her daughter's room.

With Openda's help, Joseph laid the body on the mat Eyang brought in, and he, too, joined the women in the bedroom. Eyang followed closely behind with a bucket of water in her hands. Her hands trembling, she poured the bucket of water over her daughter-in-law. Some of it soaked Rondani, who was trying to bring her daughter back to consciousness by slapping her lightly on the cheeks.

As Eyang worked hard attending to everything, the *pagne* she wore knotted above her chest came undone, revealing a big red flowery romper that drooped down just below her breasts, shaped like squeezed-out grapefruits. Bracing herself on the carpet, she started searching for her *pagne*. Surprised by such a sight, her son turned his head away and leaned over his wife, who opened her eyes at that very moment. With brow furrowed, Joseph's face looked like a mask. He stroked his wife's disheveled hair for a moment and left the room. His eyes glimmered with sparks. His neck was marked with thick veins. Bent over more than ever, Openda scanned the sitting room, letting his eyes fall and his breath deepen when he found himself facing the small corpse. The children's wailing in the next room finally woke Emilienne up.

"What am I doing here? Where is my child?"

She checked every nook and cranny of the bedroom.

"My child," Rondani begged her, "don't put yourself in this state of mind. Try to pull yourself together."

She followed her with arms outstretched. With her damp hair plastered to her face, Emilienne did not hear her mother. She pushed her away when she tried to grab ahold of her. And in spite of her weight, Rondani found herself face down. The thickness of the carpeting and surely her body mass cushioned her fall. Next to her, Eyang picked up her *pagne,* quickly tied it across her chest, and ran after Emilienne and Eva as they left, the former supported by the latter.

Seated next to her daughter's corpse, she caressed her hair, her face, her arms and legs as she rocked herself, eyes closed, back and forth. She looked vulnerable and lost at the same time. All the other women sat around the straw rug. The two men stood. The room was lit with the weak light coming from the terrace. Moaning, cries, and screams of anguish burst from within the house. Their eyes red, the two men coughed and cleared their throats in turn.

Emilienne quieted down, and the other women, too, calmed down. Pairs of red, puffy eyes stared down at the little girl's mutilated body, and sobbing broke out again, although it did not drown out the sounds of someone knocking repeatedly at the door. Joseph disappeared and came back with Dominique, Emilienne's secretary, in tow. The young man whispered something in her ear and then came back to sit down, visibly annoyed. Dominique sat down in a corner. She wore a black dress and black shoes.

Finally, Openda spoke, his voice cracking:

"What happened, where, and how was she found?"

"Police who were patrolling the industrial zone this morning, looking for a group of burglars," Joseph said, "were informed by an old woman that she'd heard a child's screams coming from the woods. They found Rékia right away, already dead."

Joseph's voice went silent. The five pairs of eyes stared at him as if, through him, they were reliving the tragic scene. Emilienne looked haggardly upon the corpse, and a frightening smile came to her lips. Joseph continued his story in a voice that was barely audible.

"Her dress was hung on a tree, and her shoes were lying a few yards from her body."

Eyang sniffled loudly as Rondani sobbed to the cadenced rhythm of her heavy breathing. Emilienne, having heard the end of the story, suddenly leaned over the corpse, lifted it up, and held it to her. With the same fervor, the two old women grasped her tightly, trying to pull it away from her. Frantically, Emilienne squirmed and thrashed around with the little body against hers. This time, they managed to unclasp her arms from the corpse. The young woman rolled around on the ground howling. Openda rubbed his eyes vigorously. Next to him, Joseph sniffled.

"I will find her killer even if it costs me my life," Joseph threatened.

All eyes turned toward him.

Coming out of her desperation, Emilienne's voice rose up, grew louder and louder until it filled the house. Her words pierced the walls before dying out into the cold, morbid air.

"I wanted a second child, and now my first has been killed. I am responsible for her death with all my wishing for another child, as if she didn't count. Before I am even buried, I'm already a wreck, and all my parts have come to pieces, even the one who managed to live independently of me. By choosing her as their victim, they have pierced my belly with their knives.

By killing her, they have killed off and buried my already dead womb. From this point on, my womb will serve as my daughter's coffin and tomb, as it has for all of her brothers and sisters who did not make it out of me alive. They will finally all be reunited in the confines of my body. We will remain together forever."

Emilienne bent over and hugged the daughter who, nearly thirteen years ago, had emerged from her body and who, before even becoming fully conscious of her existence, had left this world.

III

Drifting

For several weeks already, Emilienne had been getting home very late at night. When she wasn't staying late at the office, she was leading women's meetings for the Single Party or would spend her evenings at her sister's or her parents'. Since old lady Eyang practically never saw the couple, she took it upon herself, despite her advanced age, to take care of her grandchildren.

Tonight, however, Joseph came home to spend some time with his mother. To make the few short moments they would spend together a memorable occasion, Eyang asked the cook to prepare her son's favorite dish. Joseph was especially talkative this evening. Sitting next to his mother on the divan, he had a great time conjuring up memories from his childhood. Visibly delighted by this regained intimacy, his mother corrected him when he got a date wrong or mixed up facts.

Evoking those distant memories lasted a good two hours. In the end, his mother stopped talking so that her son could watch the evening news on TV. She was eager to talk with him about the issue that she could barely contain. Tonight the news seemed longer than usual. So Eyang got up, went to tuck in her grandchildren, who had already been asleep for a while, and then came back and sat down just as her son was turning off the television set.

"My son, we need to talk a little bit about you."

She tied the belt of her lace bathrobe, which her son had brought back for her from France before their falling out about his marriage.

"What do you want to say to me, Mama?" he asked with a smile and a simultaneous yawn.

"Don't act as though you're so tired; I am very serious. The child you had with your wife is dead, so you are in the same position today as when you first got together. As your mother, I want to know what you plan to do with your wife."

Joseph, who had been listening to his mother half asleep with his eyes half closed, became wide-eyed and sat up straight.

"What do you mean? I'm not going there with you," he retorted dryly.

"You've understood me just fine," his mother interrupted. "That woman is useless to you now, and, since you spend your nights with another, you obviously don't love her anymore. Don't tell me that you're going to keep up this double life for long."

Joseph grumbled like a child, then was very clear in his answer:

"You know, your reasoning is really simplistic. Do you think people just leave their wife like that after living together for nearly fifteen years, if I count the year we were together in college? When are you going to understand that I don't like hearing you talk about my wife with such contempt? Get it through your head once and for all that I have no intention of leaving Emilienne. Have you tried for a minute to put yourself in her shoes? She has just lost a child, and even though she's stopped saying so, I am sure that now more than ever she wants to have another one. I may be unfaithful, but I'm not a louse. Plus, so many things tie us together."

"No, Son," his mother started in again firmly, "I do not agree with you one bit. What ties you together? Memories! We don't build our lives on memories. My grandfather often said to my father that the life of a human being has worth only if he has ambition and shows his dedication through work and thought. Memories don't help a man get ahead. And I don't think your complicated studies can refute those wise words. I would like to know what you want to save in your marriage! For the sake of appearances? Be careful—you won't always be young. If you had listened to me before choosing that woman for your wife, you wouldn't be in this situation today. If your own happiness is nothing to you, at least think of that younger woman who wants only to love you. I stopped by to see her yesterday and found her very unhappy. If you don't make a clear choice between those two women, you'll lose them both. Be wary of women in love, they are capable of the meanest things when men don't give them the attention they demand."

"You never liked Emilienne, did you? And since you couldn't stop us from getting married, you're demanding our divorce. That other person in my life is perfect for you for the simple reason that she is from our region and gives you gifts, which you will very quickly forget just as you've forgotten those from Emilienne. If it didn't come from you, the argument about my double love life would be valid, because I don't believe that it is my happiness that you ultimately want. What do you want, exactly, Mama?"

Eyang was silent for a few seconds and then responded, more composed:

"If your wife were looking to save her marriage, she would not spend her evenings out. I wonder if she has a lover. She has nothing to lose since she is incapable of having any more children." Eyang's voice became more aggressive: "You want to know what I really think? Well, you're right; your wife does not suit me. What kind of a wife spends her days and a good part of her nights at women's meetings making demands for I don't know what rights, as if she's intent on changing our traditions! Do you think that she could actually make a name for herself in this country if she doesn't know how to be a good wife and cannot bear children like all the other women? Can you tell me what use she is to you now? I don't want to do her any harm, but I am certain she'll be happier without you. And if she were really intelligent, she would ask for a divorce so that both of you would be free, unless, of course, she's afraid that she won't find anyone else, and prefers the humiliation which you are making her suffer in this city."

Joseph gave his mother a penetrating stare, then relaxed and looked at his watch.

"It's late, Mama, I have to go. We'll continue this fascinating conversation very soon. Do the children need anything?"

He looked in his pocket, took out five one-thousand franc bills, handed them to his mother, and got up.

"How can you be proud of this life you are leading? Oh, what your father must be thinking in his grave! No one can say that they want others to be happy when they're not happy themselves. You'll blame your wife later for your weakness, which today you see as a sign of your fidelity or honesty." She got up and went on, this time in French: "When will you come to see us again?"

"Good night, Mama," her son said, also speaking French—the conversations between mother and son were always held in their local language. Occasionally, when Emilienne was there, they spoke in French.

He kissed his mother on the forehead and went out practically running.

Eyang sat down after she'd switched off the light in the room. The yard was bathed in natural light. Her cheeks fluttered like a half-filled balloon. She was grinding her teeth and pushed her mouth forward showing her anger. Who could blame her for thinking of her old age and the future of her child? At sixty, she felt she was living with a ghost for a son and a daughter-in-law whom she upset and who upset her. What would become of this unstable situation if she didn't take it upon herself to set it straight? Would her son be able to stand up to his wife if the latter wanted to get rid of her? Where would she go live? Not with Antoinette—her husband hated his own wife's children. "They'll end up sending me to my cousin's place in the village, and I will die alone, far away from my children. There is no way I'm going to allow this woman to take my son away from me."

When Emilienne's key clinked in the lock of the door, Eyang closed her eyes and held her breath. After a moment, which to her seemed an eternity, she started running out of breath. Holding her hand over her heart, she opened her eyes wide; then opening her mouth wide as well, Eyang let out a hoarse grumble. Emilienne had turned on the lights in the room and was standing over her. In the weighty silence that surrounded them, the two pairs of eyes confronted each other. Eyang was the first to blink, then, with her head held high, she stood up and walked with a dignified air toward her bedroom.

At 6 a.m., the old woman was sitting on the roadside waiting impatiently for a taxi to come. Over her long striped dress that fell over her rubber sandals, she wore a turtleneck sweater, so worn its original color was difficult to identify. Women and children passed by her carrying baskets and basins on their backs or on their heads overflowing with the provisions they were bringing to sell at the market a couple of miles down the road. Out of curiosity, some passersby came back to stare at the old woman then hurried on their way. It is important to know that over the past several months there had been stories of ghosts wandering around the city. People claimed to have crossed their paths in the wee hours of the morning, between three and five o'clock, some of them naked, others dressed, all of them beautiful young women with long flowing white hair, who would disappear and reappear at the city's major intersections. Although one could not compare Eyang with these mysterious young women, appearing at the crack of dawn in a nearly deserted street, she did frighten those early morning walkers, some of whom did not seem fully awake yet.

She did not wait long. The illuminated sign of a taxi appeared in the distance. Eyang rose to her feet and walked right into the middle of the road so that the driver would have to stop. And he did, coming to a sudden halt in front of the old woman.

"You trying to get yourself run over, Mama?" the taxi driver shouted.

"She is mad," one of the passengers in the taxi said harshly.

"That woman looks like a witch," said the second passenger. "You'd better not let her get into your taxi."

Eyang smiled, exposing all of her yellow teeth.

"Hello, son," she muttered deliberately. "Do you want to bring me to Nomba? Thanks, son—I knew you weren't going to say no."

The driver shook his head and then guffawed at the old woman's obsequious words.

"Mama, even at your age you still manage to charm the men! Come on, get in."

"Have her get in front next to you, then," the second passenger said sharply. "Don't be fooled by her seeming innocence.

Old women like her are very dangerous. She knows exactly what she wants and will not back down from anyone."

The driver opened the door for her. Eyang had regained her impenetrable air. Deep inside, she quivered with anger. How could people she didn't even know treat her like that, she whose son, with his diplomas and good looks, would crush those two passengers stinking of rotten cassava? "They'll pay for this," she grumbled.

"What are you saying, Mama?" the taxi driver asked.

Eyang turned her head and looked out at the passing trees, withdrawing into a silence that contrasted with her earlier smile.

"Aren't you afraid of going out alone so early in the morning?" the driver continued. "You could be attacked, or someone could snatch your purse."

Eyang held on to her small bag clutching it tightly between her legs.

SHE WAS PRACTICALLY skipping along the path to the home of her son's mistress. A moment ago, she'd nearly slipped on a stone. Luckily, her reflex had been to grab onto a clump of grass along the path's edge. The young woman, leaning against the window drinking a cup of coffee, jumped when she saw her. Looking worried, she ran to open the door for her.

"What's going on? Is something wrong at the house?"

"No, no, relax. Is he here?"

"Yes, snoring away."

"He's going to have to rent a house for you in a nice neighborhood. Well, I didn't come for that. Pour me a coffee and bring me some croissants if you've got any left."

She sat down. The young woman took two croissants out of the freezer and heated them up in the oven.

"Listen, my dear," the old woman said firmly. "He is not about to leave his wife. I was wrong to think that their child's death would cause a definite break. So, listen to me carefully. I've found another way to bring about their divorce. We're going to go after the wife. Do everything you can to become friends with her. Once you see that she trusts you, let me know, and I will put the second phase of my plan into motion. In the meantime, do as I've just told you. And I am going to do all I can to really upset her. If the two of us are not able to get her out of my son's life, I will leave this city. Try to make him love you more, too. I hope you're not already behaving like a married woman who has nothing left to give or to prove. Be careful! No fetishes. I don't want you to make him go crazy."

Eyang stared at the coffeepot and warm croissants, tapped her right foot rhythmically, then smiled, and after a long silence added:

"That would be a weapon to use later on if . . ."

"What do you mean?"

"Nothing—in any event, we'll see. Why don't you try to get close to Antoinette? She could be useful to you. If things go our way, she will be your sister-in-law."

"I think she really likes Emilienne."

"Oh! You know! Her attitude toward Emilienne will change as soon as I talk to her. Don't forget, I am her mother."

"Thank you, Mama Eyang!" the young woman said as she walked the old woman to the main road.

"Don't be in a hurry to thank me. You'll have all the time in the world to do that after my son has married you."

SHE SHUT the taxi door, and it took off. When the car had slowed down to drop her at home, Eyang asked the driver to bring her instead to the luxury housing complex where Antoinette and her husband lived. They were in an eighth-floor apartment of a modern building. The new development was only two years old and had seven buildings of ten floors each. On the ground floor, there were shops, cafés, beauty salons, butcher shops, banks, and several other businesses. There was also an enormous circular parking lot around the complex.

For the first time, Eyang had to take the elevator alone. Had it occurred to her that she would have to do this, she'd have been happy to talk to her daughter over the telephone. Until now, she'd always gone up accompanied by one of her children. Even though she knew perfectly well which button to press to call the elevator and which door to ring once she reached the eighth floor, she hesitated. What would she do if she were to get stuck in what she called the haunted box? Would she still be alive when they found her? She looked around; no, no one was heading toward the elevators. All the residents were at work and their kids at school. Just as she began to go back, regretful that she'd made the useless trip, a little girl all out of breath came toward her. She pushed the elevator button, and the door opened immediately. Eyang rushed in before the little girl even got in. The old woman smiled at her. She recognized the child now, a neighbor on Antoinette's floor. Both of them got off on the eighth floor.

"You can't live in a normal house like your brother?" her mother scolded as soon as her daughter opened the door. "You never did do anything like everyone else, and your husband is just as odd as you. You two are so afraid of people disturbing you that you prefer to lock yourself up in this can of corned beef."

"Mama," Antoinette said, smiling, "you say the same thing each time you come here. Hey! Why have you come here all alone at this hour?"

"I have to talk to you about something serious, and I need your help," Eyang said as she followed her daughter to the living room.

It was an enormous room, and all the décor and each piece of furniture seemed to have been made for its space. The old woman sat down on the brown leather armless low-back chair.

"Are you aware that your brother has a mistress?"

"Come on! He just has a 'second office' like every other man in this country, perhaps even a third. You certainly haven't come over here to talk about my brother's love life!"

"I really need to talk to someone about it. And don't make that face! I want your brother to marry his current mistress, whom I know well. Well! Of course she isn't as educated as Emilienne. She does however have something which for me trumps my daughter-in-law's supposed qualities: she is from back home. And, she is very beautiful. You know, my dear child, since I've lived under the same roof with your sister-in-law, I don't trust those women who've been to the top-notch schools as you say. What I want from you is quite simple. First, try to find out what that woman is up to."

"Which one?"

"What do you mean which one! I am talking about Emilienne, of course. Does she still want to have children? And can she? What does she think of her marriage? Once you have all this information, I'll know how to use it against her. And ask your brother to bring you to see his mistress. She's a fine girl."

"Have you finished, Mama?" Antoinette asked, her voice suddenly broken.

"What's wrong with your voice?" her mother asked, infuriated. "You're not going to start crying!"

"With good reason." Two big tears fell from the young woman's lashes. "Unbelievable. Is it really you, my mother, who just spouted out such rubbish? You are asking me to help you get rid of your daughter-in-law! Don't you know what you owe her, Mama?"

"What are you talking about?"

"Let me tell you. Thanks to Emilienne, seven years ago you were able to have your eyes operated on in France. Without that operation, you would be walking around with a cane now or you would be laid up in a chair. It's also because of your daughter-in-law that you receive free care in the most expensive clinic in the city each time you fall sick. The majority of the clothes you wear come from her. Those, dear mother, are but a few specific examples of the ways in which your daughter-in-law helps you out. Even if she hadn't been so attentive to your needs, I find it disgraceful that you are plotting to evict her from her family home. I find it intolerable that you come to ask me to assist you in your Machiavellian scheme. What would you say if my mother-in-law was doing the same to me? What kind of mother are you anyway?!"

Antoinette got up and headed toward the bay window. She stood immobile in front of it, fuming with almost uncontrollable anger. But her argument did not make her mother back down; rather, she countered harshly:

"I will not allow you to speak disrespectfully to me. It is completely normal that my daughter-in-law would help me out in the ways you've just listed. That doesn't at all change what I think of her, nor my decision to get her away from my son. My rights and duties to Joseph are most important. He may be a man, but he's still my boy. I know what's good for him, and no one can make him happy better than I can. Everything that troubles him gets me right here"—she kneaded her lower abdomen. "Everything stirs up in there if anything serious happens to you or your brother. Do you understand now why I am so hard on that woman? I suffered in order to bring you both into the world and to take care of you after your father's death. And I continue to want what's best for you. Before you insult me, try to put yourself in my place. Do you think it is easy to wage this type of battle at my age? I owe it to myself to repair the damage I caused when I allowed my son to marry that woman. I am doing it for all of us. You'll understand when your kids are grown."

She got up and concluded:

"I forbid you to speak of this visit to your brother."

Antoinette responded to her mother's words by opening the door wide.

"Did you hear what I said?" her mother asked from the doorway. "I will not give up on this, and damn you if you try to betray me. There will no longer be two women under my son's roof, and the one who replaces Emilienne will be under my orders."

The elevator closed on her. Eyang's words were still ringing in Antoinette's ears as she flopped down onto the couch. She felt dizzy. She was afraid, very afraid.

At the same time, she was already in a panic thinking of the repercussions to such machinations. Words are not so strong. Would she keep this secret? There was no question she would talk with her husband about it. He would go and tell Joseph right away, and the latter wouldn't stand for his mother's taking such steps. Talking about it with Emilienne would only cause exactly what she wanted to avoid: divorce. Moreover, she couldn't go to war with her own mother by publicly siding with her sister-in-law. "Unbelievable. Has my mother lost her head? I've got to see her again before it's too late," Antoinette concluded on her way to her hairdresser. "I will make sure that she puts a stop to this diabolical plan."

Outside in the garden where she was picking flowers, Emilienne jumped when she heard Roxanne barking desperately, followed immediately by barking that sounded almost human. Her basket slipped out of her hands, and her gladioli, acanthus, and hybrid arctotis scattered across the lawn.

She was completely out of breath when she reached the kitchen door, which she shoved open. The dog was lying under the sink in a pool of blood. She had an open wound on her right side.

Standing in the middle of the kitchen, Eyang held a machete in one hand and her scarf in the other, with which she wiped her face. Her short white hair was standing on end. Her rangy, long-limbed body rocked back and forth. She glanced unwaveringly from the animal to the machete.

Shuddering, Emilienne rushed over to the dog and shook her fiercely. The animal was weakened by the acute pain and struggled to wag her tail. Emilienne got up and sighed. Without bothering with her mother-in-law, she went out, came back in with the kennel of liana vines and put the animal inside. Still racing around, like a perfectly calibrated robot, she placed the kennel on the backseat, leapt into the driver's seat, and took off. Only as she was flying at 60 mph did she wonder whether the veterinarian, like most city dwellers who fancied sunbathing and Sunday drives, might have gone to one of the many urban wooded areas scattered around the city.

When the city was undergoing modernization, the first mayor ordered all such forests to be razed to the ground because, he said, they made the city look untamed. In order to convince the chiefs—or at least their great-grandchildren, who held the positions of the chiefs and who were boldly against the big operation to raze the ancestral forests—he used this type of language, which was recorded in the annals of history:

"We have lived in the forests for too long. Those days are gone. We must let bygone days be bygone; it is thus vital, now, that we level off our lands and rid them of all that is green."

Those few words were enough to incite outcry among the intellectual elite. The project to raze the city died right then and there. That was how the Olamba forests came to be preserved and later redesigned as small parks complete with amusement park attractions, natural and artificial rivers, bars and restaurants, benches, and fountains. Since that time, open-air enthusiasts would go there in small groups every weekend.

Fifteen minutes later, Emilienne parked her car outside Dr. Obamé's residential building. As she hurried up the stairwell, she jostled a tiny, shapeless mass, and although it surprised rather than alarmed her, it forced her to stop. In the dim shadow, she recognized the veterinarian's son crouched against the handrail, shirtless and with a ball in his hand.

"Alain, dear! I hope I didn't hurt you, did I? What are you doing in these back stairwells anyway?"

"No, ma'am," the good-looking little boy answered with a smile. "I'm going down to play outside."

"Is your father upstairs?"

"Yes! Your dog is hurt!" the boy exclaimed, leaning over to pet the animal.

Roxanne started to whimper and wag her tail.

Dr. Obamé lived on the tenth floor. When people asked why he chose to live in a building devoid of an elevator, he would let out a thunderous laugh and answer sharply that it was to force his family and his clientele—the owners as well as their animals—to do a little exercise. Then, in a serious tone, he would invariably add:

"If we're not careful, in ten years this city will be plagued by obesity, our animals included."

Dr. Obamé was an odd one. His clients nevertheless considered him the best veterinarian Olamba had, and they came to him despite the workout he imposed on them. Some even credited him for their decision to get back to a healthy diet and an active routine.

The young woman was completely exhausted by the time she got to the tenth floor. Little Alain had already opened his father's office. Emilienne struggled as she lay the dog down on the examination table, and then stroked her as she waited. Dr. Obamé, whose son had already told him they were there, came out of the adjoining room wearing a smile. He had thrown his white coat on over his jogging suit. As he examined the animal, he said, in a calm, measured voice:

"That's a nasty wound. It could have killed her. Your dog is fighting courageously for her life. I don't believe I'm mistaken when I say that her struggle against death is to spare you of your pain. Look at her eyes! It looks as if she's suffering more from the pain she sees in your eyes, from your grief-stricken face. How did she get that wretched wound?"

Emilienne remained silent for several seconds before responding in a tone she hoped would sound convincing:

"I don't know exactly. Most likely it was neighborhood children throwing stones over the fence. It would not be the first time."

"That's strange," the veterinarian remarked. "It looks rather like she's been slashed by a long, sharp object."

He disinfected the wound, then, after giving local anesthesia, stitched up the clean cut.

"They are unruly," he grumbled as he sewed up the wound. "I don't understand children's aggressiveness these days. Just yesterday I stopped at a gas station to fill my tank, and a gang of kids between six and ten years old appeared out of nowhere, jumped the attendant, ripped his shirt, undid his pants, and slashed the gas pump hose with a knife. All of the customers who were waiting, the station attendants, and even some passersby hurled themselves on those ten kids. A little while later, the police picked them up. When I was leaving, the firemen were getting there as well. In my day, we too would invent dangerous games, but never did we go that far."

"Do you think she'll make it?" asked Emilienne, to put a stop to this narrative, which, unwittingly, she had prompted with her lie.

"Yes, she will heal in no time," Dr. Obamé replied, petting Roxanne's stitched side. Buy these antibiotics no later than tomorrow," he added as he filled out the prescription, "and bring her back in on Tuesday or Wednesday. Don't be surprised if your dog takes on less trustful and more aggressive behavior around strangers who come to your place. Be sure to be very affectionate with her. Ah, yes! Pets are like children."

"Thank you, Doctor, and my apologies for coming and disturbing you. How much do I owe you?"

"We'll talk about that when she's all better." He handed her the prescription. "Wait, I'm going to help you bring her down.

My family and I were about to go out when you arrived. But I am very happy you came. A pet is as precious as someone who is dear to you. Everyone who has ever cared for an animal knows that."

"Take good care of her," he added, handing her the kennel when they were in front of the car.

Feeling reassured, Emilienne finally relaxed. Behind the wheel of her car, she planned out the speech she was going to give her mother-in-law when she saw her.

EYANG WAS LOUNGING on a folding chair, flipping through an old pornographic comic book that she had found by chance a long time ago in her daughter's bathroom and brought home. In spite of her glasses, which she never took off, she squinted with sustained concentration, her eyes lingering particularly on the nude characters in the most outrageous positions. And, although she shook her head in disapproval, she kept returning to those same images.

She didn't understand why those indecent scenes fascinated her. Could it be because of her age, the contrast to what people of her generation usually saw, that this aroused a bizarre interest in her? And yet she had refused to watch television for three months after the first time she'd seen a naked man and woman caressing each other. Later, she'd believed that she was doing a good thing by taking all the pornographic magazines her daughter and son-in-law collected, intending to burn them. Instead of following through with her threat, though, she'd hidden them in her bathroom and under her mattress. When she knew she was alone in the house, she would take them out and look at them. During those moments of intense concentration, her lower lip would become moist, she would take off and put back on her old pair of glasses that hung on black strings from her ears, and her nose would flare.

Hearing the car approach, Eyang hid the comic book on the chair and stretched out on top of it. She closed her eyes and feigned a light snore.

Emilienne sat down in turn, facing her. For a while she tried to read this face overrun by wrinkles and doubtlessly malice as well. How would this living arrangement with her mother-in-law end? she wondered. It went without saying that she was becoming a threat that weighed on her like the sword of Damocles. If anything confirmed this threat, the machete blows to her dog certainly did. What would she think of next? She'd surely already revealed how calculating she could be.

ONE DAY, when Emilienne had arrived home from work, Rékia had come to her, curled up in her arms, her eyes full of tears, and told her about the argument she'd had with her cousin and of her grandmother's mean words: after he had deliberately knocked over his cousin's bowl of milk, Nomé had said the following, word for word:

"Papa Joseph loves my brother and me more than you. And Grandma says that he's going to remarry and make Auntie Emilienne leave."

After she'd heard those words, Rékia pummeled her cousin with fierce blows. Her grandmother, who'd heard everything from the next room, came in to give the little girl a slap and lectured:

"What right do you have to hit this child? All he did was tell the truth. Don't ever forget that these two children have more rights than you do in this house!"

EMILIENNE'S WEIGHTY silence forced Eyang to open her eyes. It was just the two of them in the house that weekend. The two boys had been home with their mother since Friday evening. Eyang shot her daughter-in-law a look of resentment and said mockingly:

"I see your baby is still alive."

"I'm so sorry you won't be able to mourn her death," the young woman hissed back, pulling her chair closer to the old woman. "When are you going to have the courage to confront me openly instead of attacking an innocent animal? Enough of your provocations; let's be clear about our positions."

Eyang was evasive:

"What are you talking about? You know full well it was an accident."

"You're lying!" Emilienne yelled. "Do you realize that you deliberately hurled a machete at a defenseless animal? And you dare call that an accident? What exactly do you want from me?"

"What do I want from you?"

Eyang crossed her legs. She took off her glasses, calmly put them away in their case, and went on:

"Instead of bearing children like other women, you raise dogs and cats. As soon as they fall sick, you put them in your car and run to have them examined by a doctor, and when they die, you buy more of them. Not to mention all the cans of food you buy for them, and the vaccinations you have them get. You ought to use all that money to treat your ailing womb. There is medicine for abnormal women like you, in case you might have forgotten!"

Eyang got up, backed up a few steps, spun around, and sat back down facing Emilienne, who hadn't moved. In her state of anger, the old woman was unrecognizable. The energy of a young woman seemed to be emanating from her shriveled-up body. Her movements and gestures expressed her stern hatred.

Emilienne, barely managing to control her anger, gripped the armrests of her chair. Her eyelids fluttered rapidly over eyes reddened with fury and fixed on her mother-in-law with a piercing gaze.

Eyang kept going:

"I was right to oppose this marriage. If my son had married a girl from our part of the country, he would not have lost a child and would not be so unstable today. You have wrecked his life. Had I not been in this house, I am sure you'd have made him eat filth so that you could destroy him."

In response, Emilienne hurled herself at her and slapped her hard across the face. Eyang fell backward, her arms and legs writhing. She helped her back to her feet and then struck her down again.

"I've had it," she hissed. "As of tomorrow, you will leave this house, and take your grandchildren with you."

Emilienne stepped away from her and went to lean against the bay window.

Sitting on the cement, Eyang dusted off her arms then straightened up, shook out her dress, and declared solemnly:

"Poor girl! You have just done a very stupid thing. You just don't think things through. How can you make me leave this house! If I leave here—which I will not do—you will lose my son. And, oh! Don't think that I will stay to keep you from separating. No, no, quite the opposite, I have been waiting for this moment for a long time. I want you to be the one who leaves. And this moment has arrived."

She let out a nervous laugh, which was at the same time victorious.

Emilienne raised her hand again and then held it back just as it was about to hit the old woman's cheek. Shaking her head, she turned her back to her and headed toward the garage.

SHE DROVE AIMLESSLY through curving roads and intersections, her eyes misty with tears. She started down winding, broken roads she'd never been on before. In that respect, she was similar to those foreigners who knew only Olamba's main areas: the major banks, the big movie theaters, the supermarket, their workplace, and the main residential neighborhoods. In her case, she had to add the big open-air market and the neighborhoods where her parents and sister lived.

She soon found herself in a bustling neighborhood. There, the road was not paved but was instead a red dirt road full of bumps and crevices. The roadway belonged to vehicles as well as pedestrians, who walked indifferently along the side of the road either in front of or behind the bicycles and trucks. In order to force their way through a motley and idle crowd, drivers were beeping, screaming, and yelling insults at passersby, who yelled right back at them. Small groups of men and women were carrying on and arguing in front of the bistros crammed up against one another. From outside, you could see customers of both sexes in the cafés fluttering and twisting around.

Having forgotten her argument with her mother-in-law for a moment, Emilienne slowed down the car, in awe of the liveliness of the working-class neighborhood she was discovering for the first time. The roaring laughter and jokes all around could at times be heard above the blaring music. For the first time, she was aware of the gap that separated her from these people, so ordinary, yet at the same time radiant with a real joie de vivre.

"What good is social success when you bear the burden of a melancholy soul? One has only to look at these men and women to understand that true success is within. Surely, they know better than I how to overcome their suffering and find great joy in simple things. They know how to have fun, laugh heartily, and marvel at the sight of thousands of stars twinkling in the sky, or simply at an animal giving birth, at all those everyday miraculous things that I no longer know how to see. My senses are so limited and so deformed that they see, hear, taste, and touch only wretched things. For a minority of people, the accumulation of possessions is nothing more than a natural way to supplement an inner richness and sense of fulfillment. For others, dupery fulfills confused souls, to camouflage the reality of a cruel existence. To appease my own confusion, I've held on desperately to anything that sustained my attention, until today. I had to maintain my social status. To do that, all I had to do was appear on the arm of my dear husband—when he wanted me to—in fashionable places and at official ceremonies. What hypocrisy! And I believed it! As Rochefoucault said, 'We are all so used to disguising ourselves in front of others that in the end we become disguised to ourselves.' And so, like most people, I've gone through life from one end to the other, happy to be like them and to hide, quite well, my permanent inner madness. Forgetting that the others would someday finally see me as I am. Forgetting that they, too, wear heavy, asphyxiating masks, which eventually fall and reveal them to those around them."

For the first time in a long time, she suddenly had a burning desire to mingle with those people toward whom she had always been indifferent. At that moment, those lower-class men and women were no longer the common folk, but were instead human beings, and she needed them to calm her inner agitation.

After she'd circled Nomba Square three times, she parked on a rutted part of the sidewalk strewn with broken glass. Before she stepped away from the car, she made sure to crack the back windows to keep Roxanne from suffocating, then walked timidly into the first bistro she came across. Emilienne sat down at the only open table in a corner of the rectangular room.

Although at first she was frightened by the intoxicated, buzzing human mass, she sat down all the same, bowing her head in resolute submission. The waiter's attentive "What'll you have, Madame?" made her look up. Without giving it any thought, she ordered a beer and let her timid eyes graze slowly over the customers of this place that was so new to her.

At the bar, laughing, drunken customers grumbled or gave each other rough taps on the shoulder. Six sweaty couples were dancing the rumba, taking wide, helter-skelter steps along a narrow dance floor. Four women seated at another table were brandishing wine bottles. The first one to empty hers was applauded by the three others. As she brought her glass to her mouth, Emilienne's startled gaze lingered again upon the crowd in front of the bar, as they clinked their glasses and bottles together. In response to the catcalls of the guy sitting next to her, a woman yanked the sleeve of her dress so far off her shoulder that it exposed her drooping breast, bulging with crisscrossed veins. Then, in a fit of nervous laughter, she grabbed her breast with both hands and started caressing her aggressor with it. The audience chuckled. As Emilienne witnessed this odd spectacle, trying to take it all in, a voice rang out above the hubbub in the room.

"That'll teach you, pal," it said. "You young executives come over here to flaunt your preppy clothes in front of the poor. Tell me, your tailor wouldn't be Balmain, by any chance?"

Emilienne seemed to have forgotten her own social status and moved her chair over to the left so that she could get a better view of the scene. The guy who'd just spoken belched so loudly his head knocked the center beam that supported the roof frame. The impact was so great that the drunkard then collapsed on some chairs, which smashed to pieces. Obviously his buddies had seen this a thousand times before and looked away from the spectacle. Not wanting to draw any further attention, the young preppy exec smoothed out his beige suit and backed up toward the door. As if it were, in turn, telling him off, the 1970s record player screeched repeatedly over the scratched record. Disappointed, the dancers clamored in outrage and started shouting, "Music! Music!" A man with a pimply face and a bloated belly came out from behind the bar and leaned over the player. Half the people left; it was as if they had needed this cacophony to hide from themselves, and alcohol was no longer doing the trick.

"And what if this setting, this exuberance were another way for all these people gathered here to hide from their existential problems? So I'm not wrong to think that only a minute minority of individuals have found inner peace. I am sure, though, that *they* still know how to laugh and sing."

Emilienne did not have time to ponder her thoughts, because shouts to the owner were quickly turning to threats. Through all that commotion two young people emerged, arms around each other's waist, and it was they who in some way gave more weight to her argument.

"Man!" the hoarse voice boomed out from the little guy, "I'm saying that the best way to avoid seeing what's happening around us is to drown ourselves in alcohol. I drink and smoke weed so my family doesn't eat me alive. It's the truth: the family is what's wrong with our society. Your blood brother snatches up your wife; your mother's jealous and doesn't want you to marry; your father, getting to retirement age, can't stand the fact that you have a job and a better salary than his; your uncle can't deal with you being better educated and distinguished than his son. And that whole world is working against you in all the ways they can . . . and the paradox is they say it's 'for your own good.'"

Silence fell on the room, surely because it was rare to hear a speech in this place. The young people sat down at the bar, a few steps away from Emilienne. Not having noticed the crowd that was gathering around them, the little guy was now no doubt intoxicated by the interest he was stirring, and burst out:

"You know, my sisters and cousins think my missus is arrogant? And you know why? Simply because she's the master of the house, has everyone under her control, including my little brothers. Those boys, thinking they're so precious, don't want to demean themselves by doing household chores. As custom would have it, they consider my wife theirs and demand she serve them as if they're her husband. On the other hand, they have no problem emptying bottles of my alcohol and eating my food with their girlfriends. My mother—that mother hen—approves of that behavior and sees me as their future adoptive father, after her husband dies. No, man! Traditions and customs have got to adapt to modern times. Besides, I don't want to hear these words any more 'cause it's just a nasty way of exploiting people. Why do you think the young folks are turning to wine and whiskey?"

The semicircle of customers grew larger. The little guy, appropriately and yet simply dressed, raised his eyebrows as if it would give more weight to his question.

"Think about it. You're an intellectual—corrupt, maybe, but an intellectual all the same."

He flashed a mischievous smile. His sidekick, who hadn't yet opened his mouth, shrugged. He was about six foot five and must have weighed over 300 pounds.

"Aw, man! Let's order a drink." The giant finally put a word in in his reedy drawl.

His hands moved up and down the suspenders holding up his oversized pants.

"Take a good look at me," the short one went on tirelessly. "Since I've been drowning myself in alcohol, I've been soaring alongside the angels. With them by my side, I feel perfect bliss. They ignore the problems of Earth dwellers, problems that crush humans and drive them to an early grave. Our world is an AIDS syndrome that gnaws away at our lives calmly and surely until our last breath, and when it can no longer inhabit our unharmonious organs, leaves them. You'll go on, no doubt, and say that this world is ours for the taking, and I will answer: Yes, but we gotta get through armored glass. If you really want at all costs to have everything that it reflects back to you, break the glass. And then you'll agree with me and notice that a lot a people draw back in the face of its resistance. Are you still following me?"

"Step by step" the giant replied.

"So, our world offers up everything to us and only throws us scraps. Unless you're one of those fools who risk breaking their bones to make pacts with the devil, or that rare type of individual who crosses that bullet-proof glass barrier effortlessly and without a scratch, as if they were an exceptional race. And speaking of that type, there's something I really don't understand about God's plan. And though I hold no bias against the opinion of those who find him unjust—which is fundamentally in opposition to Tradition and Knowledge and all its benefits—I think that some divine laws have been overlooked, even if they are not mentioned in the Bible, not clearly anyway. Well, that isn't all," he concluded, tapping his friend on the shoulder. "Put in our order, man, you know what I like."

"Two gin and Cokes, boss! My friend and I want to forget this world and its unsolvable problems. Hey, ya little asshole!" the giant yelled in the direction of the waiter picking up dirty glasses the next table over. "Come drink with us. I recognize your kisser."

"No thanks! I don't drink on the job," the young waiter answered, smiling.

His massive neck folded into his rippling shoulders, like a turtle hiding inside his shell from an attack.

"I said, come," the giant growled threateningly, grabbing him by the arm.

The waiter struggled free. His smile stiffened. His neck moved in and out of his shoulders, disappearing then reappearing.

"No, sir, I will drink after work."

"What's this refusal all about? For all we know this gin is poisoned! To make sure it's not, I order you to drink with us. We all know what happens in your bistros. Cowards come here to settle their scores. Can you tell me how many of your customers have died of cirrhosis or bilious attacks? Come on, answer!"

His grip tightened around the waiter's wrist. His buddy, indifferent to what was happening around him, sipped his gin and Coke with half-open eyes. Emilienne trembled at her table.

Suddenly, the fire-brand got up, grabbed the waiter by the neck, and smashed his mouth against the rim of the glass. The drink spilled onto his white shirt. The waiter quickly whipped out a pocketknife and pointed it at the giant, who, caught off guard, backed away.

Emilienne stood up and took a step back as well.

"He's scared," someone whispered quite loudly.

Several people started laughing.

"Oh, do you believe that!" the giant hissed, rolling up his sleeves. He stared mercilessly at his opponent. "I'm going to kill him."

And with that he took out a pair of scissors and hurled them at the waiter's throat as if throwing a spear. A gush of blood spurted from his chest. The waiter grabbed his killer's neck with both hands, then collapsed on the floor. It took the latter a few good seconds before he could get out of the dying man's grasp.

Having watched the murder up to the last second, Emilienne lost consciousness as soon as the waiter fell. A heavy silence weighed over the bistro.

"Let's get out of here," one of the patrons yelled.

"*I* didn't see anything," another claimed as he ran out.

Almost everyone left, one after the other, hugging the tables and walls.

"You're all a bunch of louses," shouted another patron, who'd emerged from the adjoining room with the second waiter. "You just stood by and let them try to kill each other, and now you rush out of here to get out of being witnesses for the police. You two over there! Don't move."

He stood immobile before the killer and his friend. Emilienne slowly came to.

"Don't stay here, Madame, if you don't want trouble," the last customer mumbled to her as he helped her up. He escorted her to the door.

"What's all this violence about?" He wanted an explanation. "It is rampant at home, is spreading to public places, and is becoming the order of things between nations. When there is violence, there is anger, and anger is only one step away from hatred. It's as if man has lost all connection to his heart, where there is love."

"Who are you, Mister?" asked the young woman.

"I'm a journalist. I'm preparing an article on bistros, that's why I'm here. Don't stay here. It won't be long before they start going at it again. Do you want me to drop you off somewhere? My car is parked right next door."

"Thanks, but I have my own car."

They parted without another word.

NOT FULLY RECOVERED from the shock she had just endured, Emilienne walked toward her car. In front of her, an exhilarated crowd trailed on the heels of the police headed toward the bistro. She saw expressions of glee on all of their faces. She moved to the side of the road to let the tidal wave of people pass. Finally, she reached her car. A few yards away, her cook and secretary were babbling excitedly. The scene intrigued her.

How long have they known each other? she wondered. She was tempted to go and ask them. That would not be appropriate, she thought. So, she got into the car and started the engine. Hearing the engine rev, Dominique turned around and noticed her. And before Emilienne could take off, she was running in her direction. She carried a basket in her hand and wore a *pagne* tied carelessly around her waist over a transparent black blouse through which you could see her bosom supported by a white bra.

"Good morning, Madame, what a surprise! And what are you doing around here?" Dominique exclaimed after Emilienne had rolled down the window.

"I was going out for a drive, and I accidentally witnessed a bar fight that cost one of the waiters his life."

Dominique blinked and crinkled her almond-shaped eyes. Her voluptuous lips formed a thin line.

"The news is already the talk of the neighborhood. You know, there is on average a murder a month here. It's sad—frightening, really—but we're used to these tragedies."

"How can you live in such a state of insecurity?"

"As long as the killings happen in bars, we don't really feel threatened by them."

"Tell me," Emilienne went on, this time in a dry tone, "where did you meet my cook?"

"Your cook, who's he?"

"The young man you were chatting with a few minutes ago."

"Oh! That's your cook! He was asking me for some information." She ran her hand through her straightened hair, flung her head backward, and then added, "My place isn't far from here. If you're not in a hurry . . . that is! Do you want to have a drink?"

Emilienne did not answer right away. Her secretary seemed, like any woman in this neighborhood, so confident. Her private life had never interested her. Like everyone else, she had two lives: she wasn't just an employee; she was also a young woman with her own problems. In any case, she was very beautiful, Emilienne admitted. Why would she refuse her spontaneous invitation? Before she got out of the car, she looked carefully at her dog asleep in its kennel.

"Actually, I just bought fruit juices and alcohol."

She raised her basket.

"I live down the hill. Watch out, these stones get slippery when it rains."

The young secretary jumped with great ease from one stone to the other while Emilienne walked carefully over the huge stones, placing one foot after the other. Along both sides of the trail, small houses made of wooden planks, cement, and bamboo stood on mounds of soil eroded by bad weather. The inhabitants of the makeshift houses yelled out to one another from their homes. With whimpering infants clinging to their skirts, the women were braiding hair or patching their worn clothes on their sun-soaked porches. Walking behind, Emilienne wondered again about the nature of the relationship between Godwin and her secretary. Contrary to what the young woman had told her, she was still convinced they knew each other. Why had she lied? I will find out, she thought to herself, whisking the idea from her mind.

"Are you okay, Madame?" Dominique asked as she turned around.

Her smile, so innocent and reassuring, made Emilienne drop her suspicion. What was happening to her? For some time now, she had been obsessed with the idea that everyone was out to get her. Dominique, however, had no reason to hide the truth from her.

"Don't worry about me," Emilienne answered. Then, in a low voice: "I must be tired. It's not surprising given all I've been through since the morning."

"We're here."

Dominique opened the door to her wooden-plank house. The stylish, welcoming interior impressed her employer. The furniture was top quality. Cartoons were playing on a color television; a VCR sat beneath it. At the other end of the room, an imposing air conditioner hummed softly.

"I love cartoons so much that sometimes I forget to turn off the TV when I go out."

She pointed to one of the armchairs for Emilienne to sit down and turned off the television set.

"It's so hot outside, and it's so nice to come home to a cool house," she continued as she herself sat down. "I live here with my two children and my three brothers. They've all gone to spend the day at my elder sister's, who takes care of my parents. What do you want to drink: Campari, martini, gin, rum . . . ?"

"A simple glass of water is fine. Your house is tastefully decorated," Emilienne continued the conversation.

"Thank you," Dominique replied, smiling, as she brought her a bottle of mineral water and a crystal glass. If I weren't my little brothers' guardian—all of them are still in high school—I'd have already left this appalling neighborhood. Oh! I'm sorry, Madame. I must be boring you with my troubles.

"No, no, go on."

The two women looked into each other's eyes. There was renewed chemistry between them.

"So, the father of your children doesn't live with you?"

"No way, Madame! He's married."

"It doesn't bother you to rob another woman of her husband and to have two children with him?"

"You know, Madame, no woman can keep her husband from having extramarital affairs. Just as I, as his first mistress, cannot keep him from taking a second or a third. If every married man's lovers took pity on the plight of their legitimate rivals, a lot of single women would commit suicide from loneliness. You know, we too should be pitied."

"You think so? After all, you have the best of all worlds, as they say. These men generally come to see you when they're relaxed and in a good mood. They take pride in showering you with gifts and compliments."

"A woman, no matter who she is, cannot be satisfied merely with a man's gifts. There comes a time when she wants *him*. From then on, the gifts lose their value and the money its power."

"What stage are you at with yours?"

Dominique shot her employer a sideways glance. Emilienne's calm, even kind look loosened her tongue a little more.

"For now it's fine. Compared to other single women, I am a little spoiled. I've got his children, and I do not intend to let him leave me. In fact, he's with his children now at my parents'."

"Don't forget, you're talking to a married woman."

"Sorry, Madame. I said too much."

She lowered her head, ashamed.

"Don't be sorry."

The two women looked at each other and laughed. Then they talked about other things. Emilienne got back home at the end of the afternoon. The two women promised to meet often outside of work.

FROM INSIDE her bedroom, the door ajar, Emilienne could hear her nephews telling their grandmother about their weekend with their mother. Her husband, who'd brought them home, had left. With nothing better to do, the young woman riffled through the latest issue of a women's magazine. The alluring title of an article grabbed her attention: "How can you win back a man who is slipping through your fingers?" Curious and skeptical at the same time, she skimmed through the article.

"You think for sure he doesn't love you anymore, that it's a lost cause or that he is responsible for the downhill turn in your relationship! Don't be so sure, and don't be so impetuous. Forget for a moment everything he may have said or done. Instead, think about your attitude, your behavior, and your words. You'll see that something wasn't right on your part! You are therefore also responsible for the bad parts of your relationship. What must you do? Above all, don't give up and prejudge his feelings toward you. Make some new resolutions right now and put them into practice right away. And, unless you are a couple that has truly reached the point of no return, you will be surprised by the changes you notice in your partner . . ." Emilienne closed the magazine and had that pensive look on her face that reflected the intensity of her thoughts.

She could no longer remember when her relationship with Joseph had started to go downhill. She hadn't been made aware of it until her mother-in-law pointed out that a divide had long existed between them.

One evening several years ago, when her car was in the shop for a tune-up, she'd come home in a taxi earlier than usual, and from outside she had heard his mother talking to her son:

"Avomo has agreed that his daughter will be your second wife. Until, that is, your Emilienne asks for divorce. Yes! She plays the role of the sophisticated woman so well; she'll never accept sharing you."

"Still, I must see this girl you're talking about. After all, I am fine with being polygamous as long as my wife approves. Though it would definitely surprise me if she did."

What Eyang had proposed hadn't bothered her; it was more Joseph's comment that had horrified his wife.

Two days later, Eyang had come to Emilienne's bedroom trying to blame her for her son's financial ruin. She had even gone so far as to say that it was Emilienne's doing that she, Eyang, lacked clothing. Emilienne had to wave both of their pay stubs in her face to prove to her mother-in-law that she earned twice the salary of her husband. Later that day, when his wife repeated the bitter words she'd exchanged with his mother, Joseph was so enraged, he completely lost it:

"Just how far *will* you go to humiliate me?" Joseph howled. "Was it really necessary to show her my pay stub? Isn't it enough that the whole city knows that your company provides my housing? Did you also have to belittle me to my own mother? If you want a divorce, let's go ahead and do it. You assume this air of superiority, and I'm just about fed up with it. Get it through your head that I will never allow a woman to control me, even if it is in the interest of women's lib. If ranting and raving about it is so important to you, go live in your head. This has been going on for too long, and I've had it up to here."

She'd neither had the time to explain herself nor to talk to him about the conversation she had overheard between him and his mother. He spent that night out. For the first time, she realized that her husband reproached her for her social success and that, with his mother's help, he had considered taking a second wife. Although many a time she'd been told anecdotes about husbands who, in spite of their choice to register their monogamous marriage at city hall, ended up secretly marrying a second wife, then a third, never had Emilienne thought that Joseph belonged to that category of mean and vicious men.

Those two almost concomitant events were deeply disturbing to her. From that moment on, the complicit looks, unfinished sentences, and asides between mother and son irritated her to no end. She managed, nonetheless, to control herself and had concluded bitterly that the ship she'd embarked upon with the man whom she loved, and which she'd thought was solid, was beginning to capsize dangerously. It pained her greatly to hear that she'd given him a complex, having never, up to that point, lacked respect for him. Their professional situations were incomparable—he was a civil servant and she worked in a state-owned company—so his complex seemed unfounded, irrational, and at the same time threatening to their life as a couple.

Following that outburst, so typically male, Joseph became short-tempered, verbally abusive, and plain crude. He'd begun to drink excessively and refused to bring his wife to official ceremonies, and even to respond to their friends' invitations. Married life quickly became unbearable. Eyang had had the decency not to blatantly take her son's side. Confronted with this unbearable situation, Emilienne initiated a conversation with her husband one afternoon at siesta time.

"I find it deplorable that you've decided to turn to alcohol and odious behavior to prove your virility. And the idea of taking a second wife so that you can eclipse my social standing is ridiculous, because I do not think that I've used my superiority—and I don't really like that word—to assert my authority in our relationship. It just so happens that I have a certain understanding of marriage, which I've defended since we were students. I need you, and if we ever separate, my social standing certainly will not fill the void of your absence. And if, without realizing it, I've made you feel that money was more important to me than you, I beg your forgiveness."

On the other edge of the bed, Emilienne had started to cry. It was difficult to get out the words she'd prepared the night before. Swallowing her pride, she had felt the urgency to give some reassurance to her husband so that the potentially thickening cloud would dissipate.

Joseph, who had remained impassive from the beginning of his wife's intended intervention, now drew her awkwardly toward him and uttered through his teeth:

"No man, not even the most liberal-minded, accepts being financially inferior to his wife. Of course, I'm not talking about those who have no sense of honor, those who have a bizarre liking for being on welfare. Now, don't go thinking I'm jealous of you. When your company made you director of administrative affairs, I was very proud of you. As for me, I was hoping that my financial situation would quickly improve. You know better than anyone all the obstacles I've had to face. Not only did my application file disappear at the Ministry of Public Administration, but there was also the jealousy and numerous betrayals by some of my colleagues at the Ministry of Foreign Affairs. How can a man put up with his partner being financially superior in such conditions and for an extended period of time, especially when those not so subtle friends harp on it every chance they get?"

Having to open up to his wife in that way seemed torturous for him, which, for Emilienne, proved his love for her. Throughout his speech, which was difficult for both of them to get through, he had not loosened his embrace.

"Tell me," Emilienne spoke softly. "You still haven't answered my question. I want to know if it is my social status that is making you want to take a second wife."

"What gave you the idea that I want to become polygamous?" he snapped, moving brusquely away from his wife. "Are you listening through doors now? That does not sound like you at all."

Emilienne, who had been seated for a long time on the bed, retorted:

"Stop dismissing me and trying to evade the question. Do you intend to bring a second wife to this house, because, as your mother said, I will not consent to it. Did you ever love me, Joseph?"

Her watery eyes desperately searched her husband's averted, embarrassed gaze. She placed her hands over her face to hide the large tears flowing down her cheeks. Then, as if in an act of defiance, she suddenly raised her head and forced him to look her in the eye. Their breaths melded together then merged. They had become one . . .

"Of course I love you; I love you, I . . ."

Joseph's last words died in Emilienne's mouth. After several long minutes, which seemed very short to his wife, he pulled away from her gently:

"I promise not to leave you, whatever happens."

That promise was not a promise, and had bothered Emilienne for a long time. It was only several years later that she realized he had not sworn his fidelity to her that day.

Even so, their reconciliation had brought them closer to one another, and for about a year they lived a sort of second honeymoon.

"How did we manage to grow more distant after having had that period of happiness?" the young woman wondered, melancholic, emerging from all those memories. "Now, he collects mistresses. They must change weekly, as routine as changing the sheets. Has he finally managed to get over my so-called social status by being with all those women, obviously chosen because they're inferior to him, and next to whom he must really beam with pleasure? Unless these days his new professional duties are making him want to jump into bed with those other women. No, Joseph is no different from other men who cheat on their wives to forget their own problems or who use women to test their seductive power, or quite simply who are happy, and act out of capriciousness or subconsciously. So, when can they be faithful? Aren't they all made to constantly slip through our fingers? As for us, Joseph and me, an abyss has come between us, which we may never again cross to get back together. When our daughter was still alive, we had a human being who belonged to both of us, as proof of the strength of our love. Even a lover couldn't destroy the bond we had because of that child. A tender and affectionate look from her was enough to make us make up after our arguments. Her tears would shatter us and her joy would bring us happiness. Now, I have the feeling that when he looks at me he is faking, or else revealing his reproach and bitter regret. On those rare occasions when he smiles—he no longer knows how to laugh when he's with me—it comes in the form of a slight, fleeting gesture, as if a burdensome memory is standing between us."

Emilienne rubbed her frozen arms together briskly. She distinctly felt the energy leave her body through her legs, and her entire body became weak, then heavy. It was a strange sensation that she had never before felt so distinctly. Her body was so heavy that she couldn't lift her right foot, which had gone completely numb. Her left leg, luckily, was lighter, and so she was able to drag herself into the living room by walking her hands along the bed. She turned on the television set. Her physical weakness had also attacked her brain so she couldn't make out the images that paraded across the screen, nor could she make out the host's words even though his voice was ringing in her ears.

She groped her way over to the armchair, sat down, staggering, and then passed out. Little by little she came to, got up, and headed, this time, over to the window; with a detached gaze she moved her eyes over each of the spotlighted plants in the yard. The moon glistened in the sky. "It's time to have my fruit trees pruned," she murmured. She rubbed her arms together again, then moved away from the window and sat back down in her chair. But on her way, she'd inadvertently bumped up against the sharp corner of the glass shelf. She was bleeding profusely, and the blood was streaming down her leg.

Holding her hand over the gash, Emilienne ran to the bathroom, got the rubbing alcohol out of the cabinet, and poured a good amount of it over her wound. But the black blood continued flowing nonetheless. So she took four compresses, doused them with alcohol, and laid them over the gash, then stuck a large square bandage over it all. She sat down again, this time on the bed. And just as she did, she heard doors opening. It made her think that Eyang and her grandchildren had been locked up in one of the bedrooms since she'd gotten back, waiting patiently for her to go to bed so they could come out.

Emilienne stretched out on the bed, her hands on the nape of her neck. Once again, her thoughts kept her inside her head. "How strange it is that people who have such high regard for one another and who love each other cannot live together for long before their relationship starts to deteriorate. As if friendship and love needed space in order to last. At the same time, although that physical separation keeps intact the feelings one has for the other and embellishes memories, if that separation lasts for too long, it creates a distance between them that is everlasting. It gives the impression that the only reason people get together in this world is to accompany one another during a very specific moment in their journey and for a precise length of time before going their own separate ways and allowing each other to proceed through the labyrinth of life or before they are separated by death. What do people take away from these often painful separations? Oh, Joseph! Do we have nothing more to learn from one another, nothing more to share or to give? Has the moment come for each of us to go down our own individual path?"

A DOOR SLAMMED. Emilienne jumped, the threat she had made this morning to her mother-in-law looming in her mind. It wasn't the idea of facing Eyang in front of her son that frightened her, but rather what could transpire from the confrontation.

Emilienne had been in a quandary for a long time now, unable to guess how her husband might react. And, as if it were meant to, her predicament proved just how far apart they had grown. What remained between two people who, in spite of their love having been so strong, could no longer even predict the other's actions? What happened to the time when all she had to do was focus her thoughts on him and a few seconds later he would telephone her? Would they ever be able to transmit messages to one another merely by thinking something again! Lately, every time she tried to focus on him, a black hole came between her and his fleeting image. If love between two people was not enduring, what could be in this life? Perhaps this emotion needed another dimension.

It had been three weeks since Joseph had come home. Obviously, it wasn't the first time he had disappeared for so long. And if Emilienne was feeling apprehensive about his return, it was because she sensed that it would bring about a change in their life as a couple.

However, contrary to her expectations, Eyang had shown nothing but extreme kindness over the past week. As to be expected, being no fool, the old woman had fully considered the severity of her blunder in attacking her daughter-in-law so openly. Since it hadn't been long since she'd suggested divorce, it wouldn't take her son long to understand that Roxanne's wound had been premeditated. As he had proven by marrying against her wishes, there was a good chance that he would never leave his wife.

After analyzing at length the situation she'd just created, Eyang decided to change her tactics. She would have to make everyone forget that stupid attack against Roxanne. This sudden change in her mother-in-law could only perplex Emilienne, who had finally come to the simple conclusion that she would lead Joseph to choose between his mother and her. This was a risky approach that would appear to be a choice she was imposing on them and one that would force them all to make decisions they would most likely regret.

After pondering for quite a while the sudden change in her mother-in-law, she wondered if the latter hadn't simply returned to her senses with regard to her. If that were the case, she wouldn't take the risk of ignoring the process of reconciliation she'd begun a week before and would hope that it was unconditional and sincere. Unless Eyang wanted to grant her a reprieve as she waited with baited breath for her son to come around, in which case Emilienne would respond accordingly.

As they waited, the two women kept a close eye on one another. Nothing in Eyang's behavior, however, revealed any sort of duplicity. Several times, Emilienne turned around suddenly in an attempt to surprise her mother-in-law's gaze. And even surprised like that, Eyang remained kind and affectionate. What could Emilienne do other than trust her own judgment? Distrust could become a vice that could distort reality.

Then, one evening Antoinette arrived at the house, in a whirlwind, as usual. After saying a quick hello to her sister-in-law and greeting her two children with a kiss on each cheek, she ordered her mother to lead her into her bedroom to discuss a very important issue. They stayed in there for nearly an hour, and when they emerged, the mother and daughter appeared to have made up. They especially went out of their way to show kindness toward Emilienne, which immediately made her think that their conversation had been about her and that for once it wasn't about destroying her—even though her sister-in-law had never, to her knowledge, sought to blame her for anything.

Emilienne was not mistaken. Although she'd been hesitant to do so for more than a month, Antoinette had managed to persuade her mother to abandon the plot against her sister-in-law, which she had already set in motion. To her great surprise and without having to insist, Eyang had promised to bring the couple closer together rather than seeking to break them up.

The fact that Joseph showed up at home again, she sensed, was proof of Eyang's renewed disposition. All sweetness and light, Eyang divided her attention equally between her son and her daughter-in-law. She engaged more and more in private conversations with Emilienne. Her constant suggestions and motherly advice were disconcerting to Joseph, whose first impression of their reconciliation, the reasons for which he could understand neither its basis nor its aims, was that the women were conspiring against him.

Their apparent complicity was far too unsettling to him. He was terribly affected by it, especially since he was not able to openly reproach them for it. It might very well have given him the answer that he had always hoped to be true and now dreaded: a mother-in-law and her daughter-in-law are not necessarily enemies. Their reconciliation was totally baffling. In the worst case, he thought, it was actually dangerous for him. In hindsight, he suddenly realized that it had been reassuring to see them arguing over him and hating each other because of him as well as for him, like a leader whose subjects would fight over the privilege to serve and to please him. Of course, he couldn't say that his mother had become indifferent to him; to the contrary, she was showing more interest in him.

More so, he was bothered that his wife was progressively carving out her own space at his mother's side. She made it so obvious that he had the sensation he was already being relegated to second place. As for Emilienne, she seemed calmer to his great surprise; and Joseph came home every evening after work so that he could closely follow the development of this odd friendship blossoming under his nose.

As days passed, he became increasingly irritable; he grew angrier each time the two women hovered over him as if he were an ill patient, sulkier and sulkier when, so absorbed in their chatter, they would ignore him. His brief outings in the evening were disrupted by his obsession that they were criticizing him and sharing secrets about him.

Because what could they be talking about other than the man they shared, the one who had brought them together not only because of their love for him but also for the sake of his well-being? It is true that there is strength in unity, and Joseph felt weak and alone confronted with two women who had gotten close to one another undoubtedly because of their anger at seeing him lead a double life, each perfectly aware of what they could gain from their complicity. And as a popular singer had said, *When the wife gets angry, the secrets are out.*

To his deep regret, his presence at home did not make their relationship normal again. Instead, it produced the opposite effect. Joseph inevitably withdrew into himself, because the women in his life, and even his nephews, were so preoccupied with playing what he called their "vaudeville-like comedy." The new strategy failed so quickly that this time he disappeared even longer from the home that excluded him. If each of the women suffered from it, they both refused to share their grief.

THE CHANGE in each of the members of the family seemed to have affected Godwin the most. His transformation had actually begun at the time of Rékia's death.

Previously indifferent to Eyang's status, he now gave the impression that he answered directly to her, carrying out her orders so willingly that it took Emilienne by surprise. For her part, Eyang was overjoyed by the influence she had over the cook. But his submissiveness and her dominance ceased when they found themselves alone. Their roles changed. Eyang was terrorized by the cook's silent threats and damning looks. One day, when they were alone, Eyang had the courage to reproach Godwin for being repeatedly late. Annoyed and motivated by the delight he took in flaunting his growing confidence in the old woman's presence, the cook moved close to Eyang, and, pointing his finger at her, uttered disturbing threats:

"Listen, lady, I will not allow you to use that tone with me. You know that if I say certain things to the mister and missus, you could have serious problems."

Eyang stepped back but maintained her composure.

"Ah, yes! And what are you going to say? Be careful! Don't forget that you are a foreigner in this country. Go ahead and talk. There are planes that leave here every day; there will certainly be a seat for you. Who do you think you are?"

The cook stepped toward the old woman again, and with a mean look in his eyes, his voice booming, said:

"I am not afraid of you, because in this game it is you who have everything to lose. So, choose your words carefully before you speak to me."

"Come on, boy!" Eyang said, suddenly seeming vulnerable. "Don't get mad, you are fine here, right!"

"That's better."

Eyang backed away toward the gate and leaned against it because she was feeling weak; Godwin returned to the kitchen. For the first time in her life, Eyang was overcome by a sense of extreme panic. Or worse, she thought she was in danger.

In order to make her son happy, she had done certain things, and she would definitely do them again if she were in the same circumstances. If she had to blame herself for anything, it would be to have not acted alone. In any case, she knew one thing: her son's girlfriend would not talk. The threat came from the lowly cook, whom she thought seemed to be a bit crazy. She could not demand he be fired, nor could she tolerate his arrogance for long; those options would lead to his inevitable betrayal. What was she to do, faced with this dilemma?

Panic-stricken, the old woman pushed open the gate and found herself outside of the compound. Roxanne ran behind her and took off toward the trees, where some mangy dogs were gathered around an old bone. Eyang trotted along behind the animal, which had disappeared from her sight once he'd sniffed out the bone. Eyang retraced her steps and came back to the topic that was preoccupying her. She suddenly felt very weary and felt an aversion to everything, to herself especially. She knew well that feeling of uneasiness that would erupt in her from time to time. It came from her childhood, from the memory she had of her poor mother. She was a kind, gentle woman, but was terrified of her husband, who would beat her with a stick at least twice a week. Her whole life she had injuries and bumps and bruises all over her body. Before she had died at an early age, her husband had managed to blind her in one eye and had broken all five fingers of her right hand, making it useless up to the day her soul was laid to rest. Eyang had promised herself that she would never allow herself to be dominated by a man—which she had succeeded in doing effortlessly with a husband who was far too easily swayed—and that she would choose her children's partners according to very specific criteria. She had not managed to tame her rebellious daughter and had left her to take care of herself, and with her son it was not going to be easy. And now the cook was complicating things as well.

Suddenly, a bright glimmer lit up her melancholy eyes. She had just come up with the only solution that would keep Godwin quiet once and for all.

With a renewed sense of enthusiasm, Eyang returned to the house with a quickened pace. Frantically, she pushed open all the doors that blocked her path. When she reached her bedroom, she knelt down in front of her trunk, and with trembling hands untied the cord she kept around her waist, then pulled out an old tarnished key and inserted it hurriedly into the keyhole of the thick padlock.

With both hands, she emptied out the trunk, throwing its contents all around her. At the bottom was a port bottle filled with bank bills. She grasped it around the neck and threw it with all the remaining strength she could muster so that it crashed and shattered against the wall. Shards of glass, bills, several papers with scribbling on them, and her marriage certificate went flying. Eyang grabbed the wad of bills, took out several of them, and ran out of the room.

"Here," she said and hurled the money against the cook's chest. "This time you are going to keep quiet. Understood!"

"Oh, yes, Madame Eyang," Godwin answered, delighted, and with a look of malice. "Well, what a nice surprise; you are very rich! I swear by my mother's good name, and she is your age, not to tell anyone what I know."

"Okay! Okay!"

Eyang returned to her room calmed and with a smile.

WITH EMILIENNE, Godwin was sometimes hostile, and sometimes he displayed a false kindness, which disconcerted the young woman more and more.

That Saturday morning, when she came back from the market, Godwin came running to unload the groceries from the trunk of her car.

"You've done quite the shopping, Madame Emilienne! Have you noticed how the prices have gone up? Soon the poor won't be able to eat anymore. And we are surprised by all those store robberies and the blackmailing of the rich."

Emilienne stopped in her tracks and looked quizzically at her cook. Since he'd worked for her he had never put three sentences together in a single conversation. Godwin lowered his head, a smirk on his face, and took out two bunches of bananas and a box of sea bream, marlin, and an enormous tuna. In the kitchen, he feverishly put away the vegetables, fruits, meat, and fish.

"If you want," he went on, jumping from one foot to the

other, "I can get you some good fresh fish for a good price. I have a good connection, you know."

He straightened up and put his hands in the pockets of the new beige pants he'd put on under his work shirt so as not to dirty them.

"Is the investigation into your daughter's death moving forward?" he asked, moving from futility on to grave subjects, his facial expression mirroring the transition. It seems that the police never find the murderers of children. People don't know why. But then, what good would it be for you if they did, eh! They're not going to give back your child. And remember, those killers will never be happy."

He was getting ready to go out of the kitchen when Emilienne ordered him not to move.

"Let this be the last time you use that tone when speaking to me, and don't ever look at me in that insolent way again. Just keep to your work; the rest does not concern you."

"Yes, Madame, I do apologize."

He gave a slight disdainful smile and went out dragging his feet.

Flabbergasted, Emilienne watched him go out. Her cook's self-important air made her think of the stories she'd heard a thousand times about household staff who wielded strong influence over their employers by using fetishes.

Most cases were about cooks who worried about keeping their jobs with high society employers. In order to do so, they would mix together special concoctions and put them in the food they prepared so they could dominate and manipulate their employers as it suited them. Before long their masters were satisfying all of their needs without the slightest hesitation. The lady of the house would become the cook's lover. Having fallen in love with her employee, she could leave her husband to go live with the cook in the master's house, the latter choosing to leave so as not to bother the lovers.

Those stories had always seemed absurd to Emilienne, although now she admitted that anything was possible in Africa, this land of mysteries. She decided therefore to be vigilant, paying particular attention to what the cook tasted on the menus before serving them.

Following the euphoria after her reconciliation with her mother-in-law, an overwhelming feeling of melancholy took over Emilienne. The physical inner emptiness she felt was so profound that even the attention her other family members gave to her, and the delightful change in Eyang, could not console her.

Yet again, Emilienne had to admit that her joie de vivre and her hopes could not come from a single person, not even the one she loved and would love forever.

Her sadness carved out space first for her sinking spirit, then for mortal anguish. She felt like a prisoner with a life sentence who was destined to suffer through all her emotions in a narrow cell lit only by a small overhead window. The agonizing life Emilienne was living was unbearable. Multiple torments had accumulated and were resurfacing all at once. There was her fear of no longer being loved, the anguish of never having any more children, the fear of separating from her husband, and above all, the jealousy that was eating her up like a flame licking up dry straw.

Until this moment, she had refused to imagine her husband in the arms of another woman. In fact, she had never given the woman a face or a body. She had been a shadow which very well could have been her own—it did seem that some men looked for lovers who shared traits with their wives. And then for no apparent reason, that shadow was filling in quite distinctly and that other person did not resemble her. She saw her as more beautiful, flirtatious, charming, and very elegant. At times in her inner turmoil, she made her repulsively ugly and delighted in the fact that her husband would make such an absurd choice. Ah, if only she could surprise them in each other's arms, she would strangle the woman with her own hands. She would be the first woman to commit a crime of passion in this country where people usually settled their scores on the sly.

"What does she have that I don't?" she asked herself for the hundredth time since that morning. "Is it my infertility that is making him run away? Why does he need me to have children to love me? My illness, if that's what it is, is not contagious and should not rob us of our love. No, I cannot believe that Joseph loved me for the children I was supposed to give him after our wedding. I don't want to believe that all he saw in me was this woman who was to become the mother of his children. No, that idea is unbearable to me. I am a woman and I will be a woman no matter what happens. And I am not completely barren since I did give him a beautiful little girl. Is it my fault that she died, that it was our destiny that she be taken from us! And through all of this I have not changed, I am still me, the one he loved, I am still a woman, his wife! Am I still his wife, now that he has another woman? What is she like? I must see her. I will follow him the next time he comes around."

THIS DID NOT take long. It was 8:15 p.m. when she began tailing him, and what she saw would forever remain etched in her memory.

A few minutes before he had gone back out, Joseph had torn apart the closets, searching high and low for a silk handkerchief that matched the tie he had taken off the rack. The whole time he spewed insults left and right, swearing every five minutes. He even told his mother to go to hell when she suggested she help him look for it. Of course, Emilienne figured out right away that he was on his way to an important dinner. Clearly, he was not going alone and was going to change his clothes at his mistress's. And since for some time now people had been saying that he made a point of being seen everywhere with the same woman, it was likely she would be with him this evening as well.

After he'd taken down all the hangers and dumped out all of the drawers, even those that belonged to his wife, he left, muttering to himself.

Before he had even got into his car, Emilienne had taken the keys to her Subaru, and she waited behind the gate for him to turn on the engine; then she, too, pulled out. Her two hands gripping the wheel, she followed behind him. Joseph drove swiftly, not bothering to stop at red lights. The young woman stayed close behind so as not to lose sight of him. The smooth flow of traffic made it easier for her since, by 7 p.m., the major avenues of the city were deserted. This didn't keep Joseph from braking suddenly and coming to a halt in the middle of the road. Emilienne had just enough time to veer to the right and speed past without him spotting her.

She parked almost half a mile ahead at a poorly lit curve in the road. She knew he would have to pass by there, so she waited a good ten minutes. It started to seem like a long time, and Joseph still hadn't come. What had happened to him? Had he turned back to take another road?

Emilienne got out of the car and walked back to where the street started to curve. From where she was standing, she could see that beyond there the road straightened. A car was parked on the sidewalk, and its occupant seemed to be holding the hand of a woman who was struggling to defend herself in an argument. Emilienne thought she recognized the woman's silhouette. It was no doubt just a resemblance; certainly there were many petite women, and from this far away, she couldn't really tell. To confirm her suspicions, she decided to get closer to them. And in order to keep them from seeing her, she left the sidewalk and walked along the side of the road, which was muddy and strewn with pebbles. In the semidarkness, she tripped over a large rock and found herself sprawled on her back in the mud. Without losing her will, she bravely got back up and continued her way toward them, taking small steps.

She felt a burning sensation on her leg, where she had grazed it on the sharp corner of the low table in her living room. Her scab had definitely reopened; it didn't matter—a little wound, no matter how deep, wasn't going to stop her. She walked on her tiptoes, feeling the ground as it crunched under her shoes. In order to pick up the pace, she hiked up the bottom of her dress, stuffed it into her slip, and took her shoes off, but not for long, because walking over the loose stones hurt the soles of her feet. She continued a few steps farther and, heart beating, raised her head. There was no doubt. She recognized Joseph's metallic grey Renault 5. The woman, whom she still could not make out clearly, started yelling and fighting more aggressively. But she could see her husband's head and his shirt. What was all this about? Her legs like jelly, Emilienne ran, and fell again. She got back up just as the woman dove into the car. Emilienne started running again, and climbed onto the sidewalk screaming her husband's name. The car pulled away.

As HER EYELIDS grew heavy, urging her whole body to fall into a state of oblivion, Emilienne remembered she was still wearing the dress she'd just dragged through the mud. Too bad, she said to herself. Getting up again would make her conscious of her physical state and, consequently, relive the painful scene she had witnessed moments before. What would she gain from suffering more from a situation that had taught her nothing?

In a state between sleep and wakefulness, she continued, despite herself, to rationalize the situation and to try to be rational about it. But she would have really liked to sleep. She turned over in bed. The roughness of her legs bothered her. What had really just happened? It had all unfolded so quickly! And with that she started thinking again, which was exactly what she wanted to avoid. How then was she to stop the string of sentences filling her head and instead make her mind go blank to avoid the pain? At that moment, her brain was like an alarm clock set to go off after an undetermined amount of time, ticking away the hours, minutes, and seconds without end. They say that a man's negative thoughts are his worst enemy. They join together, invade you, and lead you to a place you don't want to go. They are uncontrollable and elusive. They torture you, tear you to shreds, and then destroy you. They are more destructive than that which provoked them. Although their effects on one's health are obvious, we cannot help but get sucked in. At that very moment, Emilienne could not stop the painful explosion that came from her heart, reached her inner core, then ran down her legs. The localized pain worked together with the muddle in her head, which she was incapable of controlling.

"What use is it, getting myself into such a state? I will not be able to change it. It's an illusion to think someone can transform a person limited by his convictions. I am sure he never dreamed of the harm he could do me. Since it is his wish to behave this way, I should, according to him, be thankful for him and happy with him. But even if I were a saint, I wouldn't be able to, nor could I avoid the inevitable effects of his love affairs."

"How strange it is the way things always happen by chance and yet so profoundly change the course of our lives! Everything that had been anticipated, planned, in the utmost detail, is crumbling like a staircase made of sand. Will I at least be able to control my own pain despite these recent events?"

She jumped at the muffled hum of a car outside. She ran to the window and saw Joseph opening the gate. She ran as fast as she could into the bathroom to put on a housecoat and leapt into bed. She settled into bed, propped up against the headboard with a book on her chest, and closed her eyes. Joseph opened the door surreptitiously. Emilienne opened one eye then closed it immediately. Though it was long enough to notice the new grey suit he was wearing and the tie and silk handkerchief as well, a handkerchief he had no doubt found at his mistress's. In a few minutes, the room was filled with a strong odor of whiskey.

"Since when do you sleep in a housecoat?" he muttered as he flopped down onto the bed.

"Oh, no! You are definitely not going to sleep here in your drunken state. So why did you come back? Don't tell me your mistress threw you out after your quarrel on the road."

His forehead wrinkled, and he wavered as he turned around toward his wife.

"What do you mean?" he grumbled. "As usual, you come up with the craziest bullshit."

His drunken breath filled his wife's nostrils, and she turned her head away, pinching her nose. Her angry voice boomed over the humming of the air conditioner.

"Listen, Joseph! Don't think I am naïve. I know that you picked up a whore on Independence Boulevard around 8:30 p.m., after you quarreled passionately with her. I want to know who she is, do you understand?"

"Screw you! Nobody can say they saw me pick up a whore on the street around 8:30 p.m. because at that exact time I was having a drink with friends. You saw Pierre. I loaned him my car. He had a date with a girl. Call him tomorrow, he'll confirm that for you."

He dozed off.

Emilienne shook her head and smiled in despair. How could she have been so naïve as to think he would admit everything to her? He wasn't lying to spare her from pain; it was purely out of habit. If they were still together in ten years, he would repeat the same lies.

Why did this man, who was so straightforward and open in other respects, love to weave a web of lies whenever it came to his relationships with his mistresses? Joseph was not the only man who cloaked his extramarital affairs in lies and enigmas. Even the most disrespectful husband lacked the courage to reveal his intimate secrets to his wife. No doubt, for them it was the intoxicating mystery of it all that they needed.

IV

Emilienne's Isolation

Weeks passed, each the same as the last. But all the same, Emilienne had noted a change in her mother-in-law's behavior toward her. You could say that her usual feelings toward her had returned.

For once, Emilienne did not dwell on the downturn in their relationship and made a deliberate effort not to try to make it better. If for a long time she had allowed Eyang's provocations to get to her, she was firmly committed to ignoring her from here on.

In order to snap out of the depressing monotony of her conjugal life, that Saturday afternoon she was going to her parents', whom she had not seen in over a month. Thanks to them and to her sister, she had been able to cope with the death of her daughter. However, she did avoid talking to them about her love life even though she knew they were aware of her unhappiness. And it was exactly because of their silence, the pity she saw in their eyes, that she had stayed away from them these past six weeks. Pity was the one feeling she could not stand, especially coming from her family.

Before she had even parked her car, her nephews had run over to greet her, throwing their arms around her neck as she opened the gate. Although they were as happy to see her as the others, the two oldest greeted her with just a kiss on each cheek.

After the warm welcome, Emilienne, surrounded by her nephews, headed into the house, where she found her sister and parents. She sat down next to her father, who was filing his nails with deep concentration.

"Papa! Since when do you trim your own nails? Is your dear, loving wife refusing to carry out her wifely duties to take care of your needs?" Emilienne laughed and gave her father a hug and kiss.

Openda grimaced. His beautifully wrinkled face transformed into a crinkled piece of fabric. His body was still muscular and solid, in contrast to his face, which showed his age. The old man was very well groomed, had his hair dyed every three months, and exercised each morning. For a long time, he had awakened every morning at five to go for a run. But he had stopped the early morning exercise routine in order to sleep later; he could now catch up on the sleep he had missed when he took care of his patients.

To prove to himself that he was still a handsome and energetic man, at times he would charm women whom he picked up hitchhiking on his way home in the evenings. Luckily for his wife, he had never gone further than uttering a few flattering words to those women, who always listened in admiration. "The day I hear that you're messing around with young girls or even old women in your car, I'll cut off your peter and your hand too!" his wife had said to him one day in front of their children.

"Save it," the mother said in response to her daughter. "If I hadn't been useful to your father, do you think he would have kept me around this long? It's time he takes care of his old body a little. Those days when he thought he was king are over. Thanks to you kids, I realize that I've been a slave to your father my whole life."

Flopped in her armchair next to her husband, Rondani stretched out. Although she was a lot younger than he, she looked older. In fact, she was quite strong, though her white hair, which she refused to dye black like her husband, was deceiving.

Openda shook his head and smiled at his wife as she took his hand affectionately.

After she'd consoled her youngest son, who was crying for a toy his sister had just snatched away from him, Eva spoke.

"Papa and Mama are getting old." Then, turning to her sister, she added: "You're letting yourself go. You're dressing very badly and you don't want to see anyone anymore, not even your nephews, whom you used to insist come over to your place every weekend."

"Your sister is right," her mother added. "Not long ago, you'd have thrown that dress you're wearing today in the garbage. Did you notice that there are threads hanging from it every which way and the sleeves are coming undone at the seams? I hope you don't go to work in that! Before you got here, I was telling your sister that I met a healer at the market this morning. I of course talked to her about the problem you have with your womb, and she would like to try to heal you."

Emilienne, who up until then hadn't taken her eyes off of her nephews as she listened to her mother and sister, looked over at her mother, suddenly sad.

"I see that you've decided I need looking after. If it's all right with you, let's not discuss my womb today."

"So when *do* you want to talk about it?" her sister snapped back at her. "We don't mean to hurt you, you know. You must know that you will never completely fulfill your destiny as a woman until you have children to raise, for those around you to watch grow up. I know it's going to hurt you when I say that your dead child no longer counts, and in a few years people will have forgotten that you were once a mother like all normal women. Don't worry; what I am saying doesn't apply to us, your family. I'm talking about your mother-in-law and society in general. I feel your pain, Emie, and I think that you should shake yourself out of it a bit."

Patrick, Eva's youngest son, started yelling at the other end of the room. His mother ran to help him.

"My dear child," Rondani said softly, "your sister is right. Do you know that, in the elders' eyes, your husband would not be in the wrong if he brought home a concubine? The day that idea hits him, he won't ask you for your opinion. Even *I* would say he were right to do so."

Having finished filing his nails, Openda looked tenderly at his daughter.

"Mama, you know how hard I've tried to cure my so-called illness. And believe me, you are no more affected by it than I; I'm the one who lives with this drama in my body as well as in my head. I know full well that it's because of my present infertility that I am losing my husband, and God knows it's the last thing I want to happen."

Eva retorted dryly:

"Finally you admit that your husband has a mistress; you know, I knew it. Count yourself lucky that you are still together after all the years he's spent waiting for you to give him a second child. For some time I'd thought that Rékia's death would make you see the reality; now I see that I was mistaken. You seem rather to be wallowing in your problems. One would even think that you're behaving defiantly toward your husband. Perhaps you want to know if he really loves you. If that's the case, it's a stupid approach, in my opinion. So what if a man loves a woman for herself or for the children she gives him, if he knows how to make her happy? When you finally open your eyes and ears, it will be too late."

"Easy there, easy," her father interjected for the first time. "Emilienne's problem is close to all of our hearts, but let's know how to talk to her. I know my daughter well, and I know that she is suffering terribly from this."

He was quiet for a moment then continued:

"My dear child, I must admit that your sister and mother are right. And I would like to add this: in spite of the level of education women of your generation have achieved and in spite of the high positions they hold across all the professional realms throughout the country, they will earn respect and consideration and be fully happy only when they manage to balance their professional life with their life as a mother and wife. I never met a single woman throughout my long career who was able to overcome her problem of infertility. Sooner or later she feels the effects of the absence of children in her life. Your sister's children are not your own. Even if it was you who raised them, once they get older, they will go back to their mother. We have seen children, how can I say, repudiate the aunt who had raised them through adulthood, and return to a mother who had shown no maternal love for them when they were born and who was incapable of mothering. Even children who never knew their father feel that unfathomable yearning to find him. Most of those children feel no remorse at leaving their mother to go live with their father. And if worse comes to worst, seeking out the father is not so bad, since the mother knows that the child is not repudiating her and that he needs the love he's been deprived of for so long. I say all of this just so you understand that you will merely be an aunt to your nephews, no matter how much you love them. What would become of us, your mother and me, if we hadn't had you? We would be dismal old people abandoned by everyone. And if we had nephews, we would have been a burden on them; we'd have been people they helped merely in order to appease their conscience."

Openda rolled up the sleeves of his heavy cotton *boubou* and interlaced his slender fingers. His expressionless gaze wandered aimlessly then fixed on an insect nest on the terrace wall.

"It's good that you are finally talking to her. Make her understand that children are treasures and a guarantee for aging parents," Rondani added after some time.

"Really, you've got to be kidding," Eva said. "If I understand what you're saying, you had us thinking about who would take care of you when you got old. I wonder if we would have been a treasure and a guarantee for you if I weren't married to a successful businessman and if Emilienne weren't in such a good professional situation. I bet we would have been useless children!"

"You've misunderstood Mama's words," Emilienne said. "You know that it is not our respective situations that interest her. Listening to the three of you, on the other hand, I am coming to understand that a woman must procreate, or she will lose her social and family identity. You are not wrong; that is exactly what is happening right here, right now. You do love me, yet you deplore the fact that I am not exactly like all of you. I will not go as far as to say that you are ashamed of me, although . . ."

"My child, what are you getting at?" her mother whispered, her eyes filled with tears.

"My sweet child," her father added, "you know that nothing in the world would keep us from loving you."

"Right, you love me, and I bet you would love me more if I had three or five children. How could I blame you for that! It seems that, even today, a woman can earn her entire family's respect and consideration only if she is a mother. We've all seen plenty of young destitute women prostituting themselves so they can feed their kids, and they don't leave those kids in their parents' care. The overwhelming majority of those parents are incapable of providing their grandchildren with a proper education. In indigent families, those unplanned children aren't properly nourished or cared for, and then we're surprised to see a rise in the infant mortality rate or a rise in the number of juvenile deaths. One of my employees at twenty-four years of age has six children, for whom she sacrifices body and soul, as they say. All of her worries, her ambition, and her desires, revolve around the comfort she must provide for her kids. Who is thinking about *her* life? She herself isn't even thinking about it. It isn't only the smiles that have disappeared from the faces of sterile women; there are so many mothers who no longer know how to laugh. Do you know the reason for this sadness that we see already in children and, later, in adults who have become parents? That widespread sadness relates to the problems and traumas that women experience during pregnancy. Children born under those conditions often have serious personality disorders that sometimes affect them their entire life. Add to that the poor conditions in which they are brought up, because obviously no one is taking care of them. And the minute we talk about it, people respond by saying that the African has no psychological problems because he lives in a large extended family. As if the family circle can cure a man of his profound distress. Those are the same people who are surprised and worried by the problems of the youth who will be the men and women of tomorrow. I am not trying to justify my infertility, I just want to make you realize that motherhood and children do not ensure absolute happiness."

Six pairs of eyes beamed at her in admiration. Emilienne had rendered them speechless. Eva was the first to find her words.

"What do we have to do with all of those broad theories? You will never be in the situation of those women you've just described. I don't think that you've been marked since you were in our mother's womb. You won't hide your yearning to have children from anyone here. And you should know that a woman's success is limited neither to her diplomas nor to her professional situation. Your intimate life, meaning, your marriage and your children, come first, or at least are equally important. When your private life is a failure, wealth and professional success lose their importance. I know I am not telling you anything new, but we had to remind you of this today. Now! I'm going home. My husband gets back from the United States tomorrow. Gather your toys, children, and say good-bye to your aunt and grandparents."

With an infernal noise, the little ones gathered up their cars, airplanes, and dolls. After hugging and kissing Rondani, Openda, and Emilienne good-bye, they went out in single file, the eldest in front and the youngest in his mother's arms.

Outside, the ash blue clouds set against the golden sun, with its rays bordering the sky, formed a magnificent scene worthy of the brushstrokes of a surrealist painter.

Rondani whimpered quietly, and in a barely audible voice said:

"You see! That is what brings a woman joy. Don't you want to experience that again, my child?"

WAS HER HEAD spinning because she was so distraught over the arguments her family had presented earlier? She sat with her hands planted firmly on the steering wheel, remembering a statement she'd read in a women's magazine that she had thought quite exaggerated: "A woman is never completely satisfied. Whereas some enjoy professional success, others build a solid marriage based on love, and then there are those who have children to feel fulfilled. No woman, however, manages to enjoy all three. And if there are women out there who are perfectly happy, who have brought these three together, they are extremely rare, and, in our opinion, if they have even two of these, that is a great achievement."

Emilienne smiled. She admitted that the author of that statement was right. To this point, no woman had seemed to enjoy those three conditions.

She was concerned that she ranked among the women who had been left in the lurch by destiny. If she had to make a choice, she would have been incapable of doing so. And then, what use was it to speculate when destiny took charge of everything? When did a man's freedom to act stop, and when did his destiny begin? What could one do to avoid the succession of miserable events that drove people down paths they hadn't chosen without the option of getting a fresh start?

She had suffered every day since her daughter's death, and although she had wished that today would be better, it ended on a sad note. Every thought and conversation with her close friends and family members had reminded her of her barrenness. It pained her even more that she had disappointed her family. And for the first time, she reflected upon the importance she attributed to her parents' and sister's opinion of her, not only because she needed their love, but also because she was responsible for the dark shadow that loomed over them and troubled their peace of mind. In fact, *she* was the dark shadow. The last thing in the world she wanted was to make them unhappy. But now what could she do?!

WHEN SHE GOT back home, Emilienne found Joseph on the divan, all excited, watching a tennis match. From the door where she was standing, she recognized Noah by his hair and silhouette, a player her husband loved—as all Africans did.

Joseph barely even turned his head when his wife slammed the door. Emilienne didn't linger in the living room. From her bedroom, she could hear Eyang reprimanding her grandchildren. Weary and depressed, she took a quick shower and got into bed. Her bed had become the only place she liked to be when she had nothing to do, or rather, when she didn't want to do anything.

Those moments of inactivity became more and more frequent. And, even though she was aware of the dangers of her physical and mental apathy, Emilienne did not want at that moment to move. What was she waiting for? Did she even know?

BY THE TIME Joseph came into the bedroom, she had already entered that half-comatose state of deep sleep. He turned on the air conditioner and plunged into the bathtub, which he had run very hot. It overflowed with green honeysuckle suds. He lathered himself vigorously. Then, eyes closed, he rested his head on the edge of the bathtub.

It had been about six months since the last time he had taken a bath at home. There was a time—now in the distant past—when he liked to make love to his wife in that very bathtub. For her it was hard work, scrunching up in uncomfortable positions trying to find a position that worked, and that would make him laugh so hard it would bring him to tears. Sometimes, when he made fun of her, he would lose his concentration, which made Emilienne so mad, though she would forget all about it as soon as he made love to her again on the carpet or on the bed. How many times had she sworn to herself that she would not let him take her in that bathtub again? But then, with each caress, she would melt further into her husband's arms. She would not complain about her knees or her backbone, because in the end, the discomfort of it all intensified the pleasure they both felt.

Places like that, which for her were reminders that they had once been happily married, for him were no longer appealing. Could he say that he had ever felt at home in this luxurious villa to which he had followed his wife? Because that was the appropriate word. He followed his wife to this superb house on this enormous plot of land that her employer had rented to her. If he had only thought it through more carefully then, he would have proposed a more modest home rather than encouraging her, as he had done, to choose a five-bedroom villa. At least he had refused a furnished house, even though it was, again, Emilienne who had bought almost all of the furniture. The man he was at the time—a man in love—had given very little importance to such details which, several years later, would assume great importance in his eyes. And their discussion on the subject had not helped his inferiority complex.

Years later, he was named secretary general at the Ministry of Foreign Affairs. His salary tripled. He put in a request to his minister to find a house for him and his family. The minister himself called him in to refuse the request outright.

For a while, Joseph thought he would change all the furniture. The idea did not stand up to the arguments he concocted in his head and stewed over in order to convince his wife. Keeping his most recent mistress was a way for him to regain his self-confidence. He could finally assume his role as a man. Also, the young lady had never behaved authoritatively, and her demands were limited to money, which he would give her without counting. Although it wasn't long before then that she had hinted at marriage, Joseph wasn't worried about it; he knew that offering her the car of her dreams would appease her for now. He was at least sure of one thing: she would remain submissive to him for a long time—if not always—given the pittance she earned.

"Emilienne, on the other hand, doesn't need financial support from any man, and that's how I could lose her," Joseph thought. "But, I don't want to leave her. She is a remarkable homemaker and a perfect mother when all is well. My dream would be for her to raise all the children I have with my lovers. That's what some wives do in her situation. Only here's the problem, I fell for an intellectual who refuses to break certain barriers. She has really made me understand why some executives marry rural women. They see the world purely through the eyes of their spouses. Stuck in their own worlds and molded by tradition, they are obedient and tolerant. Too happy to have been chosen among so many others, they know how to show their gratitude with unwavering love. I still love my wife, and I will accept her as she is if she manages to produce another child. It is not too late. And medicine advances every day. Does she still want to? Good God, why did I have to fall for a woman with issues? Giving birth is not a luxury! The most pathetic women can bear children and why not she? She has so many positive qualities! She has been refused that simple happiness, yet she is capable of assuring a good education for her children. And I'm the one who drew this losing number. Everything is against us as a couple: her sterility, this house, and even our parents, who from the beginning disapproved of our marriage."

The bath had gotten cold, the suds had dissolved, and Joseph was cold. He got out of the bathtub and dried himself off quickly and then ran into the bedroom to turn off the air conditioner. Before joining his wife in bed, he put on the only pajamas he still had in the closet.

Emilienne slept like a little child on the edge of the bed, her legs curled up to her chin. A psychiatrist would say she had low self-esteem and that she subconsciously wanted to be back in the safety and security of her mother's womb. Several things of late were revealing of her mental state. For example, she always wore white clothes when she had her period, as if to tell the world that she was a woman like any other.

Contrary to what he had hoped, the bath had not relaxed him. He got close to his wife; she whimpered quietly. He pulled back the sheet and looked at her body wrapped in a pink silk nightgown. Her buttocks and thighs had grown curves. Her stomach had thickened as well.

"Well, well, she's gained weight," he said to himself. "She was always so careful about keeping her figure despite my wish to see her gain weight. Has she finally decided to please me! Even the most stubborn women always end up giving in to their husbands' desires when they realize they are about to lose them. That's when they find themselves doing the very things they wouldn't even admit to themselves they were doing."

Emilienne's whimpers grew louder. Joseph pulled the sheet back up under her neck. Soon cries of terror filled the room. She squirmed. In her agitated sleep, she gave a few good punches to her pillow. Her tangled hair was scattered across her tensed face. Worried, Joseph shook her. Emilienne let out a scream and woke up, her face wet with tears.

"Where is my baby, I want my baby, they have killed her!" Joseph leaned over her.

"Calm down, you've just had a nightmare."

Emilienne curled up in those muscular arms in which she'd always felt protected. Outside, a gust of wind shook the trees so hard they could hear the sound of the rustling leaves. With her head buried in her husband's chest, she told him about the dream:

"I dreamed that I was carrying a beautiful baby that looked like you in my arms and that some masked men and women tore him from me and tried to kill him right before my eyes. It was awful, Joseph."

Emilienne cried.

"It was just a bad dream," Joseph said softly to her, caressing her fingers.

"A bad dream that we've actually lived. Have you forgotten, Joseph?"

"How could I forget Rékia's abominable death?"

He remained silent for a long time before continuing:

"I was called to the police precinct yesterday. They told me they've given up on finding her murderer."

"They have no right to do that!" She exclaimed. "How are we supposed to go on living knowing that our daughter's killer is somewhere in this city, unpunished? Why did he choose her, what right did he have to take our daughter from us? Who called you in? Did you try to find out who was in charge of the investigation? Let's go back to the precinct tomorrow. I want to know who the murderer is. I want him to die inside the walls of a prison."

"I had the same reaction, you know. Try to understand that they have absolutely no clue. Despite the missing person reports, no witnesses came forward. And as they say, they're swamped. Let's try to forget our loss."

All of a sudden, Emilienne appeared more fragile to him, shattered. As he looked at her, he felt that something had broken deep inside her. He hadn't thought she had been so devastated by their daughter's death. He should have realized. His silence about the traumatic event could not be mistaken for a sign that he had forgotten. Would his presence at home have soothed her suffering?

"Why don't you go back to your gynecologist? People say that Dr. Pascal treats desperate cases."

Emilienne tensed up then got out of bed.

"I don't want to rush you, but it is time that you think about it," he went on. "A miracle can always happen."

"You believe in miracles, do you? Not me," she replied dryly. "What is it with all of you asking me to get myself treated?"

"Emilienne, having a child would change a lot of things, you know?"

"Is that it! If I have a child, you will leave your mistress. If I have a child, you will love me again. If I have a child, your mother will embrace me and my family will be satisfied. In a word, everything will be back to normal. Now, I'm just upsetting you all."

"I am still your husband, and it is natural that I want you to get better. Unless you ask for a divorce, I will accept whatever you decide."

"Please, stop saying such foolish things. And why are you talking about divorce? Are you suggesting that to me? Be clear about it then. I don't want your pity. That's it! You want the breakup to come from me so that you have a clear conscience. You would consent to a divorce if I asked you for it out of respect for my rights, is that it? What are you doing about your rights! Am I to understand that you're sacrificing them for me? No, Joseph, I can see right through you."

He clenched his fists and his forehead wrinkled.

"How can someone live with a wife who doesn't understand him? No matter what you do, there are things you cannot stop me from doing. The reasons that drive me are profound. In a word, I need a certain balance that I have not found within the walls of this house."

"You want me to understand that you are doing a favor to the barren woman I am by letting me decide the fate of our marriage. You want me to understand that while waiting, you need to get away from it all and bask in the arms of your mistress, for your own equilibrium. So what are you waiting for, go ahead and leave, you have my blessing."

She left the window she had been leaning against and stepped toward him contemptuously.

"Stop wailing, you're going to wake up the whole house. Do me the pleasure of making an appointment tomorrow with Doctor Pascal. This discussion is over. I want to sleep now."

"Oh, no! That's too easy," she replied wildly, pulling him by the sleeve of his pajamas. "Is your sleep more important to you than our future?"

Joseph let his wife pull him back. He sat back down on the bed and gave her a wily look. Standing facing him, enraged, Emilienne continued:

"The thing is, you are incapable of addressing the root of the problem. Tell me! How many times can you stand the sight of a leper who refuses to take on the responsibility of a separation! I had forgotten that in our marriage agreement there was a clause that stated that the validity of our marriage was conditional upon my ability to provide you with heirs. And I bet that my not respecting this clause, by the date that you have no doubt preset, will mean capital punishment for me."

To soothe the spasms brought on by her fury, she sat down on the dresser.

"Stop your whining for a moment. I'm going to tell you once again, it is not possible to have a discussion with you. Listen! I am going to sleep in the living room," he interrupted as he got up.

"Go ahead!"

She threw the pillow at him.

Joseph went out and didn't turn back. Emilienne went to the kitchen, took a bar of hazelnut chocolate and a packet of madeleines out of one of the cupboards, and devoured them under the covers.

In the morning, she dragged herself drowsily out of bed. As she sat in front of the pile of folders in her office, she tried to concentrate so that she could forget the words she had exchanged with her husband the previous night. And again, her thoughts carried her away.

What to do now that she knew her husband took pleasure in his role as unfaithful husband? Why, actually, wouldn't she ask for a divorce? If there was one positive thing in her life, it was that she was not financially dependent upon her husband. Instead of supporting a mother-in-law and children who were not even hers, she could invest in a business. Like many women her age, she could build houses and rent them out or open up a fashion boutique. Free of her marital problems, she would dedicate herself fully to her business, her career, and her family.

"Come in," she answered to the slight rap at the door.

The handle moved, but the door did not open.

"What is happening to me—could I be losing it?"

She got up to open the door, which she had locked earlier.

"My apologies if I've disturbed you, Madame," her secretary said, examining the distraught look on her employer's face. "I finished typing up the report that you left for me yesterday."

"Put it there," the young woman replied coldly, her gloomy gaze wandering over her secretary.

Dominique pulled at her tight-fitting knit dress, clicked her heels together, and held her lips, which were smothered in several layers of lipstick.

"Do you have work to give to me?" she added hesitantly.

"You can leave," Emilienne answered.

Seamlessly, she plunged back into her inward meditation.

"How could I, at my age, start a romantic relationship with someone other than him? God, what is it that makes me love him at this point? I am getting sick over it all, and envisioning divorce is making me crazy. I can't do it. Could my sister be right? Without him, my life has no more meaning, and it is not my professional career that's going to bring me happiness."

She left her office and went to sit by the bay window, which was hermetically sealed. From her office, Emilienne tried to picture herself outside in the rain breathing in the smell of baked earth, one of those scents so specific to tropical countries. In her imagination, the deep breaths of air she took into her lungs and the drops of warm water streaming down her body gradually brought her back to life, as if each breath of air, each drop infused her cells with vitality and renewed energy. She felt so good in that new body that she forgot herself completely. For several fractions of a second, she was happy.

Her moment of bliss was interrupted by the telephone ringing. Reluctantly, she walked sluggishly back to her office.

"It's me again," her secretary announced. "Can I speak with you?"

"What is it? Is something the matter?"

"It's hard to say . . . I . . ."

"You can come."

Intimidated by Emilienne's questioning look, her secretary stood there, embarrassed.

"Sit down, I'm listening."

"I thought that after your visit at my place, I would be able to talk more openly to you."

She went silent and fidgeted, then continued:

"I wouldn't want to pry, but perhaps I could help if you're having problems."

Since that Sunday when Emilienne had agreed to go to her place, when the two women had talked for a long time, Dominique had thought that their professional relationship would turn out to be friendlier. That was a disappointment for the secretary. Instead, Emilienne was more distant and at times cold.

"What do you think of barren women?" her employer asked, without beating around the bush.

Her secretary jumped and stammered:

"I, I don't know, Madame."

"Please, be frank. Do you consider such women to be ill?"

"If I was barren," Dominique started, encouraged by Emilienne's matter-of-fact stare, "I would have made a pact with the devil to have at least one kid."

"Why and for whom?"

"To keep my boyfriend around, for my family, and, of course, for myself. You know, men cannot stand women who challenge their masculinity. And the family doesn't forgive you for that. And then, you know, Madame, a woman without a child is like a one-armed person. How do you explain that? Her whole existence, she would be missing this other life that comes from her, without which she is crippled. Her whole life, people would point at her, ridicule her, pity her."

"What do you think of women who choose not to bear children?"

"You'd have to be sick in the head to decide such a thing," the secretary said indignantly.

She held her silence for a moment and went on:

"That's not your case; you've already had a child."

"That doesn't change anything since I can't have any more."

Emilienne got up again and went over to the bay window to conceal the tears streaming down her face, although the sky had dried its tears. On the big public square lined with coconut trees, the constant comings and goings of men, women, and children caught her attention. After hesitating a moment, her secretary joined her.

"What is going on?" Emilienne asked as a group of men in military uniforms got off a truck.

Very quickly, they planted posts in the ground and tied five hooded men to them. Then, the dozen armed military men backed up several meters, formed a straight line, and stood at attention. The motley crowd swelled, kept back by police and barricades.

"Where was my head?" the young woman exclaimed. "This is of course about the execution of the five murderers the media has been talking about for the past two days."

"They were tried two days ago. Do you know that the murderer at the bistro in my neighborhood is among those sentenced to death? In my opinion, it's a good thing they're paying this way for their crime."

Emilienne shuddered and instinctively drew closer to her secretary. The two bodies brushed against one another. Outside the jubilant crowd was pushing and shoving to get a good view. A few reckless fools managed to get past the barricades.

The people condemned to death did not wait long, as the soldiers raised their rifles and fired, spraying their victims with bullets. The victims collapsed one after the other. Emilienne let out a cry, which she quickly stifled with her hand over her mouth. Dominique threw herself on her, grabbing her by the shoulders. The two women embraced. The cameramen and photographers immortalized the last twitches in their camera lenses. One head that was still moving was decapitated by a final spray of bullets. The two women's bodies intertwined and shuddered.

Those four heinous crimes, committed within the span of a week, and the capture of the biggest criminal in the country at the same time, had shaken public opinion, which had called for an exemplary sentence. A formal judgment had been delivered within a few days, and, to put an end to such murders, they had all received the death penalty.

Judging by the large crowd, the criminals did not deserve mitigating circumstances. This exemplary punishment, the first in Kampana's contemporary history, would give rise to a national polemic among the intellectuals, who would divide into two camps: those who would be fervent defenders of justice served, and others who would strongly denounce the sentence. The intellectuals of the latter group, greater in number, would ask if the criminals were not in reality those who had consciously ordered the death sentence for murderers who had acted without premeditation, excepting the thief. "Who are we," they would chant, "to calmly decide to take another's life, even a murderer's! Who gains from this? Do the murderers or their families, who will always bear the marks on their foreheads! We weigh our words carefully when we say that all of society has condemned these poor innocent victims to a slow death. We say that a society that uses the death penalty in its justice system is heading fast toward decline."

Their opponents would fiercely defend the thesis that a society cannot evolve if each individual does not respect its established rules, which are the barriers needed to avoid chaos and anarchy. The laws, above all, aim to protect the individual, to inspire respect for the other, which men left to their own devices easily forget. And the lack of respect for the life of one's neighbor deserves punishment by the law.

This passionate debate would go on for a long time, without the polemists' reaching a satisfactory conclusion.

On the public square, a dreadful silence surrounded the last of the onlookers, who wandered along with their heads and shoulders slumped.

"Hold me tight," Emilienne whispered. "I don't feel well."

Her mouth hung half open. Dominique shuddered, her lips quivering, her eyes closed. Thunder rumbled in the distance. Flashes of lightning streaked the sky, crisscrossing from east to west, north to south. The stragglers ran toward some makeshift shelters. The rain began pattering again, as if the earlier calm had been meant for the purpose of allowing the men to accomplish their task.

It rained for forty-eight hours. The public square, people say, was washed of its stains. The same was true of the whole city, its human excrement carried along toward overflowing gutters, water flooding its avenues and alleys.

In the slums, entire neighborhoods collapsed and were carried away by devastating water currents. The turbulent waters fell in cascades down the hillsides. On the second day, the flood was replaced by a blast of wind that spared neither the trees nor the old plank and bamboo houses. Looking like unidentified flying objects, branches, sheet metal, and thatched roofs flew across the sky then landed on roads and on residential areas. Inside the gutted houses, children cried and old people wailed, all huddled under their beds.

Roxanne, who had been cooped up with her owners this whole time, started to show signs of claustrophobia. She got up onto the divan, climbed up on Yvon and Nomé, and pawed at Joseph and Emilienne. She was wary, however, of getting near Eyang, who watched her out of the corner of her eye.

Joseph, who no longer often attended family evening get-togethers, was clearly ill at ease. With his eyes glued to the television screen, he crossed and uncrossed his legs. From time to time, he scratched his head frantically, as if it were covered in lice.

Then, as if suddenly attacked by an itch in his pants, he got up, went over to the little bar, and served himself a large shot of whiskey, then sat down between his nephews on the couch. Across from him, his wife stared at a spot on the wall, deep in her own thoughts, judging by the different expressions on her face.

Between two gulps of whiskey, Joseph shot furtive glances at his wife. When his glass was empty, he refilled it. Sitting directly in front of the television, Eyang turned several times toward the couple, whose behavior amused her.

As for Roxanne, reprimanded then neglected by everyone, she rushed over to the pile of newspapers stashed in the basket next to the television. With unusual calm, she scattered them around her without her owners noticing. Once she had finished, she crouched down and got comfortable, her eyes staring maliciously at Eyang, who was focused on a film starring Romy Schneider and Lino Ventura. Yvon was the first to notice the prank the animal had just played. In shock, the child watched as the dog laid down another turd, this time on the tiled floor. Satisfied with her ruse, she chewed on the pile of newspapers and was getting ready to drag it across the living room when the little boy finally shouted:

"Look! Roxanne went poo-poo, and she wants to show it to us."

Everyone stood up, except Emilienne.

"Dirty animal!" the kids screamed and chased after her.

"Look at that! How can you live in a house with a dog?" Eyang commented, curling her lips, looking disgusted.

"Mama," Joseph said, "you seem to have forgotten that this poor animal has been cooped up all day. It is astonishing that no one thought to open the door for her when she was trying to get our attention."

He got up to pet the animal, who was so overjoyed she clung to his pant leg. Then Roxanne rolled around on the floor and finally lay down with her paws up in the air, her snout dripping with slobber.

"That's a good dog; let's go take a walk outside now."

The master and his dog headed toward the door, the former reeling along thanks to the half bottle of whiskey he'd just emptied, and the latter wiggling her hips.

When the door opened, a violent gust of wind blew into the house, knocking over the flowerpot that sat on the table. This time, Emilienne got up to pick up the pot and clean the floor. Joseph and Roxanne came back almost immediately.

"I have never seen such strong wind. Several branches have been ripped off of trees, and the plants are uprooted. Still, Roxanne was able to poop a second time. She truly couldn't hold it in anymore."

He moved toward his wife, grazing her deliberately when she stood up, the scrub brush in one hand and the floor cloth in the other. The young woman stopped short when her husband's foot stomped down on the broom.

"Stop sulking," he said to her in a derisive tone.

She looked him up and down and waited for him to lift his foot. Nomé and Yvon jumped on the animal. All three of them rolled around on the floor. Joseph joined them. The children and the dog climbed all over him, the former laughing and the animal barking. Joseph cried out like Tarzan.

Emilienne sat back down and bit her lips. Eyang fidgeted as she listened wrathfully to the giggling and yells of the three rolling around. She removed her glasses, rubbed her eyes vigorously, and then pulled at her lower lip, flapping it against her chin.

Emilienne clenched her teeth, amused by the impromptu scene. Finally something out of the routine was happening in this house! *This* Joseph, rolling around on the floor, reminded her of another who, during the first years of their marriage, had been a hysterically funny, cheerful soul, who naturally attracted friends. Any person he met, whether man or woman, loved being around him. With him, the dinners with their friends were never morose. That pleasing side of his personality had disappeared over the years. The only thing that remained of the sparkle and vivaciousness in his eyes were glimmers of mockery, unless he was in a good mood and away from home. Right then, he seemed to be letting off steam.

Eyang visibly disapproved of the spectacle and Joseph's participation in it. After she'd contorted herself in vain, she made a perilous jump several inches up in the air and fell back on one foot, slipping on the other, which had gotten tangled beneath her armchair. Without meaning to, Eyang, too, had ended up on the tile floor. But since no one had noticed her fall, she immediately picked herself up. Then, with her hand on her hip, she rushed over to the chaos. The children, seeing her coming, dispersed. Even quicker than the children, Roxanne had already made it to the other side of the room. Sitting on the floor, Joseph stared at his mother, who stood immobile in front of him with a disapproving look on her face.

"Don't you think you're well past the age to be horsing around on the ground?" she shot at him. "How are your nephews going to respect you after seeing you do that?"

"You are becoming really annoying," retorted her son sharply. "Nothing can happen when you're around without you getting involved. You are not a mother; you're a policewoman, my word!"

He got up. Three lines formed on his forehead.

"When are you going to treat me like an adult? Because I don't consider myself a kid playing with my nephews."

Her hand still on her hip, Eyang raised her head to look her son square in the eye. Then, with an angry movement, the mother whisked the scarf off her head.

"Do you intend for those words to remind me that I am not in my own home? Anything I say or do in this house irritates you, isn't that right?"

She got close to the chair and leaned on it.

"My son, you forget a little too quickly that without my sacrifices, you would be a failure of a man. I want you to remember that when you speak to me. Neither the food nor the clothes you give me will make up for the sacrifices I've made to make you the man you've become."

Exhausted, she sat back down.

Troubled by her words, and at the same time feeling a little guilty, he lowered his head. He saw himself . . . He saw himself when he was a little child, his mother carrying him on her back, wrapped in a *pagne* as she gathered brush or planted manioc roots under a burning sun or heavy rain. Another more powerful image stood between him and his mother: it was after his father's death when her income had been cut off—she had to sell all of her jewelry and clothes in order to feed and clothe his sister and him.

Those memories, so alive in his mind, brought an ashamed smile to his face. He walked hesitantly over to his mother and held her in his arms.

Emilienne got up and ran into the kitchen to get a piece of cake, which she gobbled down in her bedroom.

"Don't get yourself all worked up, Mama. What did you do, anyway, that caused that swelling in your ankle and that pain in your hip you keep massaging?"

Her face set, his mother blinked her eyes.

"Don't move. I'm going to get your Chinese balm. You're right, you know, it does work miracles."

He disappeared into the bedroom and came back with a small, flat, red box. Very carefully, he rubbed her ankles and handed her the little box.

"You'll see, by tomorrow, you won't feel anything anymore. Put a little of it on your hip."

Finally, Eyang sighed, and her maternal gaze fell, reassured, on her son; she spoke in a low voice:

"My son, seeing you crawling around on the floor like a

child earlier made me remember when you were little. I think I suddenly felt bad that I could no longer pick you up in my arms, or be the only person in the world you need. I see that I am useless to you now. What will happen to me if you cast me out of your home? You are the only one among my children I can still count on; your sister doesn't care about me. Take care of me, don't abandon me for that barren woman," she whispered, kneading her hands.

Two giant tears rolled down her creviced cheeks.

V

A Decision That Comes with Time

Most of the time when we see people in the street, we are not able to gauge the sum of their pain. We often think that the rocky periods they are going through are not as bad as our own. And even when we get closer to them and learn of the tragedies they've suffered, we are still convinced our sorrows weigh more heavily than theirs.

Who, then, could understand Emilienne's self-absolution, which for those around her was merely a sign of her egocentrism? For her, her life was in all respects like climbing a mountain with sharp, jagged ridges under the oppressive heat of the sun. For a long time, she had tried desperately to hold on to those ridges, but instead had badly scraped her hands and feet.

Still, she clung to life, having decided that in order to confront all those who scorned her, she would scale that mountain again, tackling it from another side where she didn't know the obstacles. As the saying goes, we carry the weight of the world on our shoulders, and Emilienne was conscious of her own size and strength! She managed to climb that mountain, her guarded optimism leading her to regain her will.

On the morning of her appointment with Dr. Pascal, Emilienne got up earlier than usual. Through the blinds, the radiant yellow sun's light refracting through the thick foliage of the trees produced a dazzling green. Birds were singing, perched upon the fence.

She took two deep breaths and drank a tall glass of mineral water. Despite her physical and mental agony, she applied her makeup carefully and was attentive to how she dressed. Ready two hours before her appointment, to clear her head, she decided to organize her bedroom. Perhaps she would feel more at ease placing herself in the hands of the gynecologist once her bedroom, which was part of her intimate world, was in order.

She began with her husband's walk-in closet and wardrobe, which were both nearly empty. Out of forty or so ties and thirty shirts, less than half remained. Six suits and most of his underwear had been moved into the other's house, her rival's house. With the calm and composure she did not know she had, she methodically folded and arranged her husband's clothes before attending to her own. She took out a set of silk sheets for the cleaning lady, who should arrive at any minute. Today was the day she would do a full cleaning of their bedroom and iron the laundry that had been washed the day before.

It was time to leave. Satisfied, Emilienne closed the swinging doors to the closet.

She arrived at the clinic just as those who had worked the night shift were getting ready to leave. Emilienne got a little lost in the clinic, which had expanded undoubtedly in response to its growing clientele. In order to be examined by Dr. Pascal, who was renowned well beyond the city, appointments had to be made two months in advance. Emilienne had to convince the office that her medical condition was grave in order to get in as soon as possible, and that meant after only two weeks.

There were about twenty patients awaiting their turn when Emilienne sat down in the waiting room. Dr. Pascal Moukambé's examination room opened onto a long, narrow hallway in front of the waiting room. The incessant comings and goings of medical personnel, the squealing wheels of stretchers, the shuffling feet, and mumbling of the sick made the whole scene a little frightening. It was really quite a squalid place for the sick, where people would go with a feeling of guilt, fright, and the kind of embarrassment that was really an admission to others of their illness, which they viewed as a weakness.

Left in the hands of the subaltern personnel whom in normal circumstances they would look down upon, some patients showed their antipathy and acted out violently. On the other end of the spectrum was the doctor, who became the Lord savior, the one who understood them without judgment and who had the power to heal. The fear and respect he inspired were commensurate with his wisdom and his ability to perform the miracle of healing. That was why, even today, the doctor is the man or woman most respected in society and to whom one remains grateful for the rest of one's life. Even when he sometimes fails at this tall task, for the patient, he remains a special human being.

The number of women waiting to be seen increased every fifteen minutes. Some, with bulging bellies, had distressed, grievous looks on their faces. Others, more serene, seemed distracted as they leafed through the magazines that were left out for them. One of them, certainly the youngest one there, studied her elders closely, looking at them respectfully, yet with a derisive smile on her lips. How many of them wished to have a child?

Emilienne's worried look lingered on a lady with a flat stomach, over forty, who sat right next to her. She wore thick black glasses and seemed terribly troubled by the fact that she was there.

I hope she hasn't contracted AIDS, she thought. She was so thin and so tired! The young woman trembled. The campaign about AIDS that had echoed throughout Western countries lately was so frightening, it left no one indifferent. Having originated in an African country, in a certain species of monkey, AIDS had been ravaging African populations for a dozen years. In point of fact, who had definitive proof of its origin? Whatever it may be, we would no longer attribute all those mysterious deaths to witchcraft.

Emilienne wore a slightly saddened smile as she thought about the harsh words of Pastor Oyabé, a friend of her parents: "These days, people engage in sexual relations as often as they have a meal, and they use all orifices. Because of these sins, man is giving a death sentence to innocent fetuses. He has not understood that everything in this universe and in his own life rests in a balance, which, if upset, brings about catastrophe. If, to this sexual orgy, we add terrorism, crime, and perversity, how can we be surprised by man's decline! Faced with such horrors, God has but one way to purify the world: he sends all sorts of calamities. Let us not be mistaken, it is not a punishment that God is inflicting upon his creation, but rather he is showing us the impact of our thoughts and actions in the form of airplane, train, and car accidents, of drought, famine, and earthquakes. Since there is not going to be a Third World War, as some believe, there must be powerful phenomena that will force men to regain their good senses and their dignity. And that can only be done with the sacrifice of a great number of individuals. Those who are saved will undoubtedly return to noble sentiments."

"So what is it that has broken inside me that has brought on the calamity of my barrenness?"

She didn't have the time to answer the question she'd just asked herself; instead, she jumped when the woman next to her stood up. Soon it would be her turn. Emilienne was overcome with a sense of mounting panic. Twenty minutes from now, she would have to answer the embarrassing questions the gynecologist would ask, and in a few days she would know what she had until now subconsciously refused to confront: the truth. Doubt is a secure state behind which you can hide in order to protect yourself and demand the understanding of others. Knowing the truth knocks down the fortified walls you have built and leaves you to yourself and to the judgment of others.

When her turn came, Emilienne was led into an enormous office that smelled of cold rubbing alcohol. She sat down opposite the gynecologist. Above his head, on the wall, she could read this inscription: "The role of your doctor is to treat you; don't be ashamed to talk with him about your illness."

The young woman finally looked at the doctor. He was a man of about fifty years of age with a dry face, each side marked with a deep crease. His inquisitive yet reassuring look troubled Emilienne. Dr. Pascal Moukambé was one of the very top gynecologists in the country. Before buying this clinic, he had worked for a long time at the state hospital. His clientele had grown very quickly, and he took considerable business away from his colleagues, who were not at all happy with his fame. As arguments and negative reports about him multiplied, he took out a loan from the bank, added his own considerable contribution, and bought the Modern Clinic from a prominent colleague who had been trained at the Paris School of Medicine and was retiring after twenty years of loyal service in Africa. His patients followed him.

After having probed Emilienne's brain with his piercing eyes, as if to discover her most intimate secrets, which were likely to help him with his diagnosis, Dr. Pascal finally spoke in a soft and measured voice.

"Do you have a file here?"

"No, Doctor. It's my first time here."

Then began the usual preliminary questions asked at any first consultation. Trust established, Emilienne explained the reasons for her visit. The gynecologist followed up with additional, more precise questions regarding her state of health, asked if she had contracted any venereal diseases, the frequency of her menstrual cycles, and her spontaneous abortions. He noted the young woman's responses carefully in her file then told her to undress and lie down on the examination table behind a white curtain about two or three yards away from the office. Without moving, Emilienne let him examine her external genital area and take samples of her vaginal discharge. The young woman got dressed again and found herself handing over a consultation form with illegible writing on it.

"Bring me the results of these blood and urine exams as soon as possible, as well as the X-ray of your uterus and fallopian tubes. I will have your vaginal swab analyzed here in the clinic."

Emilienne left the clinic more relaxed, albeit a little ill at ease for having allowed herself to be intimately probed by a man. It was the first time she had turned to a male gynecologist, luckily one of great renown. The only female gynecologist that had followed her progress during her pregnancy and delivery of Rékia was a French woman who had returned home seven years ago. There was no female gynecologist in Kampana, to the great dismay of many husbands.

Emilienne felt relieved. As she drove her car, she began to dream of a miracle that would make her a mother again. Yes, why not, for once, place herself among those miraculously cured?

How difficult it can be for a woman to acknowledge what it is she has that's essential, whether in relation to society, her partner, or even herself. Soon, she might no longer be able to boast about motherhood. If doctors' laboratory experiments proved successful and if governments gave their okay, in a dozen years or so, men would be able to carry pregnancies to full term and give birth. As if, their reign in politics and business not enough, they were slyly attempting to rob women of their only power. The precarious equality of the sexes that we talk about today would be challenged yet again by such a medical revolution.

If one thinks long and hard, woman has always depended on man, willingly or not. Even in their life as a couple, he always had the last word. The only times she held the advantage were when he desired her or was courting her. Then she had the power to make those exhilarating moments last, during which time, in an effort to conquer her heart, he was capable of tearing down the walls, jumping over hurdles, and getting beaten. Those were the times when gifts would accumulate and his attention would intensify . . . You've got to admit that those are the most amazing moments in a woman's life. He would tell her that she was by far the most beautiful woman, and she would end up believing it. Her caprices were still qualities, legitimate demands, that he hastened to satisfy in order to neither displease nor annoy her. His amorous gaze wooing her was so penetrating and so sadly sincere that she would hasten to abbreviate his moments of suffering, although delicious for her, by the gift of her being. That was when she was the queen in his eyes.

If there was a period following his confession that was no longer so enchanting, she would not let it upset her. Because between two caresses and the intimate conversations that he would multiply and prolong delightedly, he would tell her in a soft whisper, in the hollow of her ear and in every position, of his burning desire. He would fulfill the most beautiful promises that the young woman—hopelessly in love—so liked to hear, something like: "I-will-not-cheat-on-you-will-not-hide-anything-and-will-love-you-always." He found physical and moral qualities in her faults. He was capable of fighting a duel or against an army to be sure not to lose her to another. In her arms, he becomes her lover, then her friend, her child, and, finally, her father. Coiled in his strong arms, she would throb in ecstasy and swoon with pleasure. She was to blame for all his sensual weaknesses, she was the woman he desired, and he would devour her with haste and greed. Inside of her, he became her, she became him. They were one when he was inside of her. Even in their dreams, they would meet. They reveled in the vigor of their eternal love . . . An eternity that, alas, would not last long. He got too used to this happiness too quickly, and that led to his inattentiveness and mental absence. *She* went after her dreams. She didn't want to believe for a single second that her beloved's far-off gaze, while he lay sprawled between her two breasts, indicated some kind of lassitude.

The time came when she was merely a presence to him. Of course, still sexually attractive, but no longer the focal point of his world. Through him, she could see her defects emerge, and, progressively, they became cumbersome obstacles. From that moment on, the talents he deigned to recognize in her were limited to her domestic duties. Well behind in terms of the rapid regression of his feelings, she clung to the not-so-distant memories of their love. The rare flaws she found in him were quickly excused, minimized in light of his exceptional sexual and intellectual abilities.

The beautiful dream came to an abrupt end when he called her by another name or evoked memories of time spent with another. She heard it straight from him: she was ordinary and did not excel in culinary skill. As a favor, he told her that her muscles were losing their tone and that her eyes had dark rings under them when she woke up. Those revelations coming from him hurt her deeply. So as not to lose him, she ran to the beauty salon to try to improve her skin, which was also withering. As she did some soul searching for him, he became increasingly distant; she could no longer feel his smell . . . The great love they had shared was lost, never to be found again.

From then on, she would take care of the house and the kids—if there were any. If they hadn't gone to city hall, they would have separated, promising each other that they would remain friends, if they were smart. After all, wasn't their friendship the best thing that could have happened to them, and wasn't it also tangible proof of their great love, eroded by promiscuity and time!

If she didn't stay strong, her reason for living would vanish with him. She would live with the memory of a blurred past, but the memory would always be there, and it would have no future. When she got old, she would say that after his departure, she had not lived but only survived.

And him! What would have become of him after and without her? Well, a few months after, he would have met a woman twenty years younger than she, who would make him relive the emotions and follies of his youth, having sex in the kitchen, even at the kitchen sink. He would become a young lover at the age of fifty, an excited spring chicken rather than a wilted old flower. And he would begin a new love life, everything new and fresh, whereas she would content herself with sporadic meaningless flings, unless with determination she succeeded in filing him away, too, with the obsolete memories that held no interest for her.

THIS LONG interior monologue ended as she closed the trunk of her car. Instead of heading directly home after her doctor's appointment, she had gone to do her shopping at the supermarket. She opened the door and was about to step into the car when a warm hand on her shoulder made her jump. She whipped around. Her secretary gave a stifled laugh. The two women stared at one another as if they were meeting for the first time. Emilienne's heart started pounding; at the same time, she felt immeasurable joy. Her face lit up. Dominique mustered her courage and whispered:

"Can we meet later in lovers' woods, right behind the supermarket?"

Emilienne shrugged her shoulders. Her eyes were ablaze with the fire that stirred inside of her. So as not to lose any time, she got into her car and disappeared into the Saturday traffic, which until then was like any other. Since their bodies had brushed against one another during the five criminals' public execution, Emilienne had refused to analyze the new urges of her flesh. All she knew was that her senses had discovered a strange desire, aroused by the thrill she'd felt when she first came into contact with that other woman.

So she was very excited when she arrived home. On the terrace her cook sat reading an adventure book. Without waiting for him to come help her, she took her groceries out of the trunk and unpacked all the large parcels and bags. Then she prepared some chicken with peanut sauce for herself in the pressure cooker.

Intrigued by her enthusiasm in her work and her good mood, the cook stopped washing the fruit and followed her movements attentively. Something out of the ordinary was happening to that woman, he thought. Although, he hadn't noticed anything unusual when he'd arrived in the morning. Obviously, his boss had not spent the night with his wife.

Before she left for her rendezvous, Emilienne took a cold shower and put on a pair of jeans and a blue cotton blouse. To complete her disguise, she added a curly wig. One would have to be quite clever to be able to tell it was her in that outfit.

She parked her car in the lot reserved for the supermarket customers so as not to attract the attention of curious onlookers in this city where people were watched closely and could easily identify others by their license plates. Then, a tiny bit tense, she walked the five hundred yards to lovers' woods.

She'd arrived early, a habit she was unable to break despite all the time she'd spent in Kampana, and disappeared head first, knees slightly bent, through one of the discreet entrances to lovers' woods. To be able to see her secretary when she arrived, she curled up behind the first shrub on the footpath. From there, she would have a perfect view of the comings and goings of the passersby without being seen.

Several couples, arm-in-arm, snuck in-between the trees then disappeared in the dense brush. You had to admit, the lovers' woods certainly deserved its name.

Every time someone came near her, Emilienne lay down flat on the grass. It wasn't long, though, before Dominique showed up, smiling and out of breath. She wore, with elegance and yet simplicity, a tight-fitting minidress and flats. Avoiding each other's eyes, the two women slinked between the giant trees, and could tell, at the curve of each trail, thanks to the cooing they heard, there were already men and women lying together on beds of leaves.

Dominique, who walked ahead, was the first to find shelter for them and, without turning around, walked toward it with a natural air, as if she had come alone.

Emilienne strolled past the spot her secretary had found, then backtracked and, after looking all around, leapt into the turn-off, allowing the shrubs to close the opening behind her. She found Dominique nibbling on a stem, spread out on her stomach on a mat made of dead leaves. Her minidress was hiked up so that Emilienne could see her buttocks and firm, muscular thighs. She sat down, with her head turned toward the bush.

"Your jeans look good on you," Dominique said, breaking the silence, as she got up slowly, like a cat being caressed by the sun.

"Thanks. I have a few pairs I haven't worn since I put on weight. Actually, it's a wonder I managed to get into these."

In turn, she picked up a twig that she cracked and broke into small bits.

"I went to see a gynecologist this morning," she went on.

She turned, finally, toward her secretary.

"Oh! For your childbearing issue?" asked the young woman, placing her hand delicately and hesitantly on Emilienne's thigh. "I understand," she went on, watching her impassive face closely.

"Yes, I want to try a treatment one last time."

She took Dominique's caressing hand and enclosed it timidly inside hers. A saddened shadow crossed her face. She smiled nonetheless.

Dominique came to nestle up to her and said softly:

"I see that you are determined to get your husband back. Do you know everyone in our company knows that your marriage isn't working anymore? It would be a good thing if you could prove them wrong. I think we can talk freely now about this problem that's bothering you."

The two women stared into each other's eyes. What exactly were they thinking? Emilienne was the first to break the short, troubling silence:

"I will only feel like a woman again when I am able to give

my husband more children. When he looks so tenderly at my nephews, it's as if he were piercing my heart with a dagger. I feel I am still capable of giving him the opportunity to hold children in his arms that would really be his. After all, there are women who give birth at forty and I'm not there yet."

She stretched out and then laid her head across her new friend's thighs. Smiling, Dominique lifted her blouse and walked her long painted nails delicately across her breasts as she took off her bra.

Emilienne froze, but let it happen. She closed her eyes.

"The opinion I gave the other day about barren women was very harsh; I hope you'll forgive me. But do you sincerely think that your husband will come back to you if you give him this child on whom you've pinned your highest hope? The birth of a child doesn't always bring couples closer together. It is possible that he truly is in love with his mistress and, out of malice, he might blame you for it, convinced nothing will ever change between you. And I'm sure many people feel sorry for him and don't blame him for his double love life."

Emilienne jumped up and pulled her blouse back down. Her brusqueness was in response to the ironic tone she believed she had heard in her secretary's voice. Surely, she was mistaken, though, since Dominique seemed rather sympathetic about her boss's love drama. Nevertheless, her retort was cutting:

"If a child cannot bring us closer together, then we will divorce. We will not be the first to do so, nor will we be the last."

She got up.

"You're right," furthered Dominique, completely serene. "I must say that it would be very hard for you to ask for a divorce. In my opinion, it's better to forget a man who loves his mistress than to hang on to him and probably suffer. What I can promise is that I am here for you and ready to give you whatever support you need. And I hope that nothing and nobody will undermine our friendship."

She placed her head on her neck and wrapped her arms around her. After a prolonged silence, she raised her head and asked, seeming distressed:

"Right, Emilienne? What we feel for one another cannot be destroyed!"

Emilienne smiled and leaned over her.

"Shall I drop you at home?" she was happy to ask in an authoritative, detached tone.

"Already?"

"Yes, I have to go."

"Fine!" Dominique said reluctantly. "You go first, I'll meet you at the car; I know where you parked."

EMILIENNE LIT UP as the days went on. Dominique's words, which had shocked her when they'd met that first time in the woods, now seemed more understanding and gave some importance to their relationship.

Although she could calm it at will, for a week, Emilienne lost herself to this new intense outcry of pleasure that surged in her body each time she exchanged caresses with her secretary in her office. This happy change, she believed, had come to soothe the emptiness that grew inside her when, on the same date of every month, that precious liquid she could not keep inside her flowed out.

When her husband suddenly seemed to remember her biological needs, making love to her twice in one week, part of her remained frozen. It wasn't that her love for him had lessened; it was, rather, to her great amazement that she loved him differently, in a way she could not define. At the same time, her whole body would draw back when he touched her, as if to avoid accumulating additional wounds just when she was managing to heal old ones. With that involuntary inertia, she was able to stop her own impulses and keep her body from participating in her husband's physical assaults. Because she was experiencing another love, she now thought of herself as a mere depository for her husband's waste, which she had to absorb if she were to achieve her goal. Besides, she grew less tolerant of Joseph's double life, which threatened her dignity as a woman. And, she was even less tolerant of the wrenching between her flesh, which cried out for him, and her rebellious consciousness, which flouted tradition. She could not bear submitting to him so that she could have the child she was waiting for.

Whatever she did, whatever she said, everything unavoidably brought her back to that necessity which dominated her life. Everything was tied to that obsession. Was her existence to be determined solely by a few drops of sperm? What was it that made her believe that the greatest disruption of her life would come delivering a being that would form inside of her?

Emilienne shook her head vehemently. It would be disastrous if she started doubting herself now and pushed him away out of pride before even trying the treatment that would cure her.

As she waited for her next appointment, she saw herself become another woman; in the span of a few days she became less concerned with pleasing her husband, and more so with pleasing a woman like her. For her, she made sure that each of her outfits accentuated and flattered every part of her body. Without realizing it, some kind of dynamism seemed to be dwelling inside of her, and she was in a good mood when she brought her exam results back to Dr. Pascal.

HER GAIETY did not last long, however, in the face of the gynecologist's awkwardness when he saw the results she'd just brought.

"That is impossible, Doctor," she cried out. "Where does it come from, this illness that strikes me down every time I menstruate or a fetus forms in my womb? Is that not proof that I am ill? Speak, Doctor! I am going crazy."

She got up, paced around the gynecologist's office with her hands behind her back, then sat back down in frustration. Her head fell to her chest.

Although he was used to his patients' problems, Dr. Pascal could not help sharing the suffering of this woman stricken by this terrible disappointment. He, too, got up, placed his hand on her shoulder, and said calmly:

"Let's go over it, if you'd like. You're sure you've never had tuberculosis, filariasis, or schistosomiasis? Those diseases can also make a woman sterile. Everything shows us that your ovaries are functioning perfectly and there is no specific problem with your ovulation. The tests you've just had reveal no traces of sexually transmitted diseases like trichomoniasis or herpes. Your fallopian tubes are not blocked either. Some women have high levels of acidity in the vagina, which kills the sperm, but that is not your case. In your case, the amount of cervical mucus—the fluid that carries the sperm to the uterus, where they meet the ovum—is normal. We must consider, too, if it weren't for your repeated miscarriages, we would have concluded that your husband did not have sufficient sperm in his semen due to certain venereal diseases. We must equally exclude the possibility that he is incapable of erection or any type of testicular malformation since he was already able to produce a first child with you."

"What do you mean by testicular malformation?"

"Actually, it's a congenital malformation of the testes. There are several types of malformation. I will name only one for you: ectopic testis, characterized by the absence of spermatozoa or by spermatozoa with deficient mobility. I don't believe it necessary to ask you if your husband has been castrated in an accident or if he has had testicular atrophy after a disease like the measles after the birth of your daughter, because *that* you would know."

"No, Doctor, he hasn't had any of those diseases you just mentioned."

"You must equally know that he is not diabetic. Has he had, however, tuberculosis after the birth of your daughter? Has he become obese?"

"No, Doctor, my husband is normal and he is healthy," she replied, irritated.

"It was necessary that I discuss all of those diseases, though, for in most cases, they don't allow for the egg to form."

He sat back down on his chair and added:

"Listen, Madame, the best would be for you to come back to see me with your husband, or, if you wish, he could come alone. Some questions could be embarrassing for you. I want to be sure that everything is working fine on his end."

"Thank you, Doctor! But my husband will not come," she said as she stood up.

"Wait, take these temperature charts and fill them out each morning for three months. We should be able to find something. If you're late again by two weeks, come back and see me. We could try to attach the fetus to the uterus with the appropriate treatment. Be careful, too, not to eat poorly, overexert yourself, or to abuse tobacco or alcohol, because all of those are potentially factors that could lead to secondary sterility."

After he'd handed her the temperature charts, he scribbled on her appointment chart and handed it to her.

"Go and see this hypnotist and tell him I sent you; he can help you."

Emilienne froze, stupefied.

"It's a therapy practiced by means of the laying on of hands and magnetic passes. It's still new in Africa, but it won't be for long. I often send certain patients of mine to this man, and he is very discreet. The results are often spectacular. Don't worry about the things people say; think instead of that baby you want. He will keep me informed about the progress in your sessions. Good luck. I hope to see you back here with a smile."

SHE STAGGERED out of the office, like a sleepwalker getting out of bed at three in the morning, and went down the long halls of the clinic in the black cloud of her thoughts.

"What does all this mean? What does my unique illness have to do with a hypnotist? And what is he going to cure when there is nothing to cure! Could it be my head? But I feel fine—I feel better than I have in years. And what if I retook all those same tests, since they were all completed before my new state of mind? It's possible the results would be different. If everything is in my brain, then it won't be long before I get pregnant."

She opened the car door, raised her foot to get in, and placed it back on the ground. "No, this can't be happening; I cannot be cured in a week from an organic disorder that's been plaguing me for the past fifteen years. Not to mention that it seems that my reproductive organs are normal. Could it be a blockage then that returns at delivery? What, dear God, could have happened that I haven't thought of?"

Finally, she got into the car and rested her head on the steering wheel. Her teeth began to chatter as her thoughts whirled around in her head.

"What should I do now? I can't even resort to in vitro fertilization or artificial insemination. I can see him ranting and raving about that. Such a suggestion would to him mean the loss of his virility, a shameful process for having kids when all other men simply have them like they grow corn. Not to mention, how quickly we'd be banished from society, which does not tolerate anything new or different. Though our child would not be the first to be conceived that way."

A CACOPHONY of honking horns and the blinding headlights of a car coming toward her made her start. She was driving on the left side of the road. In a panic, she steered to the right. The driver behind her barely had enough time to brake as she cut in front of him. Oblivious to the comments ringing out from people on the sidewalks and from other vehicles, Emilienne accelerated.

"Amandine, Antoine, and all the other miracle babies are all healthy. Some of their mothers must suffer from fertility problems like mine. How could I make him accept the idea of us harvesting an egg and putting it in contact with his sperm in an incubator, so that the fertilized egg could then be placed inside my uterus? No, that would never happen! There is even less chance that he would accept a donor, even if he knows she's had to undergo tests and examinations, or his resorting to a surrogate mother, even if she were African American. Well, there you go, now I *am* completely mad!"

SHE WONDERED how she had gotten to her sister's house as she parked in front of it. As soon as her nephews saw her, they ran over. Eva, who came out of the house at the same time, let the trash can she was holding drop to the ground. The garbage scattered around her.

"Emie, what's wrong?" she cried out as she ran over to her sister. "You look strange."

Emilienne practically threw herself into her arms and broke into tears.

"Go away, kids, I don't need you here."

They all dispersed, disconcerted by the sight of their aunt weeping so openly. Eva took her sister, arm around her waist, and led her into the guest room, then told her to lie down on the bed. Emilienne lay down and closed her eyes.

"Go play outside," Eva ordered her two younger sons, who were hovering by the door.

From her left breast pocket, she pulled out a tissue and wiped her sister's face, which was streaming with tears.

"Now, can you tell me what is wrong?"

Emilienne remained mute and continued to cry.

"Calm down, Emie, and tell me what is distressing you so. You know that you can count on me. Please, I beg you, say something."

She sighed. Emilienne opened her eyes, fixing them on the statuette one of her nephews had carved that was placed on the headboard of the bed. In her desperate state, the statuette appeared sinister to her. The monster's bulging eyes that she could make out through her tears seemed to be mocking her. And just when she believed she saw the monster pouncing on her, Emilienne trembled and squeezed her eyes shut as if to protect herself.

Alarmed, her sister shook her briskly.

"Emie, my dear, has something happened to you at home or at the office, do you want to talk to me about it?"

"I'm on my way back from Dr. Pascal's, the gynecologist," she murmured.

"So . . . ! Can he cure you, yes or no?"

"No, he can't do anything for me. According to the exams and the X-rays he did, I am fine. I guess I am just sick in the head."

"What! Speak more clearly."

Eva got up and sat back down; now *she* was very worried.

"What does your womb have to do with your head?"

"He advised me to see a hypnotist; I suppose it's to heal my psyche so that I'll be able to conceive." It seems this hypnotist has already cured many women who suffered from sterility."

"He advised you to go see a hypnotist so you can have children? I didn't think there were any in this country. And how can a doctor ask a patient to go see a hypnotist! It's like asking you to go see a witch doctor!"

The two sisters held one another's hands.

After a long silence, Eva continued:

"What a story! Listen, I think you should go see him. Your

gynecologist knows what he's talking about, unless you prefer going to see the healer Mama was talking about."

"I'm sick and tired of it, you know. I'm sick of not being like everyone else. How long can such treatment last? Is it going to work? Have you thought about what people are going to say?"

Eva jumped up and lost it.

"What is happening to you? You aren't the same little girl I grew up with who feared nothing. Since when are you afraid of public opinion! Are you going to stop living for others! You know as well as I do that criticism doesn't kill. And our mentalities are not going to change. For instance, for a relatively well-off person, simply hailing a taxi on the street leads to criticism and mockery, as if man hadn't been made to walk. People immediately come to the conclusion that this new pedestrian has financial problems, and some are delighted about it. No, that is bogus. Get a grip on yourself. My advice is that you go see this hypnotist right away. Let him tell you clearly what he can cure, your womb, your head, *I* don't know! That way you'll have information and can make a decision. If he seems convincing, start the treatment immediately. In three months, you will know. As for me, I am ready to bring you to see a healer when you're ready. Tell me, do you think by any chance your Joseph has given you some kind of shameful disease? After all, he's the one who sleeps with anyone. I even wonder if he picks up some of his night conquests in the streets."

Emilienne dismissed her sister's suppositions with a wave of her hand.

"Oh! Please, don't try to defend him," Eva went on. "There are rumors flying about him, and if I haven't said anything to you until now, it's been to keep from upsetting you further. And I told him right out what I thought the day we got together at Jean's colleagues' place. According to my husband, there are more and more sterile men. A lot of them are responsible for the ailments of the womb afflicting their partners. It's sad that our society doesn't want to admit their responsibility."

"I am convinced that Joseph has already been to see a gynecologist to find out whether he's fine in that respect. I think his wish to see me cured proves it."

"How can you be so sure? Your miscarriages seem bizarre to me . . . Listen, go see that hypnotist."

"I hope the treatment isn't as long as the psychoanalysts'; theirs can last several years."

"Don't be so fatalistic. Why wouldn't you be cured in no time? Remember what our father used to say to us when we were kids? I'll adapt it a little for you: 'Success belongs to those who resolutely turn their backs on fate. The world is made of two types of men: the stragglers and the soldiers on the front lines. The latter work at giving meaning to their life. You see, children, such a choice demands faith, will, and great sacrifices when chance has not privileged you at birth. The fruits of so much effort and sacrifice bring great moral strength, of course, as long as you've stayed on the right path.' Have you forgotten that speech, repeated over and over again, that we used to find so annoying?" Eva went on. "You followed through with your studies, kept yourself safe, and stayed away from the pleasures of girls your age. That behavior has served you well. Who knows what battles tomorrow will bring? Today, you're fighting another one: trying to give children to your husband and at the same time to bring him back home. Yes, I know, as everyone does, that he spends his nights at his mistress's. Don't you believe that battle is worth fighting? Although I understand your discouragement and your pessimism, I beg you not to allow those states of mind to become second nature. You risk creating other problems for yourself. You see, I didn't succeed as well in my studies, but I believe I've learned a lot by observing, reading, and analyzing each event in my life as well as the experiences of others."

"It's true, you've also gone through some difficult times," Emilienne admitted. "What is happening to me, Eva? I am so lost. What have I become!"

The two sisters hugged each other.

Emilienne left her sister's slightly buoyed. She would have gone to her office if it weren't already dark. She hadn't been there all afternoon.

She had been missing work regularly for several months

now. From time to time, she would let her general manager know that she would be out for an hour or two. Unfortunately, her problems had taken precedence over her professional life and as long as her love life wasn't in order, her work would suffer.

She turned the radio dial mechanically in order to lose herself for a moment. Because she was so absorbed by her problems, she no longer thought that others existed.

The newscaster delivered the evening news. The reports she heard didn't bring her any joy: a father who threw his six-month-old baby from the fifth floor of his building so he would no longer hear her cries, the market crash worried the leaders of industrialized countries, the Burkinabé students in Côte d'Ivoire condemned the killing of President Thomas Sankara.

Emilienne turned off the radio and was surprised to find herself crying, not about her woes, but about the disappearance of a young head of state who, despite his extravagances, had managed within a few years to awaken his people and teach them the notion of work and sacrifice. She cried, because in her eyes the dream of many Africans—to truly acknowledge the weaknesses of their states and carry out their responsibility toward history—had just vanished.

"Why must there always be a brutal halt to new momentum on this continent, which brings its people back to a state of intellectual and physical misery? What will become of Africa, incapable of self-governance, victim of natural disasters, and attacked from within by economic and financial crisis? The least one can say is that the future seems frightful. Africa's belly will soon be as sterile as mine." She blew her nose loudly.

ROXANNE, SNOOZING in front of the gate, jumped to her paws as soon as she heard the far-off noise of her mistress's car. Wagging her tail, she patiently waited for the gate to open.

Except for the dog, the house was empty. Eyang had taken her grandchildren to her cousin Germaine's, several miles from Olamba, to spend their school vacation.

Emilienne got some ground meat for her dog and prepared a steak and a tomato salad for herself. Then she served herself a wedge of Camembert and took an orange from the fruit basket for her dessert. After she'd scarfed down her piece of meat on the terrace, Roxanne went over and stretched out at her mistress's feet under the table.

Through the bay window, Emilienne's gaze lingered on the lit-up garden. Everything seemed frozen, like her thoughts at that moment. Even the plants that bordered the numerous alleys were immobilized in the night. And this house, which had been chosen for the many children they had hoped to have, how gloomy it seemed! Under the table, Roxanne licked her feet. Emilienne pet her and gave her a smile.

Her love for dogs and particularly for Roxanne had developed progressively without her even realizing it. Today, the loss of this animal would destroy her, she knew.

This attachment to her dog frightened her. Would she have loved her as much if she had had several children? In any case, she'd learned one thing from this animal: however egotistical a man could be, he could not live without the affection and tenderness of others, even if they were pets. He could only be fulfilled when he could give love and give himself to love.

Less hazy now, the young woman's gaze turned toward the starry sky. She got up to turn on the air conditioner. The weather was drier, and it had been unbearably hot for a month now. The change of season had never been so distinct. Was it a sign there was a drought coming? But there had been no other indications. The forest was still just as dense. It would be disastrous if the Saharan landscape were to extend across the entire continent. But that wind that continued yesterday had to be blowing at about 50 mph, rolling sheets of dust. It made one think of the harmattan. With the desert advancing at 15 mph each year in the Sahel region, we, too, would be affected by the drought.

The sound of a key opening the lock brought Emilienne back to herself. "Now, why is he coming home tonight? What did they do during all that time they spent together, and what is he thinking about our future?"

Walking briskly, his face radiant, Joseph came over to his wife with open arms. He pulled her to him and kissed her on the lips. He took a step back, laughed, then came back toward her and hugged her more tightly.

"I must be dreaming. What good news has he come to share with me? He obviously wants to tell me about the purchase of the new suit he's wearing and ask me my opinion of his new cologne."

"Now," he began almost out of breath, "we're going to celebrate an important event tonight. I am going to prove to you that I am not wasting my time."

Emilienne shot him a hateful look.

"Yes, my darling, you may not have noticed, but I've been planning my future."

"Well what do you know! He has already written me out of his life." Emilienne clenched her teeth. "He talks about this future as if I'll be no part of it."

"What do you say to a sumptuous dinner in the best restaurant in the city? So, I have to call and reserve a table, I hope it isn't too late. Ah, my darling, you will never guess what has happened to me."

He headed toward the telephone and came back toward his wife, grabbing her by the waist.

"Get up, come with me to call Fredo—he'll find a table for us."

He led his wife, who was trying to gather the thoughts in her head. And as he dialed the number, the young woman came back to clear the table.

"We will not be alone; there will be two other couples whom you'll meet in a little while. I want you to make yourself beautiful. You may find me secretive, but I didn't want to talk to you about this business before I was sure the deal was going to go through. Come sit down, I'll explain."

"I can hear you from here," Emilienne answered from the kitchen.

"Fine, as you wish. I set up a construction company with two friends not long ago. Not one of those little companies with a bunch of hired hands. We put out a call for experts in the field; there are Africans and two French guys. And this morning we signed our first big contracts. The first is a construction project for the African Development Bank, and the second is Deputy Yabi's clinic, you know, the doctor. With those two deals, we are off to a good start to get rich and make ourselves known across the entire country. If everything goes well, in a year from now I'll give my letter of resignation to my minister. So, what do you have to say about that?"

"That's great, Joseph! But I can't eat twice in one evening."

"I know, make a little effort anyway; the others won't understand if you're not with me to mark this occasion."

"Are you mocking me, Joseph? Why didn't you invite your mistress? It wouldn't be the first time that you included her in your business. Let me be, please. I am tired."

"No, I will not leave you be. You are my wife; don't forget it—my joys are also yours: this evening you'll come with me to dinner, otherwise I'm cancelling. You know, I try, but I still don't understand you. Another woman would have been happy about her husband's social success. Mine leaves you cold. Whatever life I lead, there are some joys I can share only with you."

Emilienne left the kitchen where her husband had joined her and headed into the bedroom. Joseph followed behind her, his endless flow of words wearing her down.

"You know, in retrospect, I don't regret all the time I've spent at the ministry. It has allowed me to establish very good connections, without which I would have missed out on the two most important deals of the year. For now I'll spare you all the details of how we landed them, as your sense of morality would take a bit of a bashing. Thanks to my relationships and my colleagues, I've learned that in order to succeed, anything goes, and, believe me, I will use all means necessary."

When Emilienne opened the door to the closet to get a nightgown, Joseph wrapped his arms around her and caressed her breasts. Emilienne took a step back, then two, and fell into his arms.

"You've gotten more beautiful, you know," Joseph whispered in her ear.

He threw her on the bed and lifted her dress, which she pulled back down, struggling.

"What has gotten into you?"

Turning a deaf ear to his wife's words, Joseph threw himself on top of her. Emilienne melted.

THEY PARKED their car in the Elite restaurant's parking lot, next to which two men in their fifties dressed in white stood stiffly. The soft light of the spotlights between the plants lit up about twenty cars, all of them quite impressive. One of the parking lot attendants swiftly opened the door for Emilienne then led the couple to the entrance of the restaurant, where two young people in white suits and black bow ties welcomed them. They both bowed respectfully before the couple. Across from the main entrance was a huge garden with short, trimmed grass, several flowerbeds, and four palm trees through which shone a soft, yellowish light. Wooden sculpted pillars supported the marble-floored terrace. Two large pots of bougainvillea were placed by each side of the double doors. One of the waiters brought them into a long hallway; on the left was a bar, also made of marble. At the same time, a young French woman wearing a black lace dress with a provocative plunging neckline came to greet them. With her ample bust protruding, she shook the couple's hands.

"Good evening, Madame Eyang, Monsieur! How are you?"

"Fine, thank you," Joseph replied. "Is our table ready?"

"Yes. Do you want to wait for your party at the bar or do you prefer to be at your table?"

Joseph turned around toward Emilienne and, very respectfully, asked:

"What'll it be, darling?"

"We'll settle in at our table and wait for them."

"Please follow me," said the hostess, smiling.

The walls and the floor were covered, the first with a red velvet fabric, and the latter with a thick carpet in the same tone. Tall plants separated the round tables draped with white embroidered tablecloths. Golden sconces lit up the two-level room. Rays of fan-shaped light illuminated beautiful frescos. The young hostess led Monsieur and Madame Eyang toward the lower part of the restaurant and seated them a few yards away from a white grand piano, where a black man with a beaming smile and a bald head played jazz. Emilienne sat across from her husband. From her seat she could see the secretary of social affairs and the chairman and managing director of the National Forestry Company.

"They should be here any minute now," Joseph said, looking at his watch.

"Would you like an aperitif?" asked the server, who elegantly sported a red bow tie and a black suit.

"What'll you have, darling?" Joseph asked as he smiled at his wife.

"A red martini with lemon and a lot of ice."

"Come now, darling, how about drinking something other than your usual martini tonight!"

He slid his hand between her legs underneath the table.

"No, that'll be it! You know I cannot stand other alcoholic drinks," she answered wrathfully.

"Give us a dry whiskey and a martini."

"Very well, Monsieur."

Although she didn't want to admit it, Emilienne appreciated being out with her husband; it reminded her of the first years of their marriage before and after the birth of their daughter. Once a week, Joseph would take her out so they could try the new restaurants. That was how they ended up sitting at all the best tables in the city. Both having an appetite for fine food, they tasted Chinese, Italian, Indian, French, and African dishes one by one. So that she didn't put on weight, Emilienne would skip the midday meal to be able to eat at night without any guilt. Back then, he was truly in love with her and his caresses underneath the table were not a game, as they were now.

Slowly, she took his hand out from between her thighs, even though she liked its soft, delicate touch. And to avoid reading an expression in his eyes that she would not know how to interpret, she fixed her attention on the neighboring tables. Above all the voices, she could hear the secretary of state and his friends as they laughed heartily and spoke with grand gestures—at least the two men she could see, the others being hidden behind the plant.

Joseph gulped down his fourth whiskey as Emilienne wondered whether her husband's friends had gone to the wrong restaurant. And, just when they decided to put in their order, two striking couples appeared. Introductions were made euphorically. Emilienne noted that the three men were more or less the same age. In contrast, the two women seemed younger than her. To show off the most attractive features of her body to the best effect, the younger of the two had chosen for this outing a silk bolero stole, twisted at the back, and a wraparound spandex skirt draped with silk crepe. Her bun at the nape of her neck was set off by a set of diamond earrings and a matching necklace. Her shoes and her handbag were from Carel, Emilienne observed, who had the same ones. She thought she recognized, too, golden jewelry from Tania Apor on the second girl. Taller than the other, the second wore a shapely bustier and a tight-fitting skirt, which was oversewn with denim above the knee.

Underneath their artfully applied makeup and elegant outfits, the two women were undeniably beautiful and alluring. Emilienne, who had also made an effort to look stunning that evening, smiled at the companions of her husband's associates. Even though she admitted they were beautiful, she did not believe that she was less attractive, not in the least. As for her, she wore a half-cup bustier that emphasized her waistline, and high-waisted dark orange knit cotton pointelle culottes, which left her legs bare, and, over them, a damask suit with satin and raw silk stripes. The white blouse was printed in matching tones. After all those years of near separation, she wanted to prove to her husband that she could compete with the most beautiful women in the city. And, judging by his attentiveness to her and his furtive looks, she was not disappointed by the effect she had produced in him.

The conversation was very lively, and the bottles of champagne kept coming every fifteen minutes. After cursory observation of the two women's behavior, Emilienne noticed that Agnes never looked directly at her husband, who clearly had nothing to say to her either. And, even though Pauline spoke loudly, which, incidentally, took away all her charm, her gaze clouded over every time it crossed her husband's.

Between a mouthful of caviar or smoked salmon and a gulp of champagne, the three men told racy anecdotes. To Emilienne, they belonged to that generation of Africans who, having succeeded the old conscripts who had carried out service in newly independent countries and taken up their positions, had decided to make the most of their power and influence. The great majority of them took delight in having an official car, cashing in on numerous bonuses, and having a housing allowance. That material comfort did not keep most of them from creating their own businesses parallel to their official functions. Joseph, whose rise to the portals of success had been slower, didn't necessarily shoot off sparks compared to his friends. He unquestionably had the look of a company CEO, enhanced by his superb sense of style.

Emilienne came out of her shell when she heard Pauline's shrill voice:

"*I* agree with Joseph. We are not going to see the creation of a Western-style multiparty system in our countries, not today. Quite plainly, it would mean the splintering of our populations, insofar as each ethnic group would want to form its own political party. Just imagine our country made up of about twenty different parties, each claiming its own regional and ethnic constituency."

"That's not all," Joseph picked up again, "let's have the courage to recognize that we are a selfish tribal people. Take a look at what is happening in the ministries and state-owned companies! First they hire a member of the family, regardless of their abilities, and, if they have none, they look among those around them from their own ethnic group. No, believe me, in order to have a real multiparty system, Africans are going to have to manage to place national interests above their own. In the meantime, the single-party system seems to be what we need. Let me explain: when a country is under the aegis of a single party, its nationals, whatever group they're from, are forced to meet, discuss, and exchange their opinions about issues that concern them all. They don't have the time to dwell on tribal issues. Collective motivations almost always win against frictions between individuals. Obviously, with such a political alliance, men learn how to tolerate one another, to love one another, and above all to work toward the same ideals. Isn't that the goal sought by our leaders!"

He filled all of the glasses and brought his to his lips. Pauline emptied hers in one gulp, and her eyes came alive. Ogoulat took advantage of the short moment of silence to put in his two cents. While he spoke, he devoured the hostess with his eyes as she passed between the tables.

"I admit that the single-party system remains our only chance to finally see all of the ethnic groups unite in tolerance and understanding. I will add though that its current form needs improvements. In my opinion, to avoid the monopoly of power by a small group of men, there must be several political opinions inside the single party, at the head of which would be a deputy secretary general. With that type of election, he would automatically become the only presidential candidate of the republic. It would have been preferable that this latter function be occupied by another member of the party, as in developed countries. Unfortunately, the experiments certain African countries have carried out show that power cannot be two-headed on this continent. Needless to say, in these circumstances, the president of the republic would have to be elected by a large majority of its people."

"Your version is too complicated," Boundi retorted, having remained attentive to the arguments his friends had been making for a while. "Tell us, the secretary general of the party would be elected by whom exactly? By the political office or by all the members of the party, in other words, the people? I am against all these political arrangements. Let's give voice to the people plain and simple. In order to avoid the harmful multiplication of political parties, a law should set their number according to the size of their population. These parties would then each present their candidate for the presidential elections. There is no other path to democracy. You know all the advantages we enjoy because of it."

"The lesser of two evils would in fact be democracy as you've just described it," Ogoulat acknowledged. "One must not believe, however, that freedom and tolerance exist unfailingly in democratic countries. Like our country, each political party in power works at placing men from its political group in all the key positions, regardless of their abilities. Those same parties will do whatever it takes to remain in power as long as possible. They, too, influence justice and bring the shady dealings of their adversaries to the public square through the media."

"As it is practiced in the majority of moderate countries in Africa," Joseph retorted, "the single-party system encourages personal initiative. A door is thus open to all initiatives for the good of our country. Single party, certainly, but colored by capitalism, which we must welcome. That said, let's raise our glasses to our construction business's good start."

Before they left, at a very late hour, all the glasses were clinked together sharply as hoarse groans ran from mouths dilated by champagne.

Transported by his new status as businessman, Joseph gave the impression he was bursting out of his skin and larger than life; intoxicated with his new authority, he manipulated the steering wheel with his left index finger. With his right hand, he took out a Davidoff No. 2 from his cigar case and smoked it with great satisfaction. Between two long draws, his lips produced the smile of a man who sat enthroned above the peaks of his success.

Her husband's confidence thrust Emilienne into deep melancholy. Although until tonight she had veiled her eyes, she had to admit that they no longer shared anything. His success and his exploding joy, which she would have welcomed not long ago, left her impassive. Oh, she was obviously capable of hiding behind plausible excuses in order to reassure herself. But, the thing was, they would not hold up for long. If it were someone she didn't know showing his contagious exultation, she knew that for a few seconds she would sympathize with him. For the man whom she believed she still loved, she didn't feel a thing. His successes, which she knew excluded her no matter what he said, no longer interested her.

Would she fear not being able to ever see him come back to her again when his fortune allowed him to display his lustfulness and all those seductive girls looking for a rich older man ran after him? Why was she losing interest in a man she didn't have the strength to leave? Would he blame her for having no idea about her sterility and involving him in it? Before she'd gotten the results of her medical tests, she was sure that he was somehow responsible for her pain. But he wasn't at all. This crucial problem did not concern him. This heavy responsibility on her shoulders had at first confounded and overwhelmed her and then left her in a weak state. Over the hours, her burden had transformed into guilt. Responsibility that is not shared is more painful when one is forced to bear it alone. The weight of it was becoming unbearable for her.

Seated next to her husband, Emilienne felt pathetic, as if she had betrayed him. If only she had the wisdom and the courage to break out of herself, turn to him to better understand, to make herself better understood and be pardoned. Yet she remained resolutely silent, as if paralyzed by her guilt. However, she would have to tell him about Dr. Pascal's diagnosis.

As soon as they got home, she mustered her courage:

"I have something to tell you," she declared calmly as she undressed, while Joseph drank one last whiskey Perrier stretched out on the bed.

"I'm listening!"

Emilienne, now in her nightgown, stood near the window.

"First of all, I'd like to congratulate you on your business, which promises to be fruitful."

She paused. Joseph emptied his glass. He was seized by a coughing fit. "Oh, my God, I don't believe a single word of what I just said." She turned toward Joseph. "This is horrible. He knows that I am lying."

Impassive, Joseph stared at his image in the mirror. Emilienne began to speak again, in a tone she hoped would sound natural.

"This morning I went, as you had advised, to Dr. Pascal. Actually, it was my second appointment. The tests I took and X-rays didn't show anything abnormal. I am fine. He said he wanted to see you."

Joseph leapt to his feet. He frowned and stared his wife down with hateful eyes.

"If I understand you, you want to make me bear the responsibility for your inability to bear children. I can assure you right now, I am healthy. And believe me, because I know what I'm talking about. You are wrong to think that I am getting some kind of pleasure out of this tension due to the absence of children in our house. When our daughter was still alive, I displayed great pride in talking about her. At times I even praised her so much that my friends would joke with me about my feelings, which they found excessive. I am not going to hide the fact that I sometimes deplored the fact that she had not been a boy to carry on my name. When she died, I, too, shed tears of sorrow every time my eyes fell on her photo in my office, and I would see her sitting again on the seat of my car or hugging me when I got home."

Emilienne looked down with tearful eyes.

"That is surprising to you, isn't it! Yes, my pain has been as intense as yours, though I've had no witness to mine."

His hands became tense in his pocket, and he stared at the tip of his shoes.

"Nine years ago, I wasn't expecting it, but one of my mistresses told me she was expecting my child."

Emilienne staggered as if she had been dealt a blow to the head.

"I wanted to tell you about the birth of my son without hurting you. I couldn't, though, because at the time our marriage was still holding up, despite the fact that I was coming home late most nights."

Emilienne had difficulty breathing. Her hands and the soles of her feet were sweating. She grabbed desperately at the window to hold up her body, which was giving way underneath her.

He stared, first at the rug, then at the silk sheets, and then continued:

"I had a daughter with the same woman eighteen months afterward. Don't think it was easy for me to accept their births. The consequences of my nocturnal escapades, which sometimes extended into the day as well, materialized through the arrival of kids that I hadn't wanted, even less so with a woman other than you."

Emilienne clenched her teeth so hard it made her jaw hurt. She flattened herself against the window and bit her lips until they started to bleed.

"After my son, naturally I wanted to break things off with his mother to minimize the impact of my betrayal. For that reason, I refused to go see my son at the hospital. For a month

I didn't answer the insistent telephone calls from his mother. And then one night, I couldn't help myself. My blood called out to me, my blood in a son. Like a thief in the night, I went to see him. He looked like me. He was beautiful. You cannot imagine how overjoyed I was."

He fell silent, aware of the wound in his wife's heart that he was enlarging with a scalpel, but he didn't want to and couldn't stop. He would deliver his narrative to the end. He was suffering from the cry he heard rise up inside Emilienne's throat and then suffocate behind her pursed lips. At that point in his story, that cry and that pain were also his. His voice almost lifeless, he continued:

"The son I had long awaited had finally come. In a few short years, he was to become my best friend and companion. That event in my life transformed me completely and threw me back into the arms of the woman who had given me this son I had hoped to have with you. Parallel to this happiness, my feelings of guilt toward you were mounting. But I could not avoid the birth of my daughter. However, after having spent an evening with them, I made the very difficult decision not to see them again so that I could try to make you happy, you and Rékia, and to end the feelings of guilt that were haunting me in my sleep to no end. Each month, though, I would send a large money order to the mother of my children. Our marriage became stronger, and for a year we were, I believe, happy, until the problems resurfaced. During those twelve months I yearned with all my heart for a second child who would strengthen our relationship. I broke down again when the mother brought our two children to my office. They had grown. The elder one ran over to me and called me papa as soon as he saw me. That was a moment of very intense emotion for me."

Sweat was dripping from Emilienne's armpits and thighs. The banging thump her heart was making resounded like a drum in her eardrums. Joseph's voice was now striking her ears like a threat coming at her from afar.

"Do you understand why I disappear from home for weeks at a time? I am attempting to assume my fatherly role. For some time now, I've been thinking about bringing them home with me, here, so that we could all be together. Their mother would not object. She would see them when she wished."

"Stop! Stop, I beg you."

EMILIENNE WENT OUT, dressed in her transparent nightgown, her hair tousled, and barefoot. She opened the door to the kitchen and rushed into the muggy warmth of the night. Incapable of controlling her panic-stricken steps, she walked in circles around the yard before planting herself in front of the lighted doorway around which little insects buzzed. On top of the iron gate white and blue lizards blithely chased each other. Emilienne rested her head on the gate's ice-cold edge. Mosquitos rushed to attack her. Insensitive to their bites, the young woman closed her eyes. Her thoughts, caught in a spiral, were a jumble inside her head.

"Nine years! So that makes ten, eleven years he has been with her! Eleven years that I've been sharing him with some stranger who managed the feat of giving him the children that I have been incapable of having. How could I have been so naïve as to believe his clever lies: 'Listen, darling, my minister worked very late, and you know how he doesn't tolerate it when his staff leaves the office before him.' Or even: 'I had to prepare a file for tomorrow's council of ministers.' And I, like an idiot, believed these lies. Better still, I was proud of having a husband who, contrary to what most of the civil servants did, showed an excellent professional work ethic. For ten, eleven years, he has been cheating on me, only a few years after our daughter's birth, before I had even wanted a second child. So it's been all those years that my husband has no longer belonged to me, that his body has not carried the exclusive scent of our intimacy. Where did he meet her? Where did they make love for the first time? On the rug in his office after he'd ordered his secretary to tell his visitors he was in a meeting? or in a hotel room under a fake name—hadn't he already done that with me in Paris? Undoubtedly, they'd passed for husband and wife, an amorous couple that needed to spice up their monotonous life a little."

Emilienne shook her head weakly to shoo away the mosquitos buzzing in her ears, and also to get rid of the film reel running before her eyes, bathed in this poignant sadness. The mosquitos dispersed and came back in greater numbers to suck her blood. Her teeth chattered. She half opened her eyes. The lights from the streetlamps and those of her garden went out. It was just one of the general blackouts that occurred at least once a week throughout Olamba's neighborhoods. She closed her eyes again so that she didn't have to stare into the dark nothingness.

"For eleven years he caressed, moaned, and curled up in the arms of this woman. I am his wife, but it is she who gets the most of him. How many times had she rocked to the sound of his soft whispers and been swept away when she heard his deafening moans as he surrendered completely to the pleasures of their lovemaking? How many times had he uttered her name before collapsing into her arms? I am his wife, yet I have not had this privilege."

Emilienne sobbed. She banged her head rhythmically against the iron bars of the gate. The rhythm accelerated, and she continued. Her skull hurt, but she did not stop. The sweltering heat of this nightmarish night crept up her nostrils. Suffocating, she brought her trembling hand to her heart before collapsing onto the concrete path. As if in a bad dream, she continued talking to herself:

"He had to have loved her to have two children with her and to still be with her today. Even if I am still his wife, he is connected to *her* for life. Although I am his wife, another came by and knew how to get him and how to keep him, and he just tiptoed away from me. Two beautiful children, he says, that he would like to see me raise so that he can cry out to the world at the top of his lungs, boasting about his domination, his victory, and his virility; my submission and my weakness. Does he think I am that stupid, that I would live my humiliation openly?"

As if this inner cry were a command coming from her brain, Emilienne opened her eyes. The night was lit up again. She got up, exhausted, and staggered toward the house. An owl beating its wings landed a few steps away from her. Emilienne trembled and tried to walk more quickly. Her heavy body refused to obey the commands of her bursting brain. After one last effort, she collapsed on the steps leading to the terrace.

At that very moment, Roxanne let out a bark from the other side of the gate and woke up the watchman snoring in the garage. He opened the gate for him. The animal headed toward the young woman at a gallop. The watchman, who had just noticed his boss sprawled out across the steps, in turn, hurried to help her. When he leaned over her, Roxanne was desperately licking her mistress's inanimate body.

"What am I doing here? I must no longer be myself. What kind of normal woman would behave as I am now, after her husband had revealed bluntly to her the existence of two children he had had with another, and dared to suggest that she raise them!?"

Seated next to her, Eva followed with sustained attention the cadenced movements of the dancers under the effect of the hallucinogenic powder. As they sang, they nodded gently and wiggled their hips to the rhythm of the tom-toms. Draped in red fabric, the head turbaned in a fabric of the same color and adorned with red feathers, a female initiate about fifteen years old let out an animal cry and then collapsed onto the dusty ground. Two of her fellow dancers exited the circle and led her with them to the exterior courtyard.

This vigil had been organized for the initiation rites of the young wife of an important personality—she too was struck with infertility.

Seated in the center of the guardhouse, the young woman wore a piece of a *pagne* over her chest. On each side of her braided head, just above the ears, was planted a red parrot feather. Her face was painted with white and red kaolin. The dancers, whose average age was thirty, formed a circle around the young woman. The "matron," a middle-aged woman, solid and supple, exuded her authority as she approached the chair upholstered in red fabric placed behind the patient. Agile, and with an impenetrable gaze, the dancers lined up along the guardhouse, at the other end of which burned an imposing indigenous torch made from the resin of a local wood. Its multicolored, sparkling flame licked the darkness then illuminated the solemn faces of the two immobile young people who closed off the two rows.

As the male and female dancers murmured a soft, melancholy chant, the matron shook her little bell and started singing a more rhythmic chant. Voices rose up. Drugged by the bark of the hallucinogenic wood, the patient stomped her feet on her stool. The haggard gaze on her ghostlike face fixed on the frightening statue attached to the center pole of the guardhouse. When the chanting and the tom-toms raised their sound, the "matron" shook the little bell again in her patient's ears. The latter became even more agitated, twisting in all directions. Her arms, like the wings of a bird, seemed to detach themselves from her body and flapped through the air. Her feet appeared to be revolving around themselves. At the moment her limbs gave in to a relentless struggle, the young woman found herself suspended in air, her body hunched up, before landing on her two knees. Her family, the numerous guests, and the curious people seated against the wall let out cries of joy. Unmoved, her husband followed her every movement. From time to time, he lifted one foot, moved his head, or pulled at his beard.

After having pierced the depths of the night and transmitted their messages to the spirits, the chanting returned languorously to reassure the audience and to die in the flame of the torch. Other chanting grew louder. A boy dressed in palm fronds ran up to extinguish the torch. The chanting reached its climax. The tom-toms rolled in the air. The wood fire in the outer courtyard, enveloped in this delirious ambience, crackled. The flames licked the darkness, and as daylight came, danced, twisted, and spun in a continual, incessant movement, then, one after the other, evaporated into the air.

A long procession of women, led by the patient, immediately followed by the matron, chanted as they headed outdoors toward a shelter made of branches a few feet from the fire. The patient sat down on another stool inside the sacred shelter. Inside the guard circle, the torch was relit.

As the women bustled around the new initiate, the men began to dance. The youngest of them, his torso nude, executed two perilous acrobatic movements then fell back on his frail legs amidst his fellow dancers. One of the tom-tom drummers left his place and joined him. Another woman, barely over thirty and in city attire, got up suddenly, shaken by strong tremors. She swiveled on that spot for a two good minutes then fell flat onto the hard earth. When she got up, she was hunched over and walked with slow steps like an old woman weighed down by her years. The dancers dispersed.

"Good evening," she cried out with a quavering voice from beyond the grave.

Inhabited by an aged spirit from elsewhere, the body of the young woman shrank even more. She circled the audience staggering. Her arms shriveled and her fingers curled, her face deeply grooved with wrinkles and her mouth twisted into a grimace, the old lady in her thundered:

"I have come to warn you about the evil spirit that is lingering among you. He inhabits the body of a man who wants to sabotage this vigil. May this person rise and leave before I expose his secrets to everyone."

She made another round around the guard circle, threatening the audience with her red eyes.

Apprehensive looks by the people seated crisscrossed the room. Frightened children clung to their mothers. The chanting and the tom-toms went silent. A long, horrible whistling sound came from nowhere. The guard circle vibrated. Enraged, the possessed spirit lifted the torch out of the ground and headed with the hesitant steps of her advanced age toward a man of about fifty, who took to his heels, passed swiftly behind the guard circle, and disappeared into the night.

Indignant cries burst forth. Some men set out in pursuit of him.

"Follow attentively everything that is said from here on," Eva whispered in her sister's ear.

After she'd awoken from her blackout the previous evening, Emilienne had gone to her sister's very early in the morning to ask her to accompany her to the seer's house for a consultation. After a brief explanation, Eva, revolted by what she had heard, grumbled as she threw on a clean dress:

"Such a bastard. And you are just finding out about it now.

He will hear it from me, that one. In that case, I'm bringing you to Mama Mbira.

"Do you think she will be able to tell me who this woman is?"

"In an instant. You'll see. She's very good. If her business is still open, she will ask us to join in the vigil she leads on Saturdays. She will also tell you what to do to unlock your womb. Whatever you hear tonight, don't do anything stupid, which means don't leave your husband. Do everything you can to get better. Have you made an appointment with the hypnotist?"

"I'll call him Monday morning. Don't forget it was only yesterday that Dr. Pascal mentioned it to me."

"You have to fight on all fronts."

So THEY LEFT Eva's after she'd told her eldest daughter to watch her brothers and sisters. After they'd driven for about an hour in the car, they took a bumpy fork off the main road. Four years ago, Eva had gone down this same stretch of road determined to win back her unfaithful husband. The witch had prepared a concoction for her in a tall flask, filled halfway with eau de cologne, a mixture of leaves, and tree bark that had the power to make her husband forget his multiple romantic flings. Before putting on this specially prepared perfume, she had to wash twice daily with water mixed with other leaves, so that she could wash her body and her spirit.

Eva was not disappointed. Her husband broke off with his mistresses only a few days after she'd begun the treatment. She realized it when he came home every evening and on the weekends, and he had not ceased paying attention to his wife and children since. Today, she seemed happy. Emilienne, who had mocked her sister for the primitive way she'd chosen to sort out her personal problems, was not laughing this morning as she went to her sister for her help in solving her own.

Luckily for both sisters, the old healer tirelessly continued organizing her vigils and healing men and women who had been struck down with illness. Tonight, Emilienne was finally going to know not only the identity of her rival but also her husband's intentions.

After the joyous cries had taken place in the courtyard, the women came back, chanting and gyrating inside the circle. Emilienne smiled sadly at this spectacle she was seeing for the first time. If certain employees of hers could see her in this strange place, they would be shocked. She was herself stunned by the path of her existence that had led her here.

Since the death of her daughter, she had been driven by events she no longer controlled. She had become a puppet on a string. Would she once more find the serenity to ward off certain blows? Could the answers she was waiting for tonight change her behavior and help her get out of this trap, her life with her husband? Would she, like all these women, have to dance for the rest of her life and forever be part of their group?

While the acrobatics multiplied to the rhythm of the chants and tom-toms, the "matron's" husband, made up with white kaolin and rigged out in a sort of raffia skirt, went into a trance. His step was quick, his eyes burned with a thousand fires, and he ran in the direction of the two sisters, then stopped in front of Emilienne, who jumped. The sorcerer turned around in place. In one hand he held the torch and with the other he shook his little bell briskly. The beatings of the tom-toms became more muted, and then stopped suddenly. After several seemingly interminable seconds, the tom-toms resounded again through the air. This time, they spoke a language only the sorcerer could interpret. The rumblings were alternately dull and threatening. They were halting, piercing, and solemn. With a frantic movement of his head, the sorcerer commanded silence. The air filled with a menacing silence. From his abdomen then came a nearly inaudible voice.

"Your situation, my child, is not an easy one. If you want to know everything about your husband and your rival, come back to be initiated next Saturday. You will see many things yourself as if in a mirror."

Eva, gesticulating in her chair, interrupted him:

"Can't you describe her rival to her? It's very important. Can you and your wife treat her?"

"No, she will see for herself when she eats the powder. She will be cured. And *you* are pregnant."

Just as Emilienne was about to interject, a reedy voice began singing a chant.

"Let's leave," she ordered her sister as she got up.

"You're crazy! We can't leave now—that's not how it works."

"Stay if you like; *I* am leaving."

"Wait a minute; I'm going to say good-bye to the matron. I'll also have to tell her to prepare for your ceremony and ask her for the list of everything we'll need to buy for your initiation."

"You're joking, Eva! Do you think I'm going to set foot in this place again? If you want to make him happy, tell him that I'm going to think about it."

Once in the car, Eva let her anger explode.

"What is wrong with you? Couldn't you wait at least a little while before getting up? That woman works miracles. I'm convinced they didn't want to reveal certain things to you in front of all those people. Besides, they can cure you and get you back together with Joseph."

"No, thanks. Do you honestly believe that I am going to start fetishizing to make my husband love me when I hadn't taken that route from the start when he was actually interested in me?"

"Nobody is asking you to cast a spell on your husband. It will suffice for you first to release him from the hold of this mysterious woman—I think *she* is under the protection of occult powers, otherwise you would have at least known who she was long ago. The second thing you need to do is to wash your body and finally protect yourself. Don't be blind on that point! Almost every woman in this country ends up consulting a healer at one time or another so that she can break the evil spell cast by her in-laws, her rivals, or even her own family. Why don't you want to use the same weapons so that you can once again find the joys of motherhood and take back what belongs to you? You will not be punished for things that are owed you and that others are trying to take from you."

"Listen, Eva, don't insist. In fact, is it true that you're pregnant?"

"I'm three weeks late. I've decided not to keep the child—that's why I haven't said anything to you about it. If there is someone who must have them, it's you."

"Have you gone out of your mind? Whatever you do, don't abort it. Don't refuse the children God gives you, please. I am very happy for you, you know. Don't deprive me of the immense joy of cuddling with that child. After all, he will also be a little bit mine."

They looked at each other and smiled tenderly.

VI

The Last Resort

Emilienne was swimming with broad strokes in the stagnant waters of apathy. Her pain had turned into paralyzing discouragement. And if from time to time she snapped out of it, it was either to drown herself in beer, wine, or whiskey, those drinks she'd always hated, or to throw herself into Dominique's arms.

At night, she would stuff herself with cakes, chocolates, and sandwiches before starting in on the hearty dishes Godwin prepared for her, all of which she ate alone, as her mother-in-law and her grandchildren had left on school vacation. She knew that she was definitely sinking into what she called her quagmire. The only way she could live with herself was to immerse herself in masochistic behavior. Since she was denied simple healthy pleasures, she relished in abandoning herself to the kind of pleasures she could find.

In that regard, she would have liked Dominique to be more available. Despite her attempts to get closer, her secretary became more evasive. Sometimes, during their most intimate moments, she would push her tender caresses away. When Emilienne would demand an explanation, they would end up in a vicious argument. The next day, Dominique would miss work, and would return several days later without even mentioning she'd returned. Alcohol wasn't enough for Emilienne anymore, and she lapsed into a state of frightful terror. That morning, she had waited, trembling, in hopes that her secretary would open her office door and throw herself into her arms. Several times she'd gotten up, run to Dominique's door, and stood still before it, raising her hand to knock, then, defeated, locked herself up again inside her four walls, listening to every little noise that came from the hallway. When her phone rang, she jumped and eagerly picked up the receiver. Finally, *finally,* after two or three hours had passed, Dominique opened her boss's door apprehensively.

She went in, then stood a few feet from Emilienne, giving her winks, half smiles, and some empty phrases, all of it sparing to say the least. And as Emilienne clung to her desk to keep from throwing herself into her arms, the young secretary walked around the table, smiling, and with a slow step and a detached air, bent down toward her employer.

Encouraged by her advances, Emilienne invited her over to her place.

The two women embraced on the big bed. The floral sheets lay on the carpet. In a voice that was calm after weeks of agitation, Emilienne asked:

"What is going on, Dominique? Why do you enjoy playing with my feelings? Would you by chance be tired of me? I demand the truth."

Moving away from her and feigning a bad mood, Dominique snapped back:

"I've had enough of this life we are leading. Do you hear me? I've had enough! Enough! I want you to be entirely mine instead of hanging on to a husband who knows how to live without you. What are you waiting for from him, anyway; do you believe that he will abandon his mistress and come back to you? I'm going to tell you the truth since you want to hear it! You're wasting your time. Soon, you'll have to choose between him and me. I want you, me, no child. You won't have *him* anymore if you don't give him one."

She sat down on the bed, looking sulky, and took a pornographic comic out of her bag.

Carried away by an indescribable hilarity, Emilienne burst out laughing. She laughed so hard that her friend put down her comic book and turned toward her, appalled.

"You should have told me sooner," Emilienne added between two bursts of laughter. "If I've understood you correctly, you are asking me to divorce so that I can live with you!"

She belched, and her intoxicated breath floated into the young secretary's nostrils, who threw her head back slightly.

"I am flattered by your request. Have you forgotten, you

little scatterbrain, that you and I don't live on a deserted island, but among our respective families and friends in a society that condemns relationships like ours?"

"Do you think I haven't thought of all of that?" Dominique snapped back, annoyed. "There won't be any problems if we know how to play our game. Since you get company housing, I will be able to move in here without shocking people. Everyone will just think that I am your protégé. Listen," she added, with a pout on her face as she caressed Emilienne's breast, "aren't we happy together?"

"And what would you do with your children and your little brothers? Are you going to leave your lover for me?"

"Oh, him, I hate him. My brothers will live with my sister and my children will come with me here. Please, do it for our happiness. I am so miserable when I'm not near you."

"Have you gone mad?" Emilienne countered. "Do you think that things are done and undone by the wave of a magic wand? You need to leave, now; we will talk about this another time."

SHE WALKED her to the gate, came back, and served herself a big glass of white wine. She carried the three-quarter-filled bottle over and sat down on the terrace. In less than fifteen minutes, Emilienne had emptied the entire bottle. If she had followed her own desires, she would have got up to get another. But she had no more energy, and, well, there was always tomorrow.

She was sorry she hadn't bought an entire case. Tomorrow, she would change wine sellers. The one from whom she was getting her supplies was starting to shoot her little looks that she didn't like at all. Did he also know that her husband was living with the mother of his children . . . ?

Emilienne grabbed the empty bottle with two hands and brought it to her mouth. Three drops fell onto her rigid tongue. Her hands trembling, she threw the bottle, and it shattered against the low terrace wall. "Where did the guard and Roxanne go?" she wondered. "May they stay far away from me tonight; I don't want to see anyone."

Emilienne sucked on her tongue and rubbed it against her

palate. She needed to drink something to calm herself down, anything. Whiskey would do it and would certainly relax her. Besides, the days were not so long when she drank. It allowed her to laugh about herself and everyone else who sought her downfall.

Emilienne tried to get up: her right leg slipped; the other folded under her. She ended up sitting back down. And as her head was spinning, she let herself slide onto the cement while singing: "On the Bridge of Olamba, We all dance there, we all dance there . . ." Then she broke out in nervous laughter.

"Who does he think he is? He can go screw himself. And this minx who wants a turn at controlling me. I wonder what's the matter with them."

She finally managed to stand up on her two limp legs. And so, staggering, she headed toward the little bar in the living room. In one gulp, she emptied the last of the gin that she'd found there, and had flopped onto the divan when her head started to throb violently. As soon as she felt better, she crawled to the kitchen and got a large scoop of vanilla ice cream from the freezer, which she devoured as she stood there, even though most of it just drizzled down her chin.

As she wiped her mouth with the sleeve of her blouse, she was suddenly overcome by a desire to vomit. And before she even had the time to bring her two hands to her mouth, the first surges of the alcoholic mixture spurted out and splattered all over the cupboards and the walls. The nauseating mixture ran pathetically down in a line, from where it fell onto the white tiles. A halting wheezing began again in her throat. This time, refusing to be taken by surprise, she ran outside. Her stomach contracted. Bent over, she let herself empty out.

As she stood up feeling light, a horrible wrenching in her lungs—unless her entire rib cage was burning—paralyzed her. Emilienne leaned farther forward, resting her hands on her bent knees. She stayed in this uncomfortable position for a long while, then again tried to stand up slightly. The pain was less acute. She could walk, although stooping, toward the bedroom, where she rinsed her mouth and face. Her ideas still muddled, she lay down on her bed and fell right asleep.

She was awakened by the heat in the early morning hours. The air conditioner had stopped. She got up and tried, in vain, to make it work.

Emilienne got undressed and went back to bed. As she lay on her back, her hands under the nape of her neck, she let her thoughts wander until her secretary's delirious words came back. Of course, she acknowledged that their relationship could become cumbersome, but she wasn't thinking of ending it for the moment, because nothing, she believed, could effectively replace her inner chaos, not even alcohol.

In any case, they wouldn't be able to appease the brutal awakening in her body. It was more of a psycho-sentimental awakening that shocked her. Masturbation was not her thing. She always felt the need for physical contact. And as Dominique's body was similar to her own, it allowed her not only to rediscover herself, but also to provide her with a certain balance. This forbidden relationship was like a drug, and she knew that its sudden withdrawal would make her completely crazy.

Time ran over Emilienne like sticky water. Every so often, fleeting thoughts about her status as an unfaithful wife crossed her drowsy mind. But they no longer affected her. It wasn't even a sign of resignation. She simply no longer dwelled in her own skin but instead was living in someone else's. She forbade herself to judge this other woman severely: one could even say that she was very lenient toward her, a feeling that led to pity, which she had always despised when it came from others.

After the black hole and the bottomless abyss, Emilienne was at an impasse, a path that led nowhere except back to the beginning. As far as she was concerned, that meant she would have to reconsider all the facts about her marital situation, which would force her to make a decision about the future, at least about what was up to her. If during the day she barely managed to clear her head, aided by an almost permanent drunken state and moments spent with Dominique, her nights were filled with nightmares.

Her state of health resisted her troubled sleep and her alcohol abuse less and less. For a few days, she was waking up feverish and her body numb. In the morning, the imprint of her body was drawn pitifully on the big bed. Her nightgown clung to her skin like a piece of clothing that hadn't completed the spin cycle. She continued to shiver and her teeth chattered, even when she turned off the air conditioner and the temperature in the bedroom got as high as 86 degrees. She ended up getting out the wool blanket and rolling herself up in it even though it was prickly. For three days and nights, her fever persisted, and even the many malaria pills she took did not manage to bring it down.

Emilienne grew weak, and her weight loss was clearly visible. She was able to get around by leaning on doors and furniture. Godwin brought her tea in bed, a good half of which spilled onto the sheets, since her hands trembled so when she brought the cup to her mouth.

Roxanne left the foot of the bed only to relieve herself or to call the cook or the night guard. One morning, when Emilienne was moaning and twisting about in her sweaty sheets, Roxanne looked sadly at her mistress and, doing a 180-degree turn that would surprise any human being, jumped outside, over the gate, and onto Charles de Gaulle Boulevard. She plunged across several streets, weaving her way through pedestrians and cars before coming to a small market in a residential neighborhood, then stopped at an intersection, and without hesitating, turned into one of the alleys just as a disabled person came hobbling along with a cane. With her momentum, Roxanne did not have time to dodge her. The disabled person's cane was knocked out from under her; she fell flat onto the loose gravel, shrieking. A young child ran to help her up. His little friend picked up a stick and ran after the animal. The latter managed to lose him, but a pack of raw-boned dogs blocked his path farther on. With a half-animal half-human stare, Roxanne gauged their strength and then started to growl. The horde approached her, determined to attack. Roxanne backed up and with a leap cleared the barrier the sickly dogs had made, and they, frightened by her, flattened themselves to the ground. She now crossed a little bridge where children waded, laughing, in a muddy river. Like an animal being hunted down, she slinked between the rows of flowers and the houses' outer walls. Finally, she recognized the imposing gate at Eva's house. Weakened from her long race, she was happy just to scratch insistently at the gate and growl. The children who were playing in the yard were stunned when they opened the door for her. One of them ran to look for their mother.

To Eva's many questions, the animal answered with groans and a tearful look. She ran to phone, first, Emilienne's office, then her home. Nobody answered. Eva then took the animal in her arms and got into the car.

Emilienne was only half-conscious when Eva had her sister admitted to one of Olamba's private clinics. According to the doctor, she had a severe malaria attack that would have been fatal if she had stayed home one more day.

A few days after her admission to the clinic, her temperature, which was oscillating between 104 and 102.2 degrees, finally went down. Although she was still weak and had lost a lot of weight, she woke up smiling and was ready to return home. The doctor decided nevertheless to keep her a little longer so that, he said, he could watch her very low blood pressure. Her family, colleagues, and friends took turns visiting her. Joseph, summoned by Eva, also came every evening to spend two hours with his wife.

To fill this long time, during which they exchanged only a few banal sentences, Joseph read his newspaper, and then went back to their home, which he had returned to since his wife's hospitalization.

Emilienne recovered rather quickly from this disease that had nearly killed her. She was very grateful to God, who had not found the moment appropriate to call her to him. And, like all those who passed so close to death, she felt the irresistible urge to live.

As soon as she felt strong enough, she got out of bed and opened the windows wide. Her arms outstretched and her head turned toward the sky, she breathed in the fresh air from the garden. The aroma of a thousand fragrances of flowers rose up to her nostrils. She breathed in deeply several times and closed her eyes. A gentle calming wind caressed her face, making it seem like her pores were also breathing. She stretched out, leaned her head forward, and smiled. She hummed along to the music playing on the radio as it drifted out of one of her neighbor's windows. She laughed at the birds that landed hesitantly on the windowsill of the bedroom above hers. She let a tiny black ant run over her arm, contemplating it with the astonishment of a child who was discovering the outside world for the first time.

"WELL, WELL! Our patient seems to be doing better today," the doctor exclaimed as he entered, followed by his assistant and a nurse.

"Good morning, Doctor. I'm doing very well. I hope you aren't going to keep me here another day."

"Don't you worry, Madame Eyang, we will release you tomorrow morning, if, of course, your blood pressure doesn't play anymore nasty tricks on us. Please, sit down. And give me your arm . . . Everything looks good, Madame," he said after taking her blood pressure. "Are you having a fever at night?"

"No, Doctor."

"Has your appetite returned now that your fever has gone down?"

"It's fine. I am eating well; I'm going to need to go on a diet when I get out of here," Emilienne said with a laugh.

"Forget about your figure for the moment," the doctor replied, very relaxed. "You need to get your strength back. I'll see you again tomorrow before you're discharged; continue with your treatment. Have a nice day, Madame Eyang."

"Thank you, Doctor."

WHILE HOME for a week on sick leave, with her cleaning lady's help, Emilienne kept busy organizing all the rooms. Every evening, she assisted the guard with his chore of watering the lawn and the plants in her huge yard, then tended personally to her vegetable garden. Thanks to her cook, she would still eat peanuts, onion, tomatoes, and good lettuce this season. These simple tasks filled her with joy.

When night fell, she listened to classical music or jazz or read a novel. Joseph slept at home every night, getting back very late in the evening. The married couple avoided brushing bodies in the large bed and still were not speaking to one another. When the situation forced them to, they exchanged measured, respectful words. One would have said that each was afraid of opening up to the other, of sharing any words that would reveal what they were thinking. In the morning, they would go their separate ways after brief greetings and fleeting looks.

This morning, after her husband had left for his construction company, Emilienne called the hypnotist, who made an appointment for her in the afternoon.

THE YOUNG WOMAN was received by Monsieur Eric Chevalier in an apartment on the sixth floor of an imposing eight-story building. The man was gigantic with white hair and a white beard. His twinkling eyes lingered on Emilienne as he led her into his spacious office.

"Please do sit down," he said, indicating a large salmon-colored armchair facing the door in front of his worktable. "I am happy that you've come," he continued. "Dr. Pascal explained your problem to me in lengthy detail."

He sat down in turn. A dozen files in salmon-colored folders were piled on his desk. To his left was a single bed covered with a beautiful white bedspread.

"Before we begin our first session, I must explain to you what hypnotherapy is, since you will be undergoing it for several months, even after you've had proven results. I am surely going to sound a little scientific to you, so don't hesitate to interrupt me and ask me questions. You see, at first people are afraid of hypnotists because we are not as popular as doctors. Before I came here, the Kampanans had never heard of our work. However, our healing method is as old as the Earth. Do you know that Jesus was in some ways one of the very first hypnotists to heal the sick by the laying on of hands?"

He stopped to answer the telephone, which had just rung. Fascinated by the hypnotist's impressive build and by his introduction to the subject, Emilienne had only given a cursory glance to the office. And so she used the phone call as an opportunity to look around.

Before her stood three tall windows, and on the other walls

were surrealist paintings, which fit perfectly with his profession. Behind her in a corner, a giant thick palm grew majestically in a black pot.

The hypnotist put down the phone and smiled at her.

"It is very important, Madame, that you have faith in your treatment, in a word, that you maintain positive thoughts throughout the whole process. Do you know that the cosmos, also known as the macrocosm, is made up of stars and planets, and Earth is one of those planets. The cosmos, therefore, is plunged into a universal electromagnetic field, and each star, each planet makes up its own force field. Man's survival depends on two forces," he went on, "the immaterial force and the material force."

"The immaterial forces come from the sky and are provided by the sun, which gives off, as you know, light, radiation, and essential vitamins. Air also comes from the sky, providing man with oxygen. As for the material forces, they come from our planet, the ground, in other words, because of the solid foods and liquids that man consumes. The assimilation of energy makes the body and mind function."

"Now you see where I am heading," he continued further. "Quite simply to this: man is a cosmo-telluric being, because his life is born out of universal fluid, along with his diet and his exposure to air and light. He is, therefore, himself a miniature universe, a tributary of the great universe. As Hermes said: 'What is above is like what is below, and what is below like what is above, the whole forming one and the same thing.' I hope I am not boring you, Madame Eyang."

"No, please, continue."

"It is therefore believed that natural radioactivity reigns in the cosmos, just as it reigns inside the body of our planet, and that uranium—which, as you know emits radiation and is one of the radioactive elements that we find in the animal kingdom—is one of its sources. The cosmos," he added, "is also endowed with magnetism, which we find on our planet in the form of magnetite (iron oxide that is naturally magnetized). This magnetite, like uranium, is found in the animal kingdom. It is a pathway for the circulation of terrestrial magnetism."

"Our globe," he added, "as I've just said, has its own radiation, its force fields, and its magnetism. Man is, consequently, a medium, because he is an intermediary situated between the sky and the earth, from where he receives, accumulates, and emits radon. He is additionally magnetic because he is influenced by terrestrial magnetism. I will finish, Madame, by concluding that man is a magnetic medium by the position he occupies on the surface of the globe and by the abundance of minerals as well as force fields that he receives from it."

"This long explanation," he concluded, "clearly demonstrates that hypnotists are not magicians. They are ordinary people who have perhaps this innate ability to produce more external waves than others, who have done nothing to get it, but decide to do some good with it."

"How do you know you have such a talent?"

"There are people who have it and who will never know. It shows up most often by chance. I realized I had magnetic powers inadvertently at the age of forty-five. My wife and I had had a dog for about twenty years whom we loved so much. One day, he was the victim of a traffic accident and was paralyzed. The veterinarian we brought him in a panic to see declared him hopeless after examining him and said he was going to put him out of his misery. My wife was strongly opposed to that. At home, the dog stayed all day in a corner. Each time we went near him, he would whimper and looked despondent, which mortified us. It was very painful for us, especially for my wife, who would lock herself up in our bedroom and cry. One evening, I started to caress his left paw, all the while talking to him, and to our great surprise, the next morning he was able to move that paw again. Intrigued, I caressed the other paw, then his whole body. In the evening, he was able to get up on his four paws. This miracle, and it was a miracle, completely flabbergasted us."

"We spoke about it to a friend, who asked me to lay my hands upon her. To convince me, she affirmed that she was very sensitive to external waves. I laid my hands over her without much conviction, on her back, head, arms, and legs. She could feel, she said, a tingling in every part of her body that I was touching lightly. The following morning, she phoned to tell us that for the first time in six months, she had been able to sleep uninterruptedly and that her rheumatism had ceased. From that day on, I began using my new powers over everyone I was close to, and they were all healed of their pain. Today, I treat practically all illnesses. And I have lived in your beautiful country for two years now, thanks to Dr. Pascal, whom I met in France."

"Does he refer many sterile women to you?"

"Yes. He is not the only doctor to send his patients to me. My clients suffer anything from nervous depression to cancer, including obesity and skin diseases."

Emilienne raised her eyebrows, skeptical.

"It is surprising that Africans trust you. It seemed to me that they preferred injections to playing games."

"You're mistaken, Madame. You are one of the races who believe the most in magical powers and supernatural experiences. It has therefore not been difficult for me to gain my patients' trust. You would be surprised to know that Westerners, the medical profession in particular, ask us for proof of our ability to heal, as if hypnosis were a branch of medicine that could be tested in a laboratory, then on patients."

"This long explanation," he said to conclude, "was necessary before beginning the long treatment that you are going to have. I'm going to wash my hands and we will begin the first session immediately."

He disappeared then came back a few seconds later.

"Stand up with your side toward me," he said, standing by the bed. "First, I'm going to magnetize you fully dressed; then you'll take off your clothes. Stand up straight, head up. There!"

He passed both of his hands again and again over Emilienne, about an inch above her head.

"What do you feel?"

"A hot flash."

"The waves are moving well. Don't be surprised that I'm starting with your head. Even though your reproductive organs are located in your abdomen, it is important to stimulate all the glands in your body, in order to get your endocrine system working again. Hypnosis has the advantage of rebalancing the whole organism while treating the localized illness."

After having made several magnetic passes over the young woman's whole body, he asked her to undress and to lie down on her back on the bed. Again, he made the same passes, returning several times to her abdomen.

"It's strange! My arms and legs are tingling," Emilienne said with wonder.

"That's normal. Half of the people who are magnetized don't feel anything, the others have various sensations: tingling on the extremities of their limbs, the feeling of vibrations or hot flashes, or accelerated heartbeats. Others feel the need to laugh when the end of their nose is magnetized. A few patients have cold sensations, and still others feel discomfort."

Monsieur Chevalier proceeded to massage the young woman's naked body, focusing on her lower abdomen. After he'd put her on her belly and repeated the same movements, he asked her to stretch out again on her back.

"Did you feel pain during any part of the session?"

"No, but I feel exhausted."

"We're going to stop for today."

To end the session, he passed his right palm quickly over Emilienne's arms and legs from the top to the bottom. The young woman distinctly felt the magnetic waves go over her feet and her hands.

"You can get dressed. Don't be worried if the magnetic shock brings on insomnia or any other kind of disturbance. It could be diarrhea, a breakout of pimples, or the resurgence of any illness, specifically asthma. These short-term reactions are signs that the treatment is working."

After she'd gotten dressed, Emilienne sat back down.

"How much do I owe you, Monsieur Chevalier?"

"Ten thousand francs," he answered, flipping through his appointment book. "Come back in a week at the same time, Madame Eyang."

As she went out of this first session, Emilienne experienced some strange sensations, particularly in her core and belly button.

"Funny way to treat sterility," she thought as she got into the car. "I'll do the whole treatment, and it will be my last attempt to cure this cursed illness. Still, nothing will prove that

I've become normal again after these magnetism sessions. Like he himself said, this treatment can't be tested in a laboratory. Whatever the outcome, his long explanations are proof that he is serious and confident. The funniest thing in all this—no, it's not funny at all, the most dramatic, I should say—is the irregularity of my sexual encounters with Joseph. It is practically impossible for me to know if after my cure any physical contact will occur at the right moment. Besides, the only way to know I am cured is to become pregnant. Otherwise, I could be doing this treatment for a very long time. How will I be able to tell I am cured? A child does not make itself, at least not in this country. Has he thought of this fundamental truth before advising me to go through the treatment? I have to believe that the second home that he created without thinking made Joseph lose his sense of reality."

"So what is the name of that African sociologist who claimed that modern man, for his equilibrium, needs three women to love at the same time? There's the wife, whom he considers as part of himself, the reflection of the mother, who reassures, consoles, and watches over his well-being; the mistress, who plays the role of his confidante and advisor, his lucky charm; finally, the girlfriend, who lets him fantasize and forget himself from time to time before returning reinvigorated to the arms of his wife. Without these three women, this sociologist says, man remains unbalanced." Emilienne was sarcastic about these words: "His virility, his machismo are threatened. We have only one life, so we might as well live it fully, right! Wouldn't they be in this way comparable to those people who do everything in excess, under the pretext of taking pleasure in life? Does Joseph, like all those of his sex, realize the great pain he has caused me? Because sooner or later, these poor women end up suffering from love the moment they refuse to stop sharing the one who counts the most for them."

Emilienne smiled sadly. Her interior monologue went on in a more biting tone. "This so-called modern man who so badly needs love and attention is wedged between three women! Like a maniac, the wife demands her legitimate rights; on their side, the mistress and the girlfriend cling to the one who had freely chosen them. This collective revolt makes man the poor victim, misunderstood and betrayed, even though the whole point was to bring these 'miserable creatures' happiness. Didn't a 'womanizer' say that thanks to men like him, single women could have an almost normal sex life and that the kids who were born of these fleeting unions would make up the necessary workforce for tomorrow?!"

With sarcasm, Emilienne continued: "It's difficult for these poor victims to give in to the egotism of these women who, after having consented to play the secondary role, clamor for first place, which, after all, is their right; they are, after all, the purveyors of well-being and comfort. They have, however, gone to the trouble of giving a long explanation to their wife that true fidelity is embedded in the heart. In regard to the other two, they had the decency—an admirable quality—to wear their wedding ring and to make them promise to respect their wife and to know their place. To their girlfriend, they didn't miss, however underlining the fact that she was not the first and would not be the last woman they would encounter. All these warnings, which can be summed up like this: 'Love me, but please do it quietly and my way,' alas, lose their weight the moment a surge of pride awakens these women. Because one fine day, they decide that they can no longer be happy with the little they want to give them. At the least, like me, they take on the huge risk of prolonging the uncomfortable situation in which they find themselves."

As THE DAYS and weeks passed, Emilienne learned to love her husband in the way she believed he wanted to be loved: silently and with great tolerance. She swallowed her fears, her suffering, and her jealousy. With all her might, she wanted to love him without demanding anything in return. She desired to love him for their love and not for what he did. In her sustained efforts to appear perfect in his eyes, she would sometimes wonder if this new love that she desired so deeply would last, and if the two of them were not maintaining it in total complicity, through normal physical relations.

At times, too, she bitterly regretted her miscarriages, which were the result of his presence in their bed and the proof of the interest—although diminished—that he held in her body.

Despite her tenacity in wanting to love him until she disappeared from the surface of the Earth, she could not refrain from hearing herself ask again and again why he rejected the idea of a separation. The answer was given to her suddenly one evening by Joseph himself, who'd come in to change his shoes.

"You must without a doubt want to know why I will not leave you! I'm going to tell you," he added with an air of provocation. "I don't see any reason for it. You ended up bending to my way of life, and, you don't bother me. And besides, you have qualities that I haven't found in any other woman. See, for example, the way you've raised my nephews even though you haven't been very interested in them the past two years. Unlike other men, you see, I will not reject you because my financial situation has considerably improved."

Emilienne, who was washing her hair, got up abruptly. Her hair flew and the soapy water ran down her face and neck. The comb in her hand fell with a clatter. With an agile hand, she gripped the pair of scissors that she had taken out to trim her nails and hurled it at her husband. With a swift movement of his head, Joseph barely dodged the scissors by a centimeter. Emilienne ran into the bedroom, slumped over, and collapsed onto the carpet, panting like her dog. Her eyes, glimmering like the lights of a deserted harbor, stared up at the ceiling.

Joseph, who absolutely did not tolerate her fainting spells, leaned over her, worried.

"What is going on with you? I wanted to be frank with you. I wanted you to finally have the answer that you were waiting for from me. Oh, and I've had enough. I'm leaving, good-bye."

"Oh, no," Emilienne shrieked, pulling herself up. "I'm not going to let you leave this bedroom this time."

She jumped up to lock the door, pulled the key from the lock, and threw it into the linen closet.

The married couple stood facing each other, he against the window and she with her back against the door.

"Give me that key," Joseph ordered, walking toward the closet.

"You will not leave this room until we've talked."

Joseph came toward her resolutely. Emilienne jumped on him and gave him two fierce slaps. Surprised and beside himself, Joseph raised his fist, and, just as he was about to swing it, his fingers relaxed. He shook his head vehemently and sat down on the dresser. He looked lost as his eyes scanned the furniture, the knickknacks, and then fell on his wife's livid face.

"Up until now," Emilienne uttered, her face tense, "I have swallowed every single grass snake that you've wanted to wave in my face. And that's enough. I am asking you to choose right now between your mistress, your children, and me. Don't forget that your kids' coming to live in this house is out of the question."

Her face, knotted up in determination, trembled.

Disconcerted, Joseph stood up and took off his jacket.

"What is it with you all of a sudden? Do you know who you're talking to?"

"Don't act high and mighty with me, please."

"I see you're not going to leave me the time to think it over," he murmured.

"Don't mock me, Joseph. You're not going to play that I-need-time-to-think-about-it game with me about a situation that has been going on for fifteen years. I can be ready to file for divorce tomorrow if you want to; if not, you're going over to your mistress's house tonight and bringing back all of your clothes. Don't smile, Joseph, I am not joking."

"Enough! I will not accept an ultimatum from you. Have you lost your head? Honestly! Do you realize how absurd you sound? Do you think I am capable of abandoning my children because it pleases you?!"

He moved toward his wife and grabbed her by the shoulders. Emilienne struggled violently to escape his hold.

"No problem!" the young woman screamed. "I want to hear you say that you want a divorce. And don't worry; I will accept your decision."

Joseph's voice dropped in tone. After a few seconds, which to Emilienne seemed an eternity, he went on faintly:

"Who do you think I set up this construction company for? And the house I am having built now, who will it belong to when I'm dead?"

Emilienne started. She had just heard for the first time that he was having a house built, that he would bequeath it to the children of his mistress before she was even out of the picture.

"Unbelievable! What else is he hiding from me? How can someone trust her husband when he is capable of hiding such a huge secret from his spouse! No doubt an open secret for his family, his mistress, and his children. It's one thing that he doesn't want to reveal to me the identity of this woman he's been with for fifteen years; I, too, have a relationship that I would never admit! But it's another thing to ever forgive him for having hidden from me the existence of two children and the construction of a visible, palpable house. This cannot be happening. He never loved me. I will not be walked all over like that."

"We will live there, obviously," he continued, "but, naturally, it will go to my children. Would you be so heartless as to deprive them of what is theirs by right: a father and an inheritance?"

Emilienne balked, her blood having already pumped a dozen times through her veins. "Oh, you are mistaken, Joseph," she said to herself. "It is out of the question that other children benefit from what would have gone to mine had they existed. If that's how it is, I will give you the son you want and I will see who snatches what is his. *Then,* we can talk about rights."

"I do believe I've given you enough time to give me more children. Your jealousy today is not justified. And to deprive me of those whom their mother has given me is a sick scheme. Don't take me away from what makes me happy and proud."

Emilienne thought long and hard. A piece of advice from her sister—"You can get anything from a man, but you've got to know how to play his feelings"—was running through her mind like a revelation. She decided to change her strategy, maintaining, however, what was essential. She smiled and moved toward her husband, embracing him.

"Darling, you have pushed me all the way. I admit I have no right to deprive you of your children. From now on, you will visit them once a week and you will spend all your nights here. For all those years, in a way I encouraged your infidelity. Now, though, I want you with me. I will never forget all the pain and suffering you've caused me, and I don't know if I can forgive you for it. I am nonetheless ready to give us a second chance."

As she whispered those words in his ear, she unbuttoned his

shirt and placed her right hand on his hairy chest and with the other dried her hair with the towel draping her shoulders.

"It would be difficult to . . . to . . ." Joseph muttered, thrown off balance.

"Yes, I know, my darling. Let's still try. In three months, we'll assess the situation. Okay?"

She slid down his pants zipper, opening it slowly.

"My career, as rewarding as it is, does not soothe my sexual desires and my maternal instinct," Emilienne said to herself as she looked for a spot to park her car in front of her hypnotist's building. "Exchanging caresses with another woman won't fill the absence of Joseph's carnal contact, nor will it replace this complicity we have had in the past. My rebellion, my anger, and my pride won't change anything in this reality. I need him, and now I know how to keep him. I won't let anyone take him from me again, and soon I will force him to reveal the name of this woman to me."

After several maneuvers, she managed to park between two cars. She was here for her eighth session. Encouraged by a feeling of serenity she hadn't felt since the birth of her daughter, Emilienne hadn't missed a single appointment. Thanks to her magnetism sessions, she was cured of her bulimia and her drunkenness. In order to detoxify her body, she drank eight glasses of water a day and rode her bicycle every morning.

She was thus very relaxed when she let Monsieur Chevalier magnetize her.

"Have you noticed that your pimples have disappeared and that you have a better complexion, Madame?"

"Yes, and I can even tell you that my hair isn't brittle anymore. I am less irritable and I feel stronger. You have transformed me, Monsieur Chevalier."

"You can see I am very happy about that, Madame. Don't forget that a sudden stop to the treatment can destroy all of our hard work. I would advise you to change to two sessions a month until you're pregnant. After that, we'll see."

After she'd been magnetized standing up, Emilienne undressed and lay down on the bed.

"Magnetism has the advantage of curing all pain," Monsieur Chevalier added as he passed both of his hands up and down the young woman's body. I have healed stuttering, mental illnesses, shyness, and so on. You aren't the first person who has talked to me about transformation. After several sessions, the patient's character changes as the illness is cured."

"It would have been good if my husband had also had a few sessions, not because he has a bad character, but just to rethink his ideas."

"You would be doing him a big favor, for it could only do him good. Bring his photo to me."

"Are you telling me that you can magnetize him via his photograph?"

Emilienne straightened up, excited.

"Lie back down, Madame Eyang. Remote telepathy is done by cosmic transmission. For that all I need is to position the photo of the patient on the bed, to visualize him lying down facing me, and to make exactly the same gestures as those I perform on a patient who's in front of me. It is not necessary to inform the patient about the process, especially if they're skeptical. It is obviously easier to remotely magnetize a patient whom you treat ordinarily, wherever he is, as long as you agree upon the place and the time he will be there. I have happened to magnetize from my office one client who was in a train and another in the United States."

"Lie down on your stomach," the magnetizer went on. "Relax completely and breathe deeply. Before you leave, leave your ovulation dates for me. I'm going to magnetize you remotely during that time. And speaking of that, I've prepared some magnetized cotton for you to put under the mattress in the spot where you sleep. If you don't feel well, take a little of that cotton and put it in your ears. When you wake up, moisten those cotton balls and then throw them out. Leave half of that cotton in a plastic bag, and apply it from time to time to your belly or any another part of your body where there is pain. I've also prepared a bottle of magnetized water. Put some in a vaporizer and vaporize your face every morning. You can also drink the equivalent of three teaspoons if you have to be at an important meeting. Turn back over onto your back."

At the contact of the magnetic waves that Monsieur Chevalier's hands gave off, Emilienne felt, first, a strong heat on her back, then an intense pain in her pelvic region. She told the magnetizer, who then, with his eyes closed, passed his hands again several times over the painful part of her abdomen. The pain intensified. Emilienne grimaced.

"There is definitely something wrong in the fallopian tubes and uterus."

He concentrated more and, with the back of his right hand, repeated the same magnetic passes, while with his left hand, he gently massaged her lower abdomen. He stopped three minutes later.

"How do you feel?"

"The pain stopped."

To conclude, he massaged the soles of her feet and passed his hand quickly over each limb from the top down to the extremities.

"You can get dressed, Madame, and don't forget to note down the dates I asked you for on the notepad on my desk," he said as he went to wash his hands in the adjoining room.

"You talked about cotton and magnetized water," the young woman reminded him when he reappeared.

"Of course."

He took them out of one of his drawers.

"For how long do I have to keep the cotton under the mattress?"

"Three to four weeks. Wet it before you throw it out so that you destroy the magnetic current."

"Thank you," Emilienne said, getting up. "I hope that with all of this it won't be long before I'm cured."

"Stay resolutely optimistic. Your sterility is without a doubt psychosomatic; your cure thus depends a lot on you. I'll see you again in two weeks," he added as he walked with her to the elevator.

EMILIENNE CAME out of Natalys with her arms full of packages. Tonight, after the UN-sponsored conference to which she was invited, she would stop by to bring them to her sister, whose delivery was imminent.

For this child who was going to be born, Eva had resolved

to reuse her last child's layette. And to be nice to her sister, she had ended up allowing her to buy a few clothes for newborns and for six months to one year. Although Emilienne had promised her not to get carried away and spend a lot of money, she had not resisted the temptation to also buy a playpen and a variety of baby products a little while ago in the toy store.

Her joy was so great that she hummed an old song she'd remembered from the last decade. At the same time, a fleeting shadow dampened her joy. She had just then thought of her relationship with her secretary. "Starting tomorrow, I'm putting an end to these lackluster sexual encounters. Hey! What if I asked Joseph to find work for her somewhere else! He could just as well hire her as a secretary in his company. I am going to have to weigh my words carefully so that I don't give the girl the opportunity to exploit this dirty chapter in my life. She is not trustworthy. How could I have fallen so low?"

EMILIENNE SAT DOWN in the row reserved for the Kampana delegation. The UN-sponsored international conference on "the emancipation of the African woman" was about to begin. The agenda items dealt with three themes:

—women and work;

—how to reconcile professional life with family life; and

—marriage legislation in African societies.

With the mass education of women came their concern for independence and their desire to be considered as full economic agents. It had to be acknowledged nevertheless that that sociocultural economic upheaval, provoked by women's entering the workforce, didn't always get politicians' support. International organizations' support of women's movements in the four corners of the continent was always needed.

The interest shown by the UN, UNESCO, and, to a lesser degree, the OAU regarding the problems of the African woman took concrete form at meetings like this one, which represented one more step toward a fair and equal society.

After the opening speech by the president, and the welcome speech by the secretary of state for women's affairs, work groups were put together, led by two representatives of each country in attendance.

Emilienne chose the subcommittee under the heading "women and work," made up of about thirty women.

The opening of the conference was broadcast on television. The president of the subcommittee, a petite middle-aged woman, invited her sisters to give the best of themselves throughout this conference in which each new idea, she stated, constituted a pillar for the edification of the continent.

Designated as a spokeswoman, Emilienne noted the proposals that came out of the heated debate. After four hours of discussion, they ended the session to meet again the following day.

Despite the evident interest the women present at the conference had, if one considered the array of proposals that had been formulated, Emilienne noticed very quickly that none of the recommendations intended to make the leaders of the countries in attendance conscious of rural women. "Because," she went on, "I am not sure that the awareness campaigns that will follow our work will reach these women, who are bogged down by certain old-fashioned traditions which bring along with them living conditions that are still difficult."

Her speech aroused applause and everyone's approval. One of the delegates proposed that when the awareness campaigns were launched, the national commissions go through every region of each country. Another suggested the creation of radio and television programs, as well as informational magazines. This task of creating awareness would be the responsibility of the Ministry of Women's Affairs or of leadership groups from the political parties.

In her report, Emilienne concluded: "There can be no social evolution without radically changing the mentalities in all categories of our population. Woman's exploitation runs counter to the process of development initiated during independence. We no longer want sectorial integration; we want to include all occupations and we also wish to hold positions of responsibility, according to our abilities, which have been reserved for men. We no longer accept the passive and verbal acknowledgment of a pseudo-influence determinative of woman in society and in her home. We are calling for the complete revision of all socioprofessional laws. We ask for the unconditional application of measures that have already been confirmed but that remain unheeded, and ask for the diffusion of legal texts by each departmental unit, which must rapidly be formed. Finally, we urge all women to take recourse to the laws of their country each time that the texts are not respected."

After reading all the recommendations to the general assembly, a dozen women, including Emilienne, were invited to a debate broadcast simultaneously on radio and TV to support the president of the African Feminist Movement of the UN and the secretary of women's affairs in Kampana.

From her armchair, Eyang could not help feeling great pride in the idea of knowing that the whole country was watching and listening attentively to her daughter-in-law. Even though she didn't understand the erudite words the latter was using, she was convinced that her ideas would one day contribute to change certain things in this country, things that were apparently important, judging by the seriousness of the debate.

Eyang waved her arms about and kneaded her fingers. She trembled for Emilienne each time she took the floor. Her smile widened. All those who knew Eyang would soon come to congratulate her. She would no longer go unnoticed, and for good reason; it isn't every mother-in-law who can pride herself on having a daughter-in-law as educated and respected as hers was.

"She is incredible!" Joseph thought, smiling at his wife on the screen.

As soon as she opened the car door, smiling faces greeted her at the door.

"My girl!!" Eyang exclaimed. "The telephone has not stopped ringing since the program began. Your parents, your sister, and even my cousins called, your friends and colleagues as well. I am sure that some members of my family who don't have telephones at home will come to congratulate us tomorrow."

"My girl," she continued, "you must be tired. Give me your purse and go sit down with your husband and the children. Ah! What a day! When I think that you didn't say anything to me about being on television. Anyway, even if I didn't understand anything, I know that you said important things."

"Give it a rest, Mama," Joseph broke in. "Go keep an eye on your pans on the stove."

He sat down next to his wife, his eyes glimmering. Their nephews in turn sat down on the divan. After they'd congratulated her, he commented on the various points she'd made. Eyang, who was moving about between the kitchen and the dining room, came beaming to announce that the table was ready.

"Sit down, my girl. I prepared that eggplant dish for you that you like so much," the old woman declared with a jaunt in her step. "I wonder why your sister-in-law, Antoinette, hasn't called; she must have gone out to eat at a restaurant with her husband."

Eyang trotted into the kitchen and came back with a bottle of champagne, which she handed to her son.

"You have forgotten the champagne that you yourself put in the refrigerator. No point in ogling the eggplant," she said to the children. "I didn't prepare it for you."

"They can have some, Mama Eyang; I won't eat it all by myself. Thank you for your concern."

Finally, Eyang sat down.

"My son, you are lucky to be married to a great lady. May the good God bless you, children." Her eyes were suddenly moist, and she looked tenderly at Emilienne.

Overcome with emotion, the young woman got up and went over to give her mother-in-law a hug. Eyang bowed her head, an embarrassed smile at the corners of her mouth.

Throughout the entire dinner, the whole household laughed and talked at the same time. The conversation constantly came back to her television performance. Moved and at the same time a little uncomfortable with everyone's sincere happiness, Emilienne felt unsettled and, so as not to burst out sobbing, left the table hurriedly and went into the kitchen.

She did not believe her eyes and ears. Was she living a beautiful dream that would end when the sun rose? And if her suffering, all of her anguish were to end with this event that had taken on the appearance of a family victory she had never dreamed of! This unexpected happiness that she had vaguely sensed since she'd gotten out of the hospital suddenly made her fearful. Her sorrows had become almost normal in her eyes. She had come to believe that sooner or later she would have to learn how to cope with them. And, although she felt revived after a few magnetism sessions, she was far from thinking that her family environment was also going to change for the better. However, she had refused to have her husband telepathically magnetized, so as not to cause a misunderstanding later.

Emilienne was shaking. This window of happiness was really unsettling to her. What was going to happen in the days and weeks to come . . . ?

For a minute she let herself get trapped in a sort of indefinable fright she had never known before. This new sensation was unbearable, because it was keeping her from living fully in the present. If only she could discipline her mind, she would live these moments intensely that she so desired.

In any case, she realized that her husband's return home would be for the long term, if not for good, if, on her part, she cleared up the dark spot that was still clouding her newfound serenity.

As SHE PARKED the company car in front of the imposing building of the National Headquarters for Administrative Building Maintenance, Emilienne was more determined than ever to put an end to the compromising extraprofessional relationship she'd been having with her secretary.

Before she'd even opened the door, Dominique got out of the back of a new BMW, a young man dressed in white having just opened the door for her. The young secretary, with a triumphant air, smoothed out the creases in the sky blue silk skirt suit she was wearing, then, flipping her head, pulled her long braids back against her neck. And, after she'd taken the car keys from her driver's hands, she ran to catch Emilienne, who was heading for the elevator.

"Good morning! Why didn't you park your car in the lot reserved for company management? Did you see mine? Do you like it? It was delivered to me with the chauffeur. It's a gift from my boyfriend."

"Bravo! I see that your boyfriend has a lot of money. Is it still the married one?"

"You have nothing to fear. He's a very rich businessman and I don't see why I shouldn't benefit from his money. Plus, he owes me this little gift; I gave him beautiful children, which I knew would make him happy."

The two women stood still as they waited for the elevator, each adopting an air of secrecy that the other tried to penetrate. Just then a young boy came out of the stairwell carrying a flowerpot in his hands.

"Five hundred francs for the flowerpot," the boy announced, planting himself behind the two women, who turned around.

"Don't you go to school?" Emilienne asked him.

The little flower vendor stared at his bare feet and answered timidly:

"I only go to school in the afternoon. Buy my flowers please, Madame; I need money to buy notebooks and a schoolbag."

He pulled at his shirt flaps, which ripped with a high-pitched screech, leaving his protruding ribs exposed for the two women to see.

"Here, now scram," Emilienne said, handing him a 1,000 franc bill.

"Thank you, Madame, thank you very much."

"Poor kid," Dominique commented as the elevator door opened.

"Come by and see me in a little bit; I have to speak with you," Emilienne said as she opened the door to her office.

"Okay, I'll open up my office and be right there," the secretary replied, intrigued by her employer's expressionless face.

"WE HAVEN'T HAD the chance to talk since I got out of the hospital," Emilienne said as Dominique sat down, her hands clenching her open bag.

"About that, I wanted to say that I'm sorry I didn't come to see you at the hospital. The thing is . . ."

"It doesn't matter," Emilienne cut her off. "I've decided to end our relationship. You and I are involved with men whom we care for, and our relationship could hurt them. Besides, it's not appropriate."

Dominique tensed up, held her bag tightly to her, and then calmly started to dig around inside her bag before placing it on the desk.

"I am not opposed to us seeing each other just as friends, and, if you're having problems, you can talk with me about them."

Dominique, who until then had contained herself, burst out sobbing.

"You don't love me anymore, is that it? What are you blaming me for? Have you managed to get your husband back? It's his fault!"

"Stop this drama, please. My husband's return is not the only reason for this breakup. In any case, for those who are dear to us, we can no longer keep our relationship going. I know that you're smart enough to see the wisdom in my decision."

Dominique sat up defiantly in her chair.

"How can you be so naïve as to think that your husband has come back to you for good? Can you swear that he is no longer making love to his mistress?"

It was Emilienne's turn to jump, tapping her hand on the table.

"Listen, little girl, this problem is my business. From now on I forbid you to meddle in it. Do you understand?"

Dominique let out a sarcastic laugh and whisked the door open violently.

"Don't be stupid and mean," Emilienne yelled after her secretary as she left her office.

THE YOUNG SECRETARY was already racing down the stairwell and running to her car. The chauffeur, sitting on the grass, caught the keys she threw at him in midair.

Fifteen minutes later, Dominique threw herself like a poisoned arrow into the elevator of a small five-story building, bumping, in her haste, into the occupant, who was stuffed into a tight dress.

When she'd arrived on the fifth floor, she shoved open the secretary's door with a bang, interrupting the latter, who was crocheting a doily.

"The boss is expecting me."

Before the secretary even had the time to inform her employer of her arrival, Dominique turned the golden knob of the padded door and then shut it right away behind her.

"What are you doing here? Get out right now—you are not at home here. I don't want any scandals."

"Don't use that tone with me," the young woman snapped back nastily. "I have something for you to listen to, Mr. Joseph Eyang," she added, taking a tape recorder out of her bag and placing it on the desk.

Then, with a contemptuous smile, she rewound the cassette.

"Sit down; otherwise you're going to have a very bad fall in a minute. I had a little conversation with your dear wife a few minutes ago, and I thought it might interest you."

"What is the meaning of all of this?" Joseph grumbled. "If you have something to say to me, do it quickly. I don't have time to lose. And you're not telling me anything new, saying that you've just seen my wife; I think you work together. And what are you doing with this cassette player?"

In response to all, Dominique pressed the button. And, as soon as he identified his wife's voice by the first words she'd spoken, Joseph jumped up, went over to the cassette player, and stopped it.

"Who do you think you are, recording my wife on a cassette player? This little joke must stop right now; leave this office."

"Sit down, Joe, the rest is more interesting, and it would be a shame to deprive you of the information I am bringing to you on a silver platter."

Joseph's curiosity prevailed over his anger. He sat down, staring at the machine, which Dominique started playing again. The crackling of the tape, no doubt old, didn't muffle the conversation, which they could hear distinctly.

Joseph let his head fall on the backrest of the armchair with a vexed look.

"There you have it," Dominique began with a threatening smile. "Any explanation would seem useless to me. So listen to me carefully. I demand that you leave your wife in the next twenty-four hours. Yes," she said smiling, "I'm leaving you a little time to get your things together. If you refuse, know that I will tell the world that your wife is a lesbian. In a month, we will marry."

As at the time of his daughter's death, Joseph let big tears run down his face, this time in front of a woman. The pen he was holding fell from his hand. His red eyes blinked nervously. His forehead creased.

"You have no choice, my dear. I will not be satisfied purely by denouncing your wife's vice if you refuse to marry me. I will make it so that you also lose her, since you still find her charming. You will not buy me with a car and not even with a house if you are not part of the package. Nothing will make me change my mind."

She sat down on Joseph's worktable, bursting with laughter.

"You are the devil in person," Joseph muttered. "What did you do to pervert my wife, because I know it was you who dragged her into the mud?"

"Oh! I didn't have to make much effort. She was so unhappy because of you that all I had to do was to be a little attentive to her problems and get close to her, very close to her."

An inhuman cackle burst from Dominique's fleshy mouth.

"You didn't actually believe that I was going to let you get back together," she added, "and be satisfied with this car that you offered to me so that I would give you up! I had a very carefully devised plan to win you back, a plan that your wife hastened without even knowing it. Think of your mother, darling. Don't worry; I know how to make you happier than you already were with me up to now."

She pulled him to her and held his trembling lips. In a brutal gesture, Joseph slapped her.

The young woman doubled over, both hands on her cheeks. She was shuddering, her look, bewildered.

"How could you believe I would marry you after such plotting? If my wife allowed herself to be sullied by you, I am responsible for it. Good God! You are the reincarnation of the devil! Get out of here before I call the police!"

He hurled himself at her again and gave her a violent kick. Dominique collapsed.

"A woman like you is not going to make me separate from my wife. And *I* had thought you worthy of being the mother of my children . . ."

In a threatening voice drowned by stifled cries, Dominique retorted:

"I'll have my revenge! Your mother is on my side. Your cook, too, for that matter. Nobody at your house wants her."

"Get out of here," Joseph shouted.

He took her by the shoulders and threw her forcefully toward the door.

Left alone, Joseph took out his cigar and swallowed the smoke as he puffed on it, until he was seized with a fit of coughing, which alarmed his secretary.

"Are you all right, sir?" she asked, opening the door wide and keeping it open.

"Fine, fine, go back to your desk."

He sat down behind his desk, then got up. Making a fist with his hands, he paced around the office.

This story exceeded all bounds; it would be beyond the imagination of anyone who knew his wife. He was so distressed that he rushed to the closet and took out a full bottle of whiskey and gulped it down straight from the bottle. His eyes half closed, staggering, he felt around the door to find the handle, which he had trouble getting a grip on, and went out.

After trying several times unsuccessfully to reach her secretary by phone, Emilienne, worried, decided to go reason with her. She opened her door and found herself in the hallway filled with about twenty employees.

"What are you doing in the hallway? Why aren't you at your desks?"

"We have decided unanimously to stop working until our grievances are satisfied."

Examining each face, Emilienne saw their great determination. Already last week, the personnel's delegates had asked to be heard by the general manager. The latter turned down the meeting in a memo sent to all.

After her secretary had explained the situation to her, Emilienne had understood that the federal employees were demanding a raise in their transportation and housing allowances, as well as their salary, which had been frozen for three years.

Emilienne knew that obviously the general manager would reject these demands. Already, during a management meeting, he had justified his decision by evoking the difficult economic conditions that had made state companies the first victims. This argument, given to employees so many times in the past, had not, apparently, been convincing.

While the young woman tried to calm the demonstrators, promising to review the situation with the general manager, whose office was on the second floor, the telephone rang in her office. She was informed by the administrative secretary that a meeting with all managers would be held immediately. And, while they were seated, the employees gathered in the large conference room. They decided unanimously not to yield until their demands were met.

A minority among them, essentially made up of the protégés of some managing directors, disassociated themselves from the movement and left the room. Tempers flared.

In the general manager's office, opinions were divided. Some directors proposed holding a general meeting, whereas others opposed any dialogue, to the satisfaction of the general manager as well as of the chairman of the board of directors, who was called at home expressly for this meeting.

After half an hour of fruitless discussion, the general manager adjourned the meeting after he'd announced the dismissal of any employee who continued to strike. His colleagues all knew that, in reality, this last measure was an order given by the minister in charge of state companies. So they backed down, some with resignation, others with satisfaction.

He went up, in any case, to announce his decision to the employees still gathered in the conference room. Following his brief and threatening speech, astonishment appeared on all their faces. In a heavy silence, the staff's delegate took the floor to call for the continuation of the strike and the immediate seizure of the National Work Union. There was a burst of applause and loud cheers.

"You're wasting your time," the general manager yelled as he left the room followed by his colleagues.

Throughout it all, the foreign aid workers had remained cooped up in their offices and continued to work.

Disturbed by it all, Emilienne went home. Her cook ran to open the gate for her. He informed her, even before she got out of the car, that her sister had been hospitalized.

"What happened? She wasn't supposed to go into labor for another month."

"I believe, Madame, that she's had some complications."

"Which hospital did they bring her to?"

"To Dr. Pascal's clinic. It was your mother who called; she wasn't able to reach you at your office."

"Okay, I'm going. Tell my husband to join me there."

She took off.

In the room with her sister were two of her children, her husband, and their relatives.

"What's wrong, Eva—don't tell me that your child is growing impatient in your womb?"

Eva started crying. Her mother leaned over her.

"Emie, it's awful. My baby has been dead for two weeks in my womb. Can you believe it! And I didn't believe it. You cannot know how horrible that is!"

"What are you talking about? What does all this mean?"

Emilienne in her panic started screaming.

"Let's go out for a minute," her sister's husband said.

"This isn't happening," Emilienne added, crying now too. "You're not in your first pregnancy. How can such a thing be happening!"

The two sisters held each other tightly. Jean left the room, and Emilienne followed.

"About ten days ago," he explained, "your sister complained about not feeling the baby moving. I asked her to tell Dr. Pascal about it immediately."

"Then why didn't he take the necessary steps at that time?"

"She didn't tell him. You know how she is. She assured me there was nothing to be alarmed about since it wasn't her first pregnancy."

"You should have called the doctor yourself anyway. This child would have definitely been saved ten days ago."

"I was convinced she was right . . ."

He took his handkerchief out of his pocket and blew his nose loudly. Despite his height, his body appeared to have been diminished by his sorrow. His barrel-shaped paunch rose and fell to the rhythm of his loud breathing.

"So it was only yesterday that we went to see Dr. Pascal. And this morning, after the ultrasound, he told her to stay so that he could induce the birth right away."

"If the child died two weeks ago, it doesn't seem to me that an induced birth is the best solution. The baby is obviously decomposing. Why doesn't he do a cesarean on her?"

"He told me he wants to avoid that; a hemorrhage could be fatal to her."

"Oh my god! This is not happening."

She collapsed again.

Her brother-in-law pulled her to him. They clung to each other until a nurse brought in another drip bag.

"Don't worry," she said to reassure them. "Everything will be okay. It is better that the child die, rather than the mother."

"She's right," Emilienne muttered. "Let's go to her. The most important thing now is to save her."

The family members present helped put the second drip bag in place. Eva relaxed and began to joke.

"If you want to lift my spirits, try to smile. Dear, just because this time I'm not going to bring our baby home doesn't mean I lose the consideration due to a mother, and I want us to make another one as soon as I get out of here. We will use the layette that Emie bought for us. As for you, Papa, Mama, I promise you that I will give you a grandson soon."

Everyone finally smiled. Her two children gave her warm hugs.

"The doctor will be in to see you in a minute," the nurse said as she went out. "He will deliver you at nightfall."

"Do you need anything, dear?" her husband asked. "I'm going to take the kids home, and I'll come back right afterward."

"No, I'm fine. Give them a hug and a kiss for me and come back quickly, please."

"Come, children, your place is not here."

"I'm going to stop home, too. I won't be long. Papa, Mama, you stay. Shall I bring you something to eat?"

"No, my child, I'm not hungry, and I don't think your dad will eat at all until this nightmare is over."

"Okay! See you later," Emilienne said as she kissed her sister on both cheeks. "You'll see, everything will be fine."

Emilienne parked her car in front of the gate and ran toward the kitchen door. Hearing the voices of her husband and mother-in-law arguing, she stood there motionless. Intrigued, she headed stealthily to the terrace, where she could better make out their words. From inside, Eyang's voice boomed.

"What has gotten into you? The mother of your children just told me that you broke up with her. How could you have made such a decision?"

"Let me lead my life my way! Any way I choose is fine!"

"I've had all the time in the world to think it over! Your wife doesn't deserve you, period, that's all. And let me tell you that you have gone completely mad."

"Let's end this conversation right there, okay!" Joseph growled.

"I've merely begun, and you will hear me out. What is going on, Son? Do you realize that you have just abandoned beautiful children and a woman who loves you for that . . . ?"

"Oh, will you stop!"

"No! I will not stop. What do you find so extraordinary in a woman who spends all her time with witch doctors? Wasn't it you yourself who confided in me a week ago that she was getting fondled by a white witch doctor?"

"You're twisting my words! I never told you that it was a witch doctor nor that she was being fondled. You know perfectly well she wants to give me a child! It's what she still wants!"

"Oh! But *you* don't want that anymore! So leave her! I'm going to tell you. Do you know how many years it will take her to give you another child? Have you forgotten that she's been seeing quacks and doctors frequently for over ten years? And now she's turning to white witch doctors. That woman is leading you in a merry dance. What will she come up with the next time she fails?!"

Emilienne clung to the iron grate outside the bay window. In the house, Eyang's voice became more menacing.

"Son, you are casting me out by leaving the mother of your children. If you don't call her right now and tell her that you're sorry, I'm warning you, I will not stay one more minute under this roof."

The guard passed in front of Emilienne, a rake in his hand.

THE YOUNG WOMAN pushed open the bay window and climbed inside very quietly. The mother and son jumped.

"Ah! You're here?" Eyang asked, giving a slight smirk.

Serene, Emilienne sat down facing them.

"I listened with great interest to a good part of your conversation," she began, staring into her mother-in-law's embarrassed eyes. "I don't know what decision your son would have made after your threats, and in any case that doesn't matter anymore. I urge you to take him with you wherever you would like, tonight. That also goes for your grandchildren, obviously. When I come back, I want to find the house empty; that would be in one hour."

"What is with you?" Joseph intervened, "I thought I was quite clear with my mother!"

Openly ignoring her husband, Emilienne added, directing her comment at the mother:

"Now you can have him all to yourself."

"Don't let yourself be humiliated anymore, Son. She has done enough harm already. We are finally going to be able to breathe! I have been working on this for a long time."

"Very well," Emilienne added, "start clearing your things out of this house right now."

She got up and walked resolutely toward the door. Roxanne, who was waiting for her in front of the car, jumped onto her lap as soon as she got into the driver's seat. Emilienne took off.

In the corridor of the clinic, she met Dr. Pascal; he avoided her gaze. She could hear screams coming from one of the rooms. Emilienne ran and opened the door to her sister's room.

Before her, her mother was trembling and scratching at the tile floor. Four of her nieces and nephews were screaming. Her father and brother-in-law stared, in shock, at Eva's inert body, bearing a half smile.

Emilienne threw herself onto her sister. From the other end of the room, she could hear Jean's muffled voice:

"Her body couldn't take to the drip. She died before the doctor got here."

Emilienne felt nausea rise up to her mouth as it had every morning for a month. Collapsed on this anonymous bed with immaculate sheets where Eva lay, she held one hand to her belly and with the other caressed her sister's, inert.

"I so much would have wanted you to be by my side to attend the birth. I promise you, if it's a girl, I will give her your first name."

Her gaze was lost in the dense foliage of the trees in the courtyard, drenched in a blazing sun. There, in the distance, was a house, her house, which now sat empty.

Afterword

Cheryl Toman

Few women writers, if any, have played a more significant role in the development of a national literature than Gabon's Angèle Rawiri. Although literary history may reveal one woman in particular as the first female novelist of any given country, such pioneering women have traditionally published long after their male counterparts, for a variety of reasons often beyond the woman writer's control. In countries considered among the first literary "powerhouses" of francophone Africa, such as Cameroon, Côte d'Ivoire, Senegal, and Congo, male authors typically were producing critically acclaimed novels nearly two decades earlier than were female novelists. Although the novel in Gabon had a late start if considered alongside comparable works emerging from former French colonies in sub-Saharan Africa, it is nonetheless remarkable that Angèle Rawiri overcame the tremendous obstacles that had challenged her African sisters only thirty years earlier to become not only Gabon's first published woman writer but, more notably, the first novelist of her country—either male or female—with the initial printing in 1980 of her novel *Elonga*.

Indeed, some may find it hard to believe that Gabon, home to renowned genres of epic poetry such as the *mvet* and the *olendé*,[1] produced no novelists of French expression prior to 1980. Neighboring Cameroon, by comparison, is home to pioneering African francophone writers such as Mongo Beti, who published *Ville cruelle* (*Cruel City*, 2013) in 1954 under the pen name of Eza Boto, and Thérèse Kuoh-Moukoury, who has the honor of being the first female novelist of the country—and more important, perhaps, of all of sub-Saharan Africa—with her long-awaited publication of *Rencontres essentielles* in

1969 (*Essential Encounters,* 2002). Actual publication dates, however, usually reveal a "history" of African women's writing as opposed to a "herstory." The dearth early on of published women novelists in francophone Africa is a result of both a lack of critical interest in and a total ignorance of what these women writers had to say. These early works became part of an "empty canon," as Irène d'Almeida eloquently expressed it in the introduction to her anthology *A Rain of Words* (xxii)—empty because "no one has bothered to look inside" (xxiv). Thus, this perceived delay in novelistic creation by African women writers should not be regarded as proof that such early works lacked quality. In fact, many of these early novels have withstood the test of time and consequently are more well-known today than when they were first published. Such is the case with Kuoh-Moukoury's *Rencontres essentielles,* a novel that the MLA Texts and Translations Series reprinted in its original French in 2002 for a primarily North American francophone audience while simultaneously introducing its companion volume, *Essential Encounters,* marking the first time ever in print for its English translation. In francophone Africa and in France, *Fureurs et cris de femmes* eventually became Angèle Rawiri's best-known novel of the three she published, and Sara Hanaburgh's translation in English, *The Fury and Cries of Women,* is certain to bring long overdue critical acclaim to this novel from English-speaking readers and specialists in African studies with a range of experiences and perspectives, as well as ignite fresh interest in the novel among a new generation of scholars and students in francophone studies. Hanaburgh's published translation should also heighten interest in the literature of Gabon, whose rich and diverse works arguably deserve the same standing attained by those written in other African francophone countries but that have in the past found themselves within the "empty canon" to which d'Almeida refers.

The Gabonese novel's relatively late entry onto the world literary stage may also be explained in part by a lack of a solid infrastructure in the formal education system pre-Independence compared to those that were long in place in other former French colonies of sub-Saharan Africa such as Cameroon or Senegal. The first secondary school in Gabon, Lycée National

Léon Mba, was not established until 1958, and it remained the only lycée in the country for several years, forcing some Gabonese students to head to Brazzaville for their secondary school education (Mba-Zue 48), and leaving others who had the financial means to do so to continue their studies in France. In the post-independence period, Gabonese nationals who had received higher education and who were determined to return to Gabon were then recruited almost exclusively for political positions, and little emphasis was placed on forming a Gabonese intellectual elite as was done in other African francophone countries (Midiohouan 221). Today, a substantial number of Gabonese women writers are also university professors—Justine Mintsa and Honorine Ngou among them.

Although times are different, Université Omar Bongo in Libreville, founded in 1970, still remains Gabon's only university where degrees in literature are awarded, and students who wish to earn the equivalent of a doctorate in literature still need to pursue such studies abroad. Although higher education is certainly not a requirement for being a novelist in any country, rare are authors in francophone Africa who do not at least possess the baccalauréat, the diploma inherited from the French school system marking the completion of secondary school (Mba-Zue 49).[2] Considering these realities, one is not surprised that novelists of French expression emerged much later in Gabon.

Angèle Rawiri's Personal Journey

Angèle Ntyugwétondo Rawiri was born on April 29, 1954, in Port-Gentil, the economic capital of Gabon and home to its largest petroleum companies. Port-Gentil has also long been considered Gabon's epicenter of political opposition, and growing up in such an environment perhaps inspired Rawiri's rebellious spirit as a novelist. Even though her father, Georges Rawiri, was president of the Gabonese senate in Omar Bongo's administration,[3] this did not deter Angèle from criticizing in her works broken aspects of African political systems. Rawiri did not necessarily point out names, but it was obvious that her fictional African countries and cities often were inspired by real-life experiences in Gabon. It is to be expected that a writer's homeland influences in some way his or her works, but Rawiri was also generally critical of aspects of African society that are oppressive or corrupt. Thus, her use of the fictional name "Kampana" in *The Fury* is less about masking Gabon's identity and more about Rawiri going beyond borders of a homeland similar to others on the continent. Although the political and social climate of Rawiri's semifictitious country are important in *The Fury,* rebelliousness in all of her novels, however, is most evident in the words, actions, and everyday lives of her protagonists.

Although Rawiri rarely spoke about her private life in public, it is well known that she was greatly affected by her mother's death when she was just six years old. Her father, himself a published poet in addition to being a government official, naturally moved on with his personal life after his first wife's death and eventually started another family, and it was said that Angèle suffered profoundly from this, battling feelings of isolation and exclusion from her father's new life. Traces of these emotional wounds are clear in the way Emilienne's family interactions are depicted in *The Fury.* Rawiri's feelings may have been exacerbated by her separation from her homeland to complete her baccalauréat and postsecondary studies in translation in France. After a short stint as an actress and model in Great Britain, Rawiri returned to her native Gabon and to her hometown of Port-Gentil at the end of the 1970s, where she accepted a position with a major oil company translating and interpreting into English. With the encouragement of her brother, it was during this period that she wrote her two first novels, *Elonga* and *G'amérakano,* before leaving Gabon for France definitively and finishing there her third and final published novel, *Fureurs et cris de femmes,* at the end of the 1980s.

It is interesting to note that Rawiri published her first two novels under her given Omyènè name, Ntyugwétondo Rawiri, and thus only on the cover of *Fureurs* was she identified as Angele Rawiri, having dropped Ntyugwetondo, which translates from Omyènè as "the beloved day."[4] This modification of self-identification may have been a reflection of how Rawiri felt torn between cultures, continents, and families. In a 1988 interview for the African women's magazine *Amina,* Rawiri gave the impression that she was never able to rid herself of this sense of alienation, calling herself a "déracinée," or a woman uprooted, and stating, "I never felt at home on African soil, and at the same time, I didn't feel at home in Europe either" (Bikindou and Baker 13).[5] Writing was obviously cathartic for Rawiri, a means to deal with sentiments of perpetual exile that had plagued her since childhood and a way of coming to terms with aspects of culture and society that escaped her comprehension. Her important but relatively short career as a published novelist lasted just ten years. Although in the aforementioned *Amina* interview she referred to a manuscript in progress that was to become her fourth novel (16), and while she alluded to material she had written for three others (12), these novels, if completed, were never published. Rather surprisingly, Rawiri disappeared from view seemingly without explanation even while her works continued to gain a fair amount of critical attention well into the 1990s from influential scholars of francophone studies in Europe and North America, such as Jean-Marie Volet and Odile Cazenave, among others. Although Rawiri had been out of the public eye for some time, admirers of her work were particularly shocked to hear of her premature passing in the autumn of 2010 at the age of fifty-six. She was laid to rest in the cemetery at the foot of the Grande Arche de la Défense just outside of Paris.

Although it may be unrealistic to say that Rawiri encountered no difficulties on her path to becoming Gabon's first novelist, she undeniably gained unparalleled respect even early on from her fellow Gabonese, and the fact that she was a female author was seemingly not the handicap to her that it had been to her predecessors.[6] For thirteen years before the first publication of *Rencontres essentielles,* potential editors told the Cameroonian writer Thérèse Kuoh-Moukoury, for example, that they preferred the style of writing of the male writers who produced politically charged novels attacking French colonialism to her indirect references to and nuances of a troubled yet historical time. In an era well before the popularization of the Western feminist rallying cry of the late sixties and seventies "the personal is political," Kuoh-Moukoury had already introduced her subtle but ever-present approach to condemning colonialism and hegemony through her female protagonists, who overcame trials and hardships despite the weight of customary beliefs, practices, and rituals; the realities of colonialism in a changing, conflict-ridden world; and the lack of role models who dared to venture beyond women's traditional roles. In the period prior to independence from European colonization, this approach did not gain the attention of literary critics, and it was not considered marketable by editors in France, where African francophone novels were being published almost exclusively.

However, perhaps it was the advances made years earlier by fellow women writers in neighboring countries that allowed Rawiri to become recognized relatively easily in her country as the first novelist despite the publication of an earlier work in Gabon in 1971—a heavily autobiographical fifty-nine-page piece entitled *Histoire d'un enfant trouvé* (The story of a recovered child) by Robert Zotoumbat. Considered to be Gabon's first novelist by a significant number of scholars of Gabonese literature (Ambourhouet-Bigmann, "Où est le roman gabonais?" 18; Kassa, "La femme" 27; Mendame), Rawiri distinguished herself from Zotoumbat by writing a work that one of the earliest critics of Gabonese literature, Magloire Ambourhouet-Bigmann, has called the "début de création imaginaire" ("Naissance" 47), or the advent of creative writing in French in Gabon.

Fortunately, Rawiri was spared the experience of a drawn-out journey to publication, and her work was well-received by many Gabonese intellectuals and scholars from the beginning. As Jean-René Ovono Mendame states, "When *Elonga* appeared in 198[0],[7] Ntyugwétondo Angèle Rawiri's 261-page novel, the Gabonese public greeted with enthusiasm the zeal of the first woman writer to dedicate herself to writing. The event commanded respect especially during those years when few men, academics or those self-taught, ventured into writing" (2006).

Angèle Rawiri has had a tremendous impact on African literature in general and was a strong voice in particular amidst her female contemporaries of the 1980s, such as Mariama Bâ,

Calixthe Beyala, and Ken Bugul. Recognized as an important figure in the literary history of her country, Rawiri has also been a source of inspiration for numerous women writers in Gabon who have followed in her footsteps, such as Justine Mintsa, Honorine Ngou, Sylvie Ntsame, and Chantal Magalie Mbazoo Kassa. A new generation of Gabonese women authors has grown up reading Rawiri's novels as part of their general studies, and as a result, her influence is apparent in the works of young writers such as Edna Merey Apinda, Nadia Origo, Mélissa Bendome, Alice Endamne, Charline Effah, and Miryl Eteno following in her footsteps. Considering this solid history of women's writing in Gabon that began with Angèle Rawiri's work, it is no surprise that the country's female novelists are equal in number to their male counterparts,[8] a rare finding in any given country.

The Fury and Cries of Women *and Other Writings*

Rawiri's three novels, *Elonga* (1980), *G'amérakano au carrefour* (1983), and *Fureurs et cris de femmes* (1989), have little connection between them despite the fact that they are often grouped as a "trilogy."[9] Yet a specific aspect of Rawiri's life resonates in each work in an intriguing way. Rawiri's first novel, *Elonga,* is the story of a young male professor, Igowo, who decides to leave Spain, where he has grown up, in order to make a life for himself in the African country of his mother's birth. Except for some initial tensions with his maternal uncle, it appears that Igowo is doing well for himself; he meets Ziza, a young, dynamic fashion designer, and the couple eventually marries, and their daughter, Igowé, is born. From this point, a series of tragedies in the novel provokes a discussion about the role of witchcraft in African society, the main element driving the narrative. Although the young, modern family denies that their misfortunes can be attributed to evil spirits and the jealousy of others, it nonetheless remains inexplicable why Igowo ends up as the only surviving member, and this only after battling a mysterious, life-threatening illness. Of Rawiri's three novels, *Elonga* is perhaps the least focused on women, even though Ziza is clearly the portrait of the new African woman of the 1980s for whom career and family are both important, if not essential.

Rawiri takes a more decisive feminist approach in her second novel, *G'amérakano,* the story of Toula, a dismally paid secretary who, at the encouragement of her mother, undergoes a transformational makeover with the hope of enhancing her physical beauty in order to increase opportunities for wealth and success for herself and her family. Toula eventually becomes the mistress of Éléwagnè, a powerful banker, although her heart is reserved for one of Éléwagnè's employees, Angwé. Despite the lavish lifestyle Éléwagnè has provided her with, Toula still continues to see the man she loves until Éléwagnè is tipped off and promptly fires Angwé, provoking the young man's suicide. Toula is also rejected, and her life subsequently crumbles and she is forced to return to a life of poverty, disgrace, and prostitution while grieving the loss of the man she had loved. *G'amérakano* readily fits the Westernized description of a feminist novel, although it is interesting to note that the Gabonese novelist and scholar Chantal Magalie Mbazoo Kassa reserves the distinction of "feminist novel" exclusively for *The Fury.* Concerning *G'amérakano,* Kassa describes the work as one that "emphasizes the problematic relationships between men and women in African society" (28–29). She continues to explain that the word "carrefour," or "crossroads," in the full title refers to the complexity of relationships impacted by notions of gender-appropriate roles that often lead to dysfunction within society. Those who refuse to "play the game" and to follow such prescriptions assigned to gender are left to pick up the pieces of their shattered lives. Because Kassa focuses more on the belief that man and woman are complements, and chooses to analyze both genders instead of focusing her analysis solely from a feminist perspective, one understands why Kassa has made this distinction between *G'amérakano* and *The Fury.* In Kassa's view, *G'amérakano* is more of a critique of society as a whole—where men and women both find themselves in powerless positions, and Toula is the lens through which we see a society in trouble. Kassa emphasizes, "To study woman is to study the society to which she belongs" (12). In direct contrast to certain ideas within Kassa's analysis, however, Jeanne-Marie

Clerc and Liliane Nzé state emphatically in their book *Le roman gabonais et la symbolique du silence et du bruit* (2008; The Gabonese novel and the symbolism of silence and noise) that certain declarations within *G'amérakano* smack of "radical American feminism" (263) and that Toula's words such as "I want to feel my body with every pore of my skin" (176) are indeed "rare in African women's writing" (263).

There is less of a dispute among critics, however, with regard to *The Fury.* Kassa, for example, does not hesitate to label the work as a feminist novel (30). In her analysis, she posits that in this novel, "man is no longer master. It no longer suffices that man merely possesses the attributes of power to rule, he still needs to exercise it effectively. Thus, Joseph's wife places him in a situation of inferiority. . . . Just as man defines himself through the phallus, it matters for a woman to possess an attribute that is just as important: having a child. . . . Motherhood for Emilienne is thus a sign of power and achievement. . . . Here, sexual and economic power is no longer masculine but feminine" (34–35).

Unlike early Western feminism that tended to view motherhood as enslavement for women, based in part on theories brought forth by Simone de Beauvoir in *Le deuxième sexe* (1949, *The Second Sex,* 1953, 2012),[10] one finds the opposite in Rawiri's novel—the empowerment of women through motherhood—and this idea is essential to African feminisms and thus is typically found in African women's writing. These conflicting ideologies provide ample reasons as to why African and Western feminisms have traditionally clashed. It is not surprising that Rawiri accentuates this fundamental difference within feminism through the voice of Emilienne describing what she perceives to be a threat to women's exclusive power: "If doctors' laboratory experiments proved successful and if governments gave their okay, in a dozen years or so, men would be able to carry pregnancies to full term and give birth. As if, their reign in politics and business not enough, they were slyly attempting to rob women of their only power" (122).

Although she does not always see it this way, Emilienne is nearly always in control of her situation within her family and society, and indeed, there are few female protagonists in African literature like her. Admittedly, this does not mean that everything can come without sacrifice or feelings of isolation. One of the few protagonists in African women's writing worthy of comparison to Emilienne is perhaps Esi found in the novel *Changes: A Love Story,* written by the celebrated Ghanian author Ama Ata Aidoo. Like Emilienne, Esi is a well-educated and career-oriented woman, in addition to being a wife and mother, who has more than sufficient finances to take care of herself and her family. Emilienne and Esi both earn more than their husbands, and both harbor feelings of guilt at times concerning their daughters, Rékia and Ogyaanowa, respectively, whose affective needs may not have been met because of the time-consuming positions their mothers hold.

Like Emilienne and Joseph, Esi and her first husband, Oko, have grown distant over the years. In *The Fury,* Emilienne herself tries to understand this "drifting away" a couple can experience: "How strange it is that people who have such high regard for one another and who love each other cannot live together for long before their relationship starts to deteriorate" (80). In *Changes,* Esi eventually divorces Oko after he resorts to marital rape in an attempt to show her who is boss, a scene reminiscent of one in *The Fury* in which Rawiri describes one of Joseph's rare returns to the house: "He had made love to her like a drunkard throwing himself on a prostitute he'd picked up off some obscure roadside" (28).

Having always felt that her monogamous marriage takes away too much time from her professional responsibilities, Esi eventually decides to enter into a polygamous marriage as a second wife, reasoning that this might allow her to love a man while simultaneously reserving time for her career and for herself.[11] Both Emilienne and Esi realize in the end that marriage and the presence of an extended family offer no guarantee as cures for loneliness. Both women come to the conclusion that it may well be preferable to continue on one's own in a pursuit of true happiness. Concerning Emilienne in particular but certainly applicable in theory to Esi as well, Odile Cazenave states in her book *Femmes rebelles* (1996; *Rebellious Women,* 1999), "Rather than put up with an unhappy marriage and suffer her husband's infidelities and her mother-in-law's rebuffs, the young woman opts for a new beginning, alone and without marital constraints, a new life in which she can be committed to her own professional development" (33).

Both Rawiri and Aidoo render very credible accounts to which most women can fundamentally relate regardless of culture. Each author sends a most realistic message—unfortunately, women may not be able to "have it all." After a particularly trying day with her family, Emilienne recalls a quotation from an article in a women's magazine that speaks to her: "A woman is never completely satisfied. Whereas some enjoy professional success, others build a solid marriage based on love, and then there are those who have children to feel fulfilled. No woman, however, manages to enjoy all three. And if there are women out there who are perfectly happy, who have brought these three together, they are extremely rare, and, in our opinion, if they have even two of these, that is a great achievement" (100).

In addition to societal pressures that every woman faces, it is also the human being's ultimate need to be loved and the fear of living and dying alone that explains why women like Emilienne and Esi feel obliged to make compromises regarding their feminism. Rawiri and Aidoo do not wish to diminish the power of their protagonists by uncovering this truth, but rather do so to paint an accurate picture of what life really holds for the modern African woman, a reality not unlike one lived by any successful, career-oriented woman. In this manner, these examples of African women's writing continue to be instructive for readers from any culture.

Rebellion and Disobedience

Emilienne is more than a rebellious woman; she is disobedient—a protagonist who does an about-face and ultimately does what she wants, disregarding or circumventing reactions from family and society and deciding that she cares little in the end about appearances, for she realizes that the impressions of others have for too long been a determining factor of her behavior. During the most troubled times in their marriage, Emilienne's general disobedience leads her husband, Joseph, to reevaluate their future together: He reasons, "She is a remarkable homemaker and a perfect mother when all is well. My dream would be for her to raise all the children I have with my lovers. That's what some wives do in her situation. Only here's the problem, I fell for an intellectual who refuses to break certain barriers" (103). Emilienne refuses the traditional family of her society—that is, the extended family plus the mistress—even in the context of her infertility, a situation in which even her own mother agrees it would be acceptable for Joseph to find another woman to give him children (96). As Emilienne does not consider her infertility to be the prime source of conflict in their marriage, she refuses to see polygamy as justifiable in this or in any case. She attempts to explain to Joseph just how flawed such reasoning is, shouting in frustration: "Is that it! If I have a child, you will leave your mistress. If I have a child, you will love me again. If I have a child, your mother will embrace me and my family will be satisfied. In a word, everything will be back to normal" (105–6).

The distinction between a rebellious woman and a disobedient one is indeed intriguing and worth analyzing here. In literature, one can cite countless examples of the rebellious woman who may seem more defiant in thought than in action. In Simone de Beauvoir's *La femme rompue* (1967; *The Woman Destroyed,* 1969), Monique appears to be a subservient housewife, but we see her displeasure with what society dictates for women through notes in her personal diary. Similarly, by means of a series of letters written to a friend in *Une si longue lettre* (1986; *So Long a Letter,* 1989), the Senegalese author Mariama Bâ has her protagonist, Ramatoulaye, explain her shock at her husband's taking on a much younger second wife after twenty-five years of marriage together. Few protagonists, however, can earn the distinction of "disobedient" in the way Rawiri's Emilienne does. The rebellious woman struggles against certain realities and nearly always gains the respect of the reader in doing so. The disobedient woman goes a step further, setting herself apart from the rebellious woman in that the former ultimately chooses to opt out of the lifestyle that will gain her respect or make her existence in society more comfortable. The disobedient woman is strong, but she is not necessarily a winner. She may not even win over the reader in all cases, he or she who is the ultimate interpreter of her life. Ultimately, readers will not cast negative judgment upon Monique or Ramatoulaye for being devoted mothers. However, the same readers may be disappointed in Emilienne for linking her affection for Rékia to the status of her relationship with Joseph (31), or they may be shocked when Emilienne physically assaults her elderly mother-in-law (63), even though the latter certainly provoked a strong response. The disobedient woman is perceived as aggressive, frank, distant, and unforgiving at times, and while these characteristics may be interpreted as signs of strength and determination in men, history proves that women who exhibit these traits are not seen in the same positive light by society. The Martinican writer Fabienne Kanor gives two important reasons as to why this is so through the words of her protagonist, Louise, in the novel *Anticorps* (2010; Antibody). First, when it comes to any relationship within the family, woman is simply not allowed to be "fundamentally selfish" (37), and second, even if she manages to be, "only the most terribly courageous of women will be able to find it easy to finish her life alone" (117). Perhaps this is why Rawiri chose to end her novel with the revelation that her protagonist is pregnant (194), as this leaves the reader somewhat relieved that Emilienne no longer risks ultimate loneliness after evicting her husband and extended family from the house. The pregnancy thus spares Emilienne from failure and pity. Odile Cazenave also offers an interesting interpretation of the ending of *The Fury*. That is, failure lies not with Emilienne but rather with Joseph and Eyang, who are ultimately thrown out of the house (Cazenave 32). Ironically, they will never enjoy the child Emilienne is carrying; she will see to it that they are deprived of this for all the suffering they have imposed upon her. Cazenave also posits that closing the novel with a pregnant Emilienne is indeed significant: "According to tradition, [Emilienne's] pregnancy means that she has returned to normal" (32).

Although Emilienne's disobedience is most apparent at the end of the novel, she has from the beginning exhibited signs of intolerance of family and societal values that she has deemed oppressive and archaic. Emilienne imposes the same standards of behavior for in-laws as for her own parents, as all were initially against her interethnic marriage with Joseph. Of course, she is the most disappointed in her own mother's reaction, and she insists, "I am saddened to have to go against you, Mother. I don't expect Father will approve either. When you change your mind, you'll know where to find me, if I haven't gone back to France. Good-bye!" (16). Emilienne's relationship with her parents improves only because they come to accept and respect her choice of husband, something that her mother-in-law, Eyang, at no time is sincerely willing to do.

According to Jean-Marie Volet, Emilienne chose the man whom she was to marry and would have continued to love him unconditionally if only he had continued to treat her with respect and dignity (135). Likewise, Emilienne's abysmal relationship with her mother-in-law, Eyang, has at its core the elder woman's disappointment that Emilienne does not conform to her vision of a suitable wife for her son. Emilienne remains unapologetic for this, however, and refuses to treat her mother-in-law with respect if the respect is not reciprocated. The only time this happens is when Eyang decides on a brief truce with her daughter-in-law, one that ironically becomes threatening to Joseph, who fears for his power in the household if his wife and his mother join forces in solidarity against him (83). His fear is short-lived, however, as Eyang's dislike for Emilienne soon resurfaces as before.

At the end of *The Fury,* Emilienne overhears a conversation between Joseph and Eyang during which she is made aware of just how much her mother-in-law has been involved in the couple's private affairs. Although Joseph defends his decision to stay with Emilienne instead of conceding to his mother's wishes (that is, living exclusively with his mistress and their two children), this conversation proves more than Emilienne can tolerate (192–93)—the proverbial last straw. As a final act of ultimate disobedience, Emilienne gives the entire family (Joseph, his mother, and her nephews) until that same evening to vacate her home (193). After all, it is her home, purchased with her salary from a coveted government position as director of administrative affairs. Her earnings far exceed Joseph's meager salary as a civil servant. Emilienne has financially supported not only Joseph and their daughter, Rékia (that is, until her tragic murder), but also his mother and two nephews, who live with her as well. African literature has provided many portraits of women in vulnerable positions, especially widows who stand to lose their home and belongings to the family of their deceased husband, or worse yet, face being "inherited" by a brother-in-law as if they were a possession, as is the case for Awu in Justine Mintsa's *Histoire d'Awu* (2000; Story of Awu). But relatively early in African women's writing, *The Fury* provided us with the rare example of a female protagonist who makes the decision to "repudiate" her husband (Kassa 135). The novel ends with a triumphal image of Emilienne returning home that evening after the departure of the family: "There, in the distance, was a house, her house, which now sat empty" (194).

The power that Emilienne exhibits at the end of *The Fury* has many dimensions, and therefore it is difficult to define. Emilienne's professional and financial success automatically accord Rawiri's protagonist some power, even though it may not be exactly what Emilienne had hoped for after so many years of work and marriage. As Jean-Marie Volet explains, "If one considers power to be not only the simple ability to impose one's will to achieve a predetermined goal, but rather the ability to challenge others and their limited vision of numerous and contradicting forces that influence and justify exchanges and social behaviors, Rawiri's heroines in this case have considerable impact" (145). Volet continues to explain in the chapter on Rawiri in his book *La parole aux Africaines* (1993; African women speak out) that Emilienne's power is a defensive one that protects her from her husband's selfishness and from his need to dominate (149). Volet states, "Her power represents rather her right to speak: her capacity not only to be heard but to be listened to; and also to withdraw and to pull out of the game when the other players try to lock her into a discourse that works to their advantage alone" (149).

So the question remains, is *The Fury and Cries of Women* pessimistic or is Rawiri's novel quite simply an example of African realism? If a self-declared feminist in words and actions cannot manage to have a near-perfect life despite her financial and intellectual advantages, what hope is there for women of lower classes who will never enjoy such a status? Why does Rawiri exhibit this desire to remind us, as Volet explains it, that "even at the top of the pyramid, the possibilities are limited" (133)?

Presenting an interesting comparison, Phil Powrie emphasizes in his essay "Rereading between the Lines: A Postscript on *La femme rompue*" that feminists had criticized Simone de Beauvoir for giving "such a pessimistic view of women's situation" (328). In *Tout compte fait* (1972; *All Said and Done,* 1974), Simone de Beauvoir responds to this criticism by explaining, "I did not feel compelled to choose exemplary heroines. To describe failure, error, insincerity, this, as it seems to me, does not betray anyone" (145). Powrie continues by saying that Beauvoir "could not have done other than present a pessimistic view, given the absence of a strongly articulated tradition of women's writing" (328), a context that can certainly apply to Angèle Rawiri as the first female novelist of Gabon. Powrie then explains how contemporary fiction is problematic and therefore doubly so for the woman writer, making her "no less entombed than her heroines" (329).

Innovations and Questions

The Fury and Cries of Women is a gem not only of African literature but of women's writing in general. Rawiri raises important questions and speaks frankly about issues that had never been touched on before in African writing, especially by a female author. Even when Rawiri does raise subjects that have been commonly discussed, such as infertility, she comes at these from new angles, adding to the innovativeness of the novel.

The consequences of infertility for an African woman regardless of her social class was a subject first presented in Kuoh-Moukoury's *Rencontres essentielles* in 1969. The fact that Rawiri also chose to contribute to that discussion some thirty years later shows how timely and urgent the matter has remained.[12] Indeed, there are some similarities in the handling of the subject by these two authors. Both Kuoh-Moukoury's

Flo and Rawiri's Emilienne are highly educated, progressive, and urban-dwelling African women. Yet all these advantages do not necessarily prevent these contemporary women from perceiving their infertility as catastrophic. By all appearances, Flo and Emilienne have abandoned traditional roles and thinking. Yet their desperation causes them to pursue every possible avenue of traditional and modern medicine. Flo and Emilienne are persuaded by family members to seek out traditional healers, although both women are embarrassed by this decision in the end. The rituals associated with these consultations are described in great detail in both novels, and readers may wonder what these two authors had to gain by reinforcing stereotypes that make African practices appear "primitive." However, it must be pointed out that Kuoh-Moukoury and Rawiri also show the repeated failures of modern medicine in each protagonist's individual case. In fact, at the end of *The Fury,* Emilienne's sister, Eva, dies in labor because of the incompetence of the hospital staff and her doctor. Although the novel closes with the revelation that Emilienne is pregnant, the reader is not so certain that this is to the credit of the expertise of her renowned gynecologist, who has also advised her to consult a hypnotist—a suggestion that provokes a predictable reaction from Emilienne's sister: "He advised you to go see a hypnotist so you can have children? I didn't think there were any in this country. And how can a doctor ask a patient to go see a hypnotist! It's like asking you to go see a witch doctor!" (133).

Thus, far from reinforcing negative stereotypes about Africans, Kuoh-Moukoury and Rawiri are merely pointing out the imperfections of both worlds, the traditional and the so-called modern. Their representations also point to the weight and influence of customary beliefs and traditions in many contemporary societies, demonstrating how individuals may resort to these cultural references especially in times of hopelessness and crisis, seeking a solution to problems from within instead of from outside. Flo and Emilienne are constantly reevaluating the old and the new, trying to extract what is positive, and it is this mentality in particular that makes these protagonists forward-thinking.

Despite the similarities found in the two novels, Rawiri's

discussion of infertility goes a step further. Initially, Emilienne's infertility seems as tragic as Flo's in *Rencontres essentielles.* In Kuoh-Moukoury's novel, the conclusion drawn is that motherhood takes precedence over a relationship with a man in the end. However, as *The Fury* progresses, the reader eventually starts to question if, in an ideal world, Emilienne really would have bothered with children at all. Her desire for children may actually be a longing for power. In this case, especially when visits to the gynecologist reveal no somatic problems to explain Emilienne's infertility, the reader realizes that it is perhaps Emilienne's true, subconscious desire not to have children for the sake of others that makes her body rebel, provoking miscarriages and making it difficult for her to conceive. Emilienne gives readers much to consider in her reflection on her own infertility and its true consequences on her marriage with Joseph: "Is it my infertility that is making him run away? Why does he need me to have children to love me? My illness, if that's what it is, is not contagious and should not rob us of our love. No, I cannot believe that Joseph loved me for the children I was supposed to give him after our wedding. I don't want to believe that all he saw in me was this woman who was to become the mother of his children. No, that idea is unbearable to me. I am a woman and I will be a woman no matter what happens" (88–89).

Perhaps the only element of *The Fury* that might be labeled a possible shortcoming is Rawiri's handling of the subject of lesbianism as depicted through Emilienne's relationship with her secretary, Dominique. As the author of one of the first African novels to touch upon this subject, still taboo for many African writers even today, Rawiri had the potential to go well beyond the stereotypes concerning an intimate relationship between two women, and unfortunately, at times, it seems Rawiri's own moral judgments prevented her from doing so.

Emilienne's homoerotic relationship with Dominique is complicated, and even troubling, on many fronts, especially because it is part of an elaborate strategy. Citing Emilienne's infertility as a primary motivation, Eyang devises a plan in which Dominique—who, the reader discovers later, is not only Emilienne's secretary but also the mistress of Joseph, with whom she has two children—is to secure Emilienne's trust so that Eyang's primary objective to separate the married couple can be realized. However, Eyang is not specific in how Dominique should go about securing her boss's trust. Eyang says only this: "I've found another way to bring about their divorce. We're going to go after the wife. Do everything you can to become friends with her. Once you see that she trusts you, let me know, and I will put the second phase of my plan into motion. In the meantime, do as I've just told you" (53–54). However, in the end, Eyang has very little to do with the homoerotic nature of Emilienne and Dominique's relationship. In fact, it is uncertain whether Eyang even knows about the specifics of the relationship, as at the end of the novel, Eyang tells her son only that Emilienne is not worthy of his devotion because she spends all her time "with witch doctors" and, in particular, consults "a white witch doctor"—her preferred term for a hypnotist (192). Eyang finally issues an ultimatum to her son, saying she will leave the house if Joseph does not apologize to Dominique for their breakup: "Son, you are casting me out by leaving the mother of your children. If you don't call her right now and tell her that you're sorry, I'm warning you, I will not stay one more minute under this roof" (192).

Dominique is seemingly the one responsible for initiating an intimate relationship with Emilienne. While Emilienne is attracted by Dominique's physical beauty early on in the novel—the first reference to this being her description of "this young woman whose complexion and body were so nearly perfect" (19)—she never overtly exhibits a hint of interest sexually toward her secretary, nor is she the first to make her desires known. The relationship seems to have an identifiable starting point, however, and this occurs, strangely enough, as the two women witness together the capital punishment of five men just below Emilienne's office window. Although Emilienne and the reader are both unaware of Dominique's insincerity at the time, the secretary takes advantage of the horrifying scene to become physically close to Emilienne: "Dominique threw herself on her, grabbing her by the shoulders. The two women embraced. . . . The two women's bodies intertwined and shuddered" (110). Although there is nothing particularly homoerotic in this first physical interaction between the two, it is nonetheless essential, as Dominique is aware that her boss maintains a strict level of hierarchy with regard to her employees. Dominique needs to break this down if she hopes to win over Emilienne. Although the reader suspects Dominique's malicious intentions more and more throughout the novel, Dominique's true motivations are not revealed until her ultimate confrontation with Joseph near the end of the novel: "I had a very carefully devised plan to win you back, a plan that your wife hastened without even knowing it" (187)—a plan she sees as a weapon to blackmail Joseph into leaving his wife so that she will have him exclusively for herself. Dominique asserts, "I demand that you leave your wife in the next twenty-four hours. . . . If you refuse, know that I will tell the world that your wife is a lesbian" (186).

Emilienne views her relationship with Dominique very differently from the beginning, as she concludes that she has never lived such intimately fulfilling moments with a man. However, the relationship seems less about a sincere love for a woman and more about three things—revolt, a "psycho-sentimental awakening" (162), and narcissism—but not a healthy narcissism that is associated with and essential to romantic love. Although Emilienne may seem more genuine about the relationship than Dominique, realistically, both women are using each other selfishly, and each has little consideration for the feelings of the other in the end. Rawiri writes about Emilienne, "Masturbation was not her thing. She always felt the need for physical contact. And as Dominique's body was similar to her own, it allowed her not only to rediscover herself, but also to provide her with a certain balance. This forbidden relationship was like a drug, and she knew that its sudden withdrawal would make her completely crazy" (162).

Indeed, Rawiri's words, "forbidden relationship," reflect the taboos associated with homosexuality in African society (taboos that still exist, unfortunately, to a greater or lesser extent in most societies), but considering the fact that Rawiri presents Emilienne as a rebellious and even disobedient protagonist in terms of what society dictates, the reader is left to ask himself or herself at the end why Rawiri did not seize the opportunity here to defy yet another taboo. It is surprising, actually, that Emilienne comes to feel ashamed about her relationship with Dominique, calling it a "dirty chapter in my life" (179) and asking herself, "How could I have fallen so low?" (179). These sentiments seem inconsistent with the character that Rawiri has presented to the reader thus far. At the point where Emilienne decides to break off her relationship with Dominique, the former is still completely unaware of her secretary's ruse. Yet, Emilienne's manner of breaking up is far from sensitive. She immediately reinstates the social hierarchy between superior and secretary and gives only minimal, matter-of-fact reasons for the breakup, stating that the relationship is not "appropriate" and that it negatively affects others close to them. "In any case, for those who are dear to us, we can no longer keep our relationship going" (185). When Dominique protests, Emilienne treats her as an insubordinate employee: "Listen, little girl, this problem is my business. From now on I forbid you to meddle in it. Do you understand?" (185).

If one looks at other examples of intimate relationships between women in African writing, such as in the Cameroonian author Calixthe Beyala's earliest works, *C'est le soleil qui m'a brûlée* (1987; *The Sun Hath Looked upon Me,* 1996) and *Tu t'appelleras Tanga* (1988; *Your Name Shall Be Tanga,* 1996), one finds that Beyala's style of writing offers a more objective view of these relationships and leaves the freedom of interpretation to the reader without imposing the author's own moral judgment. This does not imply, however, that Beyala has no strong feelings about the subject. In fact, Beyala has often categorically denied that relationships between Irène and Ateba in *C'est le soleil* and between Tanga and Anna-Claude in *Tu t'appelleras Tanga* are examples of lesbianism. In an interview with Eloise Brière and Rangira Gallimore,[13] Beyala stated with conviction, "I think that those who see lesbianism in my writings are quite simply perverted, because tenderness between women doesn't necessarily imply lesbianism. How can one explain to Westerners that in traditional Africa, intimate relationships between people of the same sex are not defined in terms of homosexuality?" (199).

While there is no shortage of scholars who have spoken

about lesbianism in Beyala's two works (Ndinda; Bjornson),[14] others, such as Rangira Gallimore and Nicki Hitchcott,[15] have placed Beyala's writings within Adrienne Rich's "lesbian continuum," which, according to Rich, includes a range "of woman-identified experience, not simply the fact that a woman has had or consciously desired genital sexual experience with another woman" (317). Indeed, one can also apply this same analysis to the relationship between Emilienne and Dominique in *The Fury.* However, unlike Beyala, who never specifically uses the term "lesbianism" in either of her works,[16] Rawiri takes away this ambiguity by having her characters state the term unequivocally—to cite just one example, "I will tell the world that your wife is a lesbian" (186). Scholars as well as general readers are thus forced to address Rawiri's precision in terms in their analyses. Kassa, for example, labels the relationship "circumstantial lesbianism" (139). Clerc and Nzé once again cite the inspiration of radical American feminism that motivates Rawiri to take on the "problem of feminine homosexuality" in *The Fury,* but they claim that more than anything else, such intimacy is "a way of compensating for a loss of tenderness on the part of the husband" (263). Cazenave also speaks of a "lesbian relationship" between Emilienne and Dominique, stating, "Lesbian love is presented as a dead-end, since the liaison is shown only in its relations to social taboos and mechanisms" (32). However, Annie-Paul Boukandou provides perhaps a multifaceted interpretation of this particular relationship and what it contributes both to *The Fury* and to the African feminist novel in general. In her essay "Personnages et discours féminin dans le roman gabonais" (Characters and feminine discourse in the Gabonese novel), Boukandou applauds novels like *The Fury* that are open to change. That is, despite the shortcomings one may find in the way Rawiri chooses to handle the homoerotic relationship between Emilienne and Dominique, such a novel "produces a new type of woman free in her emotions, and free in the way she uses her body" (122). The fact that Rawiri can touch on such a subject in her novel at all proves that open-mindedness is becoming more the norm in a new, modern age. Women, in fact, can and do have loving relationships with each other (Boukandou 122–

23). Thus, taboo subjects need to be raised. Although not every reader will be pleased with the end result, the fact that Rawiri has introduced the topic is in itself radical, especially in 1989.

In addition to the issues mentioned above, Rawiri also briefly touches upon public health issues such as malaria (163–64) and HIV/AIDS, two afflictions that continue to ravage the African continent today. Although HIV/AIDS does not directly affect any of the major characters in *The Fury,* Rawiri finds a way to present the subject through a frail-looking patient Emilienne observes in her physician's waiting room (119). Although it is never confirmed whether the young woman Emilienne sees suffers from the disease, the encounter starts a chain of reflections: "AIDS had been ravaging African populations for a dozen years. In point of fact, who had definitive proof of its origin? Whatever it may be, we would no longer attribute all those mysterious deaths to witchcraft" (119). HIV/AIDS is yet another taboo subject that has surfaced in African literature only recently. Perhaps Rawiri's novel was a precursor to those whose protagonists are specifically victims of this disease, such as in the case of Chantal Magalie Mbazoo Kassa's 2005 novel *Sidonie.*

Finally, Rawiri must be applauded for her detailed commentary on the problem of tribalism in former African colonies. Tribalism is more commonly the domain of male writers, but in this instance, Rawiri has again distinguished herself among female authors along with her compatriot Honorine Ngou, author of the essay "Le tribalisme: Le virus qui tue la paix" (2003; Tribalism: The virus that kills peace). The interethnic marriage of Emilienne and Joseph serves as the backdrop for this serious discussion that takes up the better part of the first chapter in *The Fury.* Rawiri draws many conclusions throughout, most lauding the richness of multiculturalism and praising those citizens "motivated by the same spirit in the interest of our country" (16).

The Fury and Cries of Women is a novel that continues to ignite debate and passion. While Rawiri's work is a true representation of the African novel, it will nonetheless have international appeal as it is reintroduced in English translation to a twenty-first-century audience. On a personal level, readers will relate to its depictions of complicated relationships (heterosexual and same-sex), infidelity, and love triangles affecting everyday lives. Emilienne's story functions to show that education and career do not necessarily guarantee personal happiness and emphasizes the often superficial interactions of the nouveaux riches. In an increasingly globalized world, government and corporate corruption, interethnic conflict, violence against adults and children, malpractice, and extortion are ever-present, universal realities of which readers are also aware. The novel's ability to capture the interest of a new generation of readers attests to its originality and versatility. Thanks in part to the publication of Sara Hanaburgh's new translation as part of the CARAF series of the University of Virginia Press, this novel has certainly reserved itself a place among other essential works in African literature.

Notes

1. The *mvet* and the *olendé* are both rich oral traditions, from the Fang and Mbédé ethnic groups, respectively, offering some of the most renowned epic poetry in Africa.

2. Werewere Liking is virtually the only well-known exception to this rule. A resident of Abidjan for more than thirty years, Liking is self-taught in French language, literature, and culture, having received a traditional Bassa education during her childhood and adolescence in her native Cameroon.

3. El Hadj Omar Bongo Ondimba was Gabon's president from 1967 until 2009. Gabon's speaker of the senate at the time of Omar Bongo's death, Rose Francine Rogombé, was appointed interim president for three months until elections were held. Omar Bongo's son, Ali Ben Bongo, allegedly won these elections, but the results were disputed in some regions of Gabon, especially in Port-Gentil.

4. My gratitude to the Gabonese writer Edna Merey Apinda, who translated the meaning of Rawiri's name, Ntyugwétondo, from the Omyènè into French, "le jour qu'on aime," which I in turn translated into "the beloved day."

5. With the exception of quotations from *The Fury and Cries of Women* that come from Sara Hanaburgh's translation, all quotations from the French in this afterword are my own translation, unless otherwise noted.

6. When asked during the 1988 *Amina* interview if she encountered any difficulties publishing, Rawiri answered, "No. I must admit that it was rather easy. Friends who were journalists helped me out by putting me in

contact with an editor" (10). Rawiri was also asked whether during the writing of her first novel she was aware that she would become the first novelist of Gabon, to which she replied, "No, I hadn't thought about that. I was rather taken up by my reflections, my doubts, my worries, my fears. When the novel came out, I found out that I was the first novelist" (10).

7. In his essay, Mendame actually notes *Elonga*'s publication date as 1985, and thus I have corrected it here. One finds such mistakes quite commonly because the first printing of *Elonga* was not well-distributed, and it was not until the novel's second printing that scholars began to take notice; some were even unaware of the first printing, and thus the confusion over its publication date.

8. A March 2011 interview in Libreville with the author Sylvie Ntsame, who was at the time the president of the Union des Écrivains Gabonais (UDEG), reported fifty known published authors in Gabon, and half of this number was female.

9. In his essay entitled "Le roman gabonais des origines à nos jours" (The Gabonese novel from its origins to the present), Jean Léonard Nguema Ondo refers to Rawiri's three works as "sa trilogie romanesque," or, "her novelistic trilogy." The various announcements in the Gabonese press of Rawiri's death in 2010 also consistently identified her works as a trilogy. To cite just one example, see the article "Gabon: Le soleil s'est définitivement couché sur Angèle Rawiri" (Gabon: The sun sets forever on Angèle Rawiri) on the website of *Gaboneco* for 29 November 2010, describing Rawiri as "the author of a novelistic trilogy that led us to reflect upon the status of women in contemporary African societies." Many literary critics tend to group the three novels together in their analyses, focusing more on their similarities than their differences. Nicolas Mba-Zue states, "The three novels of Ntyugwétondo (or Angèle) Rawiri walk us through this same universe of literary devices" (44).

10. In *Le deuxième sexe,* Simone de Beauvoir speaks about "la servitude de la maternité" ("the servitude of motherhood") (56).

11. The well-known Nigerian feminist novelist Buchi Emecheta wrote an essay entitled "Feminism with a Small 'f'," in which she compares monogamy and polygamy in terms of the time women devote to a husband, concluding in the end that in a bad marriage, polygamy would at least allow for a woman to have time for herself while her husband is away with a cowife as opposed to her being alone with him all the time. In the essay Emecheta advocates neither polygamy nor monogamy specifically but writes a brilliant essay dramatically different from those that predictably compare a bad polygamous marriage with an idealistic monogamous one, with the logical conclusion being, of course, that monogamy is always preferable.

12. I state that Kuoh-Moukoury searched for a publisher for *Rencontres essentielles* for thirteen years before the novel was finally published in 1969. Kuoh-Moukoury actually completed the manuscript in 1956. Thus, there is

a more significant time gap to be noted between the actual writing of *Rencontres essentielles* and the publication of Rawiri's *Fureurs*.

13. In the same interview, Beyala quite aggressively denies the existence of homosexuality in traditional African societies. Her comments represent a very common reaction among African writers, especially at the time of this interview in the late 1990s. When pressed about her implying that traditional African society excluded all homosexual activity, Beyala's reponse was, "As I already told you, I can't claim to hold universal truth in regard to certain data. I therefore cannot know if other African societies indulge in homosexuality. I am convinced however that my own doesn't practice it" (199).

14. In "Écriture et discours féminin au Cameroun" (Writing and feminine discourse in Cameroon), Joseph Ndinda states, "Ateba's homosexuality is an extreme reaction of those who no longer want to be exploited" (12). In *The African Quest for Freedom and Identity*, Richard Bjornson states, "Beyala's lesbian approach to the reality of contemporary Cameroon is unusual within the context of the country's literate culture" (420).

15. Gallimore's work *L'oeuvre romanesque de Calixthe Beyala* (The novels of Calixthe Beyala) discusses this on page 132. Hitchcott's work *Women Writers in Francophone Africa* discusses this on page 138.

16. For a more thorough analysis of Beyala's two works cited here, refer to Toman's *Contemporary Matriarchies* (2008), and specifically to chapter 4, which is dedicated entirely to Beyala.

Bibliography

Ambourhouet-Bigmann, Magloire. "Naissance d'une littérature." *Notre librairie.* 105 (1991): 37–39.

———. "Où est le roman gabonais?" *Africultures.* 36 (March 2001): 18–19.

Aidoo, Ama Ata. *Changes: A Love Story.* New York: Feminist Press, 1993.

Bâ, Mariama. *So Long a Letter.* Trans. Modupe Bode Thomas. Portsmouth, NH: Heinemann, 1989.

———. *Une si longue lettre.* Dakar: Nouvelles Éditions Africaines, 1986.

Beauvoir, Simone de. *Le deuxième sexe.* Paris: Gallimard, 1949.

———. *La femme rompue.* Paris: Gallimard, 1967.

———. *Tout compte fait.* Paris: Gallimard, 1972.

Beti, Mongo. *Cruel City.* Trans. Pim Higginson. Bloomington, IN: 2013.

Beyala, Calixthe. *C'est le soleil qui m'a brûlée.* Paris: Stock, 1987.

———. *The Sun Hath Looked upon Me.* Trans. Marjolijn de Jager. Portsmouth, NH: Heinemann, 1996.

———. *Tu t'appelleras Tanga.* Paris: Stock, 1988.

———. *Your Name Shall Be Tanga.* Trans. Marjolijn de Jager. Portsmouth, NH: Heinemann, 1996.

Bikindou, F., and L. Baker. "Angèle Rawiri Ntyugwétondo, Première femme-écrivain du Gabon." *Amina.* 224 (Dec. 1988): 12–16.

Bjornson, Richard. *The African Quest for Freedom and Identity: Cameroonian Writing and the National Experience.* Bloomington, IN: Indiana University Press, 1991.

Boto, Eza. *Ville cruelle.* Paris: Présence Africaine, 1954.

Boukandou, Annie-Paule. "Personnages et discours féminin dans le roman gabonais." *Les écritures gabonaises: histoires, thèmes, et langues.* Ed. Pierre Ndemby-Mamfoumby. Yaoundé: Éditions Clé, 2009. 101–24.

Brière, Eloise, and Rangira Gallimore. "Entretien avec Calixthe Beyala." *L'œuvre romanesque de Calixthe Beyala: Le renouveau de l'écriture féminine en Afrique francophone sub-saharienne.* Paris: L'Harmattan, 1997. 189–204.

Cazenave, Odile. *Rebellious Women: The New Generation of Female African Novelists.* Boulder, CO: Lynne Rienner Publishers, Inc., 1999.

———. *Femmes rebelles: Naissance d'un nouveau roman africain au féminin.* Paris: L'Harmattan, 1996.

Clerc, Jeanne-Marie, and Liliane Nzé. *Le roman gabonais et la symbolique du silence et du bruit.* Paris: L'Harmattan, 2008.

d'Almeida, Irène Assiba. Introduction. *A Rain of Words: A Bilingual Anthology of Women's Poetry in Francophone Africa.* Eds. Irène d'Almeida and Janis A. Mayes. Charlottesville: University of Virginia Press, 2009. xix–xxix.

Emecheta, Buchi. "Feminism with a Small 'f'." *Criticism and Ideology.* Ed. Kirsten Holst Petersen. Uppsala: Scandinavian Institute of African Studies, 1988. 173–85.

Gallimore, Rangira Béatrice. *L'œuvre romanesque de Calixthe Beyala: Le renouveau de l'écriture féminine en Afrique francophone sub-saharienne.* Paris: L'Harmattan, 1997.

Hitchcott, Nicki. *Women Writers in Francophone Africa.* Oxford: Berg, 2000.

Kassa, Chantal Magalie Mbazoo. *La femme et ses images dans le roman gabonais.* Paris: L'Harmattan, 2009.

———. *Sidonie.* Libreville: Maison Gabonaise du Livre, 2005.

Kuoh-Moukoury, Thérèse. *Essential Encounters.* Ed. and trans. Cheryl Toman. New York: MLA Texts and Translations Series, 2002.

———. *Rencontres essentielles.* Paris: Adamawa, 1969, 1981. L'Harmattan, 1995.

———. *Rencontres essentielles.* Ed. Cheryl Toman. New York: MLA Texts and Translations Series, 2002.

Mba-Zue, Nicolas. "Une littérature en quête d'identité." *Notre librairie.* 105 (1991): 46–49.

Mendame, Jean-René Ovono. "Gabon: Naissance d'une littérature: Chantal Magalie Mbazo'o Kassa, une romancière en pleine croissance." http://www.africultures.com/php/?nav=article&no=4348]. 10 March 2006.

Midiohouan, Guy Ossito. Interview by Chantal Magalie Mbazoo Kassa. *La femme et ses images dans le roman gabonais.* Paris: L'Harmattan, 2009. 219–21.

Mintsa, Justine. *Histoire d'Awu.* Paris: Gallimard, 2000.

Ndemby-Mamfoumby, Pierre. *Les écritures gabonaises: Histoires, thèmes, et langues.* Yaoundé: Éditions Clé, 2009.

Ndinda, Joseph. "Écriture et discours féminin au Cameroun: Trois générations de romancières." *Notre librairie* 118 (1994): 6–12.

Ngou, Honorine. "Le tribalisme: Le virus qui tue la paix." Libreville: Multipress, Gabon, 2003.

Ondo, Jean Léonard Nguema. "Le roman gabonais des origines à nos jours (2005)." http://crelaf.tigblog.org/post/34503?setlangcookie=true. 25 January 2006.

Powrie, Phil. "Rereading between the Lines: A Postscript on *La femme rompue*." *The Modern Language Review.* 87, no.2 (April 1992): 320–29.

Rawiri, Angèle. *Fureurs et cris de femmes.* Paris: L'Harmattan, 1989.

Rawiri, Ntyugwétondo. *G'amérakano: Au carrefour.* Paris: ABC, 1983.

———. *Elonga.* Paris: Editaf, 1980.

Rich, Adrienne. "Compulsory Heterosexuality and Lesbian Existence." *Feminism in Our Time: The Essential Writings, World War II to the Present.* Ed. Miriam Schneir. New York: Vintage, 1994. 310–26.

Toman, Cheryl. *Contemporary Matriarchies in Cameroonian Francophone Literature: 'On est ensemble.'* Birmingham, AL: Summa, 2008.

Volet, Jean-Marie. *La parole aux Africaines ou l'idée de pouvoir chez les romancières d'expression française de l'Afrique Sub-Saharienne.* Amsterdam: Rodopi, 1993.

Zotoumbat, Robert. *Histoire d'un enfant trouvé.* Yaoundé: Éditions Clé, 1971.

Recent Books in the Series

CARAF Books
Caribbean and African Literature Translated from French

Jacques Stephen Alexis
In the Flicker of an Eyelid
Translated by Carrol F. Coates and Edwidge Danticat

Gisèle Pineau
Exile according to Julia
Translated by Betty Wilson

Mouloud Feraoun
The Poor Man's Son: Menrad, Kabyle Schoolteacher
Translated by Lucy R. McNair

Abdourahman A. Waberi
The Land without Shadows
Translated by Jeanne Garane

Patrice Nganang
Dog Days: An Animal Chronicle
Translated by Amy Baram Reid

Ken Bugul
The Abandoned Baobab: The Autobiography of a Senegalese Woman
Translated by Marjolijn de Jager

Irène Assiba d'Almeida, Editor
A Rain of Words: A Bilingual Anthology of Women's Poetry in Francophone Africa
Translated by Janis A. Mayes

Maïssa Bey
Above All, Don't Look Back
Translated by Senja L. Djelouah

Yanick Lahens
Aunt Résia and the Spirits and Other Stories
Translated by Betty Wilson

Mariama Barry
The Little Peul
Translated by Carrol F. Coates

Mohammed Dib
At the Café and *The Talisman*
Translated by C. Dickson

Mouloud Feraoun
Land and Blood
Translated by Patricia Geesey

Suzanne Dracius
Climb to the Sky
Translated by Jamie Davis

Véronique Tadjo
Far from My Father
Translated by Amy Baram Reid

Angèle Rawiri
The Fury and Cries of Women
Translated by Sara Hanaburgh